Shadow Lane
Volume 5

The Spanking Persuasion

by
Eve Howard

CCB Publishing
British Columbia, Canada

Shadow Lane Volume 5: The Spanking Persuasion

Library and Archives Canada Cataloguing in Publication
Howard, Eve, 1953-
Shadow lane : volume 5: the spanking persuasion / written by Eve Howard – 2nd ed.
ISBN 978-1-926585-39-0
Also available in electronic format.
I. Title.
PS3608.O82S535 2009 813'.6 C2009-904448-X

Cover artwork by Tarsis: www.briantarsis.com
Interior artwork by The Contessa

Shadow Lane Volume 5 was first published by Blue Moon in 1999,
Copyright © Eve Howard.

Publisher: CCB Publishing
              British Columbia, Canada
              www.ccbpublishing.com

Dedicated for

my sister Jeannie

Patricia Fairservis

Shadow Lane
Volume 5

The Spanking Persuasion

ℰℴ

Contents

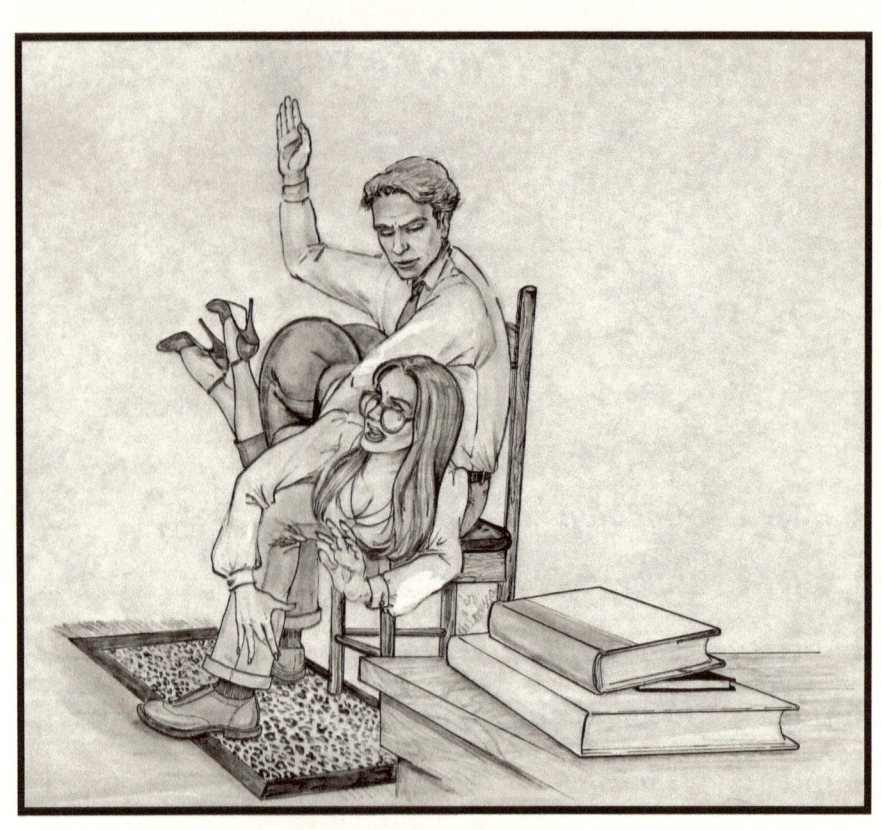

Marguerite Alexander

Chapter One

Ambition

Anthony Newton, normally the friend of every living creature, had taken an unaccountable dislike to Patricia Fairservis whose best friend, Laura Random, was lodged as a perpetual guest in his house.

"I hope your friend Mrs. Fairservis is out of town," he remarked to Laura over breakfast that rainy Friday morning in early October.

Laura gave a guilty start. "Actually, she is coming by for an instant this morning," she admitted. He looked at her in exasperation. "I couldn't stop her when she found out you were in town."

"Well, never mind. I'll leave word that I can't be disturbed."

"Okay."

"You'd better see to it that I'm not disturbed either, young lady."

"Oh, Anthony, what have you got against Patricia?"

"Laura, I don't wish to insult your friend, but she strikes me as someone who should be living in L.A."

"But, Anthony, doesn't the fact that Patricia's in the scene count in her favor?"

"Not unless I get to personally thrash her."

Patricia arrived in a flurry of perfumed fur and silken, straight blonde hair the instant their exchange was concluded.

Anthony greeted her civilly, then drifted over to the piano to practice preludes while the girls chatted over coffee. Patricia's bright blue eyes kept drifting over to him, but the composer affected total absorption in the keyboard, forcing her to abandon any plan to engage him in conversation.

"Michael's going to some jackbooted, motorcycle cop convention in Boston tonight and I haven't been invited. What are you doing?"

Patricia asked Laura at length.

"I'm having dinner with my ex-husband," Laura replied with a smile.

Anthony wished Laura had not said that, for it left him bufferless against an onslaught from Patricia. And sure enough when he looked up he caught the editor of Cape Cod Style eyeing him again. He began to pound the keyboard. Patricia had just relocated to Random Point and was still unpacking. She would become restless alone in the lighthouse tonight and remember that he lived only a half mile up the road. Anthony sighed.

Patricia and Laura exchanged a glance. Laura shrugged and Patricia looked disappointed. It was apparent that Anthony Newton did not like her and this hurt Patricia's feelings. She prepared to depart in dejection, admonishing Laura to call her. "Good-bye, Mr. Newton," Patricia called respectfully, having stopped a bare seven minutes.

"Oh, good-bye Patricia," he said pleasantly, suddenly stricken with guilt for not having been more polite.

Perversely enough, the moment Patricia left, Anthony began to miss her. All day the thought of her returned to him and he now considered what a joy it might be to feel that light, resilient girl across his lap.

By dinnertime, after Laura had left for her date and Michael had roared out of town on his motorcycle, Anthony began to think that if Patricia did stop by that night, he would not instruct Dennis to send her away.

When William Random placed Patricia as his tenant in the old lighthouse, which surmounted Lilac Cove, she suddenly acquired the best view and most isolated playroom in all of Random Point. It was especially atmospheric on a stormy night.

Although she hadn't paid for any of it, Patricia's new domain was furnished with handsome pieces from Hugo Sands' shop; including a pretty little piano he'd just gotten hold of at an estate auction. Remembering the proximity of Anthony Newton, she'd begged for this particular piece.

When Hugo put pencil to paper after Patricia had ransacked his shop, he figured that Cape Cod Style owed him a year of full-page color ads. Hugo didn't ask Patricia how she was going to explain this to her publisher, Randy Price, but knew that if her scheme backfired he could always reclaim the furniture and redeem the cost of his aggravation in some imaginative way.

Anthony's instincts about Patricia were regrettably correct. Much that she did was in questionable taste and some of it downright unethical. Like promising Hugo free ads for the furniture.

Because Patricia had only ever seen her boss, Randy Price in a good mood and because he sometimes flirted with her, she felt confident of being able to get around him with sex should the need arise. Meanwhile, he liked what she was doing with the magazine, liked her, and was made of wealth, both old and new. The chances were he wouldn't even notice the free ad space going to Hugo's shop in Cape Cod Style.

Patricia had thought of calling Anthony Newton that evening, but the chilly reception she'd received that morning caused her to suppress the urge and organize her wardrobe instead. Anthony called her at eight-thirty.

"I just realized that you're new in the neighborhood," he confessed pleasantly, "and I was wondering whether you needed anything."

"Well," she stalled to gather her thoughts, "you might bring a corkscrew."

"That all?"

"And some computer cabling."

"How about dinner?"

"Sure. And bring that gorgeous English boy to serve it."

Anthony looked at the phone and shook his head, wondering if it was too soon to start regretting this. Nevertheless, an hour later he arrived with Dennis, dinner from the inn, wine from his cellar and all the computer cabling necessary to connect her equipment.

Meanwhile Dennis laid out dinner and spent the rest of the evening happily unpacking and putting away Patricia's shoes.

"How come you're being so nice to me tonight?" she asked as Anthony sat down at the fine old piano. "I thought you didn't like me."

"Who told you that?"

"I figured it out."

"I like you tonight," he candidly admitted, beginning My Reverie.

"But not this morning?"

"I apologize for my rudeness this morning. It's been bothering me all day." He stopped playing to give her his full attention and Patricia was shocked to realize for the first time what a really youthful millionaire he was.

"You did hurt my feelings," she reproached him. "I suppose you were afraid I was going to ask you about profiling the Cliffs again."

"Yes."

"You know, it's not easy filling a magazine every month," Patricia pointed out. Anthony sighed. "And I haven't had a really great celebrity house in three issues," Patricia continued. "Oh, please, Mr. Newton, won't you reconsider?"

Anthony started playing again. At length he coolly asked, "Besides the inconvenience, what's in it for me?"

"Publicity?" she answered lamely.

"Don't need it."

Patricia began to think that she would never gain her objective and had only succeeded in sanitizing a sexy moment when he suddenly startled her by saying, "Why don't you offer me something good?"

Taken aback she stared at him. "Okay. What did you have in mind?"

"Come over here," he said, pushing the piano bench away from the piano and sitting in the middle of it. When she came to him he took her by the hand. "Did you know that you need a good spanking?"

Patricia felt her face grow very warm as he gently pulled her down across his lap.

"I understand that our own Detective Flagg generally tends to you," Anthony patted her bottom lightly through her clinging black Capri pants. "Is that so?"

"Yes," she replied, suddenly breathless.

"He must spank you lightly, however," Anthony remarked, bestowing a few warm up smacks on her taut, upturned behind.

"Oh no!" she disagreed.

"Are you saying you receive proper discipline?"

"Well, yes!"

"Then why don't you have better manners?"

Patricia had no answer for a question, which made her feel ashamed. Anthony gripped her firmly by the waist and spanked her vigorously for several minutes, warming the entire surface of her bottom through the thin woolen pants with the palm of his hand.

"This spanking is from me and every other celebrity you've ever plagued in your life," he told her, sliding her pants down over her hips to her knees. Patricia's perfect bottom was wrapped in sheer black briefs through which her peach skin blushed. "You do have a beautiful bottom," he praised her, while stroking it.

"I hope you won't be very severe with me," Patricia flirted, wriggling on his lap in such a way as to provoke him.

"Why shouldn't I be? You annoyed me, didn't you?" He pulled her panties down.

"Oh! I'm very sorry!" She tried to cover her bare bottom with her hand but he firmly pushed it away.

"Really? I don't think you're a bit sorry. Especially as now you're going to get what you want from me."

"I was brought up to believe that I should have whatever I want."

"Then you were brought up very badly," he declared, proceeding to spank her soundly. Anthony's arm was tireless and he spanked her for a very long time, with increasing firmness, until a rosy glow suffused the entire surface of her exposed skin and Patricia began to feel the punishment.

"Anthony?" she presently stopped him.

"Yes, my love?" he said with unexpected warmth, enchanted by her reactions. He had seldom met a woman who arched her bottom up to be spanked in quite the way Patricia did, or parted her legs so prettily to reveal her bedewed pubic mound.

"Have we begun?" she asked.

Patricia was not in a position to observe whether her impertinent remark amused him, however, after a delay of about five seconds he deliberately renewed his grip on her waist and began to spank her again, significantly harder and faster than before.

Now a disciplinary element had been infused into their game. He had no idea of how much really hard spanking Patricia could sustain but he estimated her capacity at no more than three minutes at the current tempo. Patricia broke down and begged for mercy in one.

"Oh god, please stop! I'm sorry for whatever it is you think I did!" she yielded.

"You call that an apology?" he paused to examine her bottom and found it tinged a deep, rosy red by his hand but scarcely marked. She was obviously seasoned to this.

When he released her she pulled her pants and panties back up in a moment, then gave her entire attention to hugging him hard enough to make his ribs creak.

"That was so good!" She wriggled her well-spanked bottom on his lap as he held her and enjoyed her girlish warmth.

"Then why did you put your pants back on?" he asked, patting her bottom through the capris and for the first time cupping her firm, little bosom through her cropped dove grey cashmere polo sweater. She caught her breath and squirmed on his lap, encouraging him to slip his hand up under it to caress the satiny skin of her flat midriff.

"Should I not have put my pants back on?"

"That depends on what you want."

"What do you want, Mr. Newton?"

"I want to send Dennis home."

"Dennis!" Patricia was suddenly shocked to realize that the English boy was still in her bedroom below them arranging her closet. "But, what if he heard..."

"Oh, he's heard it all before," said Anthony with a smile, leaving her briefly to dismiss his driver for the evening. After his departure Patricia was thrilled to observe that Dennis had unpacked every box.

"Where did you find that boy? I'm in love." Patricia marveled at the organization.

"He was working as a valet in a London hotel when I found him about four years ago."

"But, doesn't he question the strange noises Mr. Newton makes with his lady friends?"

"I think he finds it intriguing," Anthony confessed. "Of course, he's a great favorite with the girls."

"He does know how to make himself useful. Should I tip him?"

"Let him give you a foot rub."

"Really? He'd enjoy that?"

"Take a look in your closet at the shoes."

Patricia saw and was duly impressed by the meticulous arrangement of her hundred pair of shoes.

"So you keep a submissive man on your staff," Patricia observed with journalistic interest.

"He's just a kid," said Anthony, wickedly accepting a cigarette when she lit one for herself. They were sitting in the window seat overlooking the surf-beaten cove as the storm continued to pelt the lighthouse.

"Most dominant men I've met have an aversion to submissive ones."

"That's silly. Who else can you trust your submissive with but another submissive? Not that I trust Susan to leave Dennis submissive for that much longer," Anthony sighed.

"You're a funny one," she smiled at his relative lack of concern. "But I suppose it does come in handy to have someone around to do all those tedious things for ladies they might ask you to do otherwise."

"You mean like setting up an entire desktop publishing system in 29 minutes?"

"I do mean to officially thank you for that," she replied with a blush.

"You mean Dennis isn't the only one to get tipped?"

"Anything. Just name it," she promised, ready to go down on her knees to him in an instant.

"Take your clothes off," he told her, still lazily enjoying his annual cigarette. Patricia stripped with alacrity, fully displaying her willowy body to him for the first time.

"Come over here and turn around. Let me look at you. You are something though." Anthony was greatly aroused by her willingness to spread her legs and expose herself to him. "I think you must be the naughtiest girl I've ever met," he told her, inserting his middle finger into her wet pussy up to the knuckle.

Presently he made her kneel on the window seat to take his cock from behind. The entry was made smooth by her excitement, and the precision pistoning that followed conformed exactly to Patricia's notion of what a ravishment should consist of. She only had to whisper, "Take me hard and fast," once, for Anthony to fasten his hands to her waist and plunge in to the hilt, for she was an accessible girl. He fucked her for a long time, during which she climaxed beautifully for him and he for her.

After the inevitable conclusion of the window seat engagement, Patricia stretched out face down on the rug in front of the fire to slowly come to her senses. He was calmly stuffing his still throbbing organ back into his pants when she lifted her head to cry, "We forgot to use a condom!"

Anthony was taken aback by her just accusation and flushed with shame at his own irresponsibility.

Being Patricia she sat up and panicked. What was it about being in Random Point that made her forget everything sensible she ever knew about sex?

"God knows how many people you fuck!" she exclaimed, anxiously lighting a cigarette and pulling on a smoky blue silk wrapper. "I mean, you're in the theatre world, which is absolutely teeming with homosexuals!"

"Sure, but I'm not one of them," he calmly replied.

"How do I know that? I mean, you're pretty kinky," she accused, remembering the male submissive employee.

"Patricia, relax. I pulled out before I came."

"Have you or have you not fucked pretty boys?"

"Patricia, you're getting hysterical over nothing."

Patricia looked sullen.

"Look, you're just as much of a risk as I am," Anthony pointed out.

"Why do you say that?"

"Well, you've got a husband, an alley cat of a boyfriend and I understand you also play with Hugo Sands."

"Why do you say alley cat? Who has Michael been fucking besides Marguerite?"

"Around this time last year he had an affair with my little Susan."

"Susan?" Patricia drew a blank.

"My girlfriend. Cute little blonde. You must have seen her at the Pandora orientation meeting."

"That must have happened just before I met him," mused Patricia, her face burning with indignation. How dare these men of nearly 40 disport themselves with college girls!

"You did know about Michael and Susan, didn't you?" Anthony demanded, for he relished sexual gossip more than protecting Susan's reputation.

"No," she exhaled with resentment. "He never told me."

"I can see why. You're a bit volatile."

"You think so?"

"Borderline uncivilized," Anthony sadly replied. "First thing I'd do with you if you were mine would be to teach you better manners."

"Oh? And how would you do that?"

"Constant correction by the rod, my dear."

"And I suppose this little Susan Ross has impeccable manners?" Patricia felt ill at the memory of running into Susan in New York during the first trip with Michael. If what Anthony said was true, Michael had already had the little brat and the two of them were dissembling outrageously as they stood there before her and pretended to be no more than acquaintances.

"Susan's manners are dreadful," Anthony replied, "But her intentions are good. And since she's only 22, she has something of an excuse. You, on the other hand, should know better."

"So, tell me, do they still see each other?"

"Perhaps not recently. She's been through two more boys and a girl since that adventure."

"And none of this bothers you?"

"I've had one or two adventures of my own," he smiled.

"I hope you took better precautions than tonight."

"You won't believe me, but I generally do."

"So you and Michael have shared two women," she mused.

"Three if you count Marguerite."

"Oh? You've been on that ride too, have you?"

"Don't be vulgar," he admonished her.

"I've never been surrounded by so much competition in my life."

"Think of them as friends instead," he counseled mildly.

"Thrash me until I understand that," Patricia suggested mischievously.

"Whenever possible, I will," he agreed.

Patricia found Anthony witty and warm and wanted very much to keep him with her all night, to which he had no objection. The following morning, while she was giving him coffee and they were waiting for Dennis to come by with the car, she climbed onto his lap to give him a hug.

"Do you like me just a little bit now?" she asked.

"I like you a lot now," he frankly replied. "And you can shoot my house any time you like. The one in New York too."

"I can?" she hugged him harder, thrilled by the unexpected bonus.

"Well, of course," he replied, adding with the modest gratitude of a satisfied male, "after all, you gave me everything."

"So I can count you as my friend now?"

"Now and forever."

This was a promise that Patricia Fairservis was very glad to have obtained approximately one month later, when in the last week of October, she was summoned to Boston by the publisher of Cape Cod Style.

Patricia wasn't sure what to expect as she drove into town on that wet, chilly day, but she knew that it wasn't going to be good. Randy had his secretary arrange the meeting and the language of her message had been terse.

Patricia had dressed exquisitely in a wasp-waisted suit that enhanced every elegant curve. Her shoulder length hair had never looked more like that of Veronica Lake and her face would have seemed quite as lovely if not for the anxiety reflected there.

One who has entered a grim, old, office building on Water Street, Boston, in the rain, knows an existential desolation only to be found in the works of Franz Kafka. Patricia stayed away from the corporate offices as much as possible, usually managing to arrange meetings with her boss at Maison Robert. But today he'd sent for her.

As soon as she walked into Randy's 8th floor office, she knew that all the perfect suits in the world were not going to move him. He glowered at her from behind his massive desk, the color keys for this month's issue of Cape Cod Style spread out in front of him. She noticed the spread on the lighthouse on top, along with the full color ad for Hugo's shop. Now her heart contracted, for she knew exactly why she was here.

"What the hell is this?" Randy picked up the spread on the lighthouse and flung it across the desk at her. Randy Price was a sharp, calculating, young entrepreneur who had inherited a good deal of money and made even more on his own. One of his enterprises was the magazine that Patricia had been editing for the past three years. As a moneymaker it broke even, but he liked being a publisher with the unique power it brought. Randy was an arrogant Harvard business school predator whose manners were far worse than Patricia's. A gangster could not have spoken to her with more contempt.

"It's a spread on the Random Point lighthouse. Is there a problem with that?"

"Yes, there's a fucking problem. I hate William Random and everything that relates to him, and his name appears on every other line."

Patricia looked at him with amazement. "How could I have known that? I mean, he's an architect on the Cape, we do a magazine on the Cape; he renovated a great house, I photographed it. I was just doing my job."

"Doing your job, huh? Does that include living in his damned house, like you say here in the article?"

"Well, I've just left my husband and I needed a place to live."

"So you entered into some sort of sweetheart deal where you'd get the house and he'd get the publicity. Is that it?"

Patricia colored. "No, not at all. I'm paying rent to live there. And I honestly thought the spread would be nice for the magazine. Randy, how could I know you hated William Random? This isn't fair."

"Stop whining and explain this," he threw the ad for Hugo's shop across the desk.

"It's an ad," she slowly replied, trying desperately to think of a legitimate reason why it had ever found its way into the issue. By now she was so flushed with adrenaline that she could barely stand on her legs. She sat down to gaze at the color keys, numb with desolation at her probable fate.

"Yes, I know it's an ad. It's a goddamned full-page color ad that hasn't been paid for. Now what's it doing in the issue?"

Patricia felt faint as her brain tried to work. She'd never expected him to personally review the advertising receivables for the magazine. But now that she was forced to think of the ad in terms of dollars and cents, she realized that if the magazine had gone to press she would have effectively robbed approximately five thousand dollars from her boss. What in the world could she have been thinking of by promising Hugo full pages color ads?

"Oh, the ad is paid for," she told him within three seconds that seemed like a month to her tortured nerves.

"Oh? Where's the check?"

"I ... have it in my files."

"Why hasn't it been turned in?"

"I thought I had turned it in. I'll bring it in tomorrow," she promised hastily.

"And what about this?" he indicated the lighthouse spread. "You have something else to fill the space?"

"Anthony Newton's letting me shoot his house. It'll only take me a couple of days to do the photos," she replied shakily.

"Anthony Newton's house will do. Okay, you've got two days to get me some prints and the story. And you'd better produce that check for the ad at the same time. Otherwise, you're not only getting fired, but I'm going to have you prosecuted for accepting payola while in my employ. Now get the hell out of here."

Patricia had not been hit with a bag of oranges, as in The Grifters, she only felt that way as she stumbled back out of the building and found her car. Where was she going to get five thousand dollars to give Hugo in order to make him write the check to Randy? Michael was moonlighting just to make his bills. Patricia's soon to be ex-husband would have given her the money, but Fairservis was a gregarious creature that loved to wine and dine his friends and always ran in debt.

Patricia sobbed at the wheel half way back to Random Point as she reviewed all of the humiliating and nearly insurmountable tasks before her. First, she had to find five thousand dollars. Then she had to admit to Hugo Sands that her boss had demanded payment for the ad. Hugo would be furious and require the return of his costly furniture immediately. Then she had to go to William Random (to whom she had not yet paid her first month's rent) and admit that the spread on the lighthouse would never appear in Cape Cod Style because her boss appeared to hate him. Then she would have to quickly come up with some rent (and the rent was high for the tower duplex) to prove to William that she wasn't scamming him as well.

Hugo and William. Two painful interviews. And, of course, she would have to immediately get her cameraman out to Newton's house to shoot and rush the film back to Boston the next day, while writing the article overnight. And what a dreadful night that would be as she tried to think of what she could do to raise the money she needed to prove to Randy that the so-called sweetheart deal between herself and Hugo had been merely a figment of his imagination.

By the time she got back to Random Point Patricia was dry-eyed but still on the edge of tears whenever she thought of the ordeals she confronted. Choosing between the least of the evils before her, she went to see William first.

William, whom she found working at home, was astonished to learn that the publisher of Patricia's magazine was his old enemy Randy Price. He explained that he had been at odds with Randy since prep school. In recent years, Randy's unscrupulous business practices had led to the corruption of one of his most trusted employees, namely Damaris Perez Flagg.

"You mean Randy had dealings with Michael's ex-wife?" Patricia cried in astonishment.

"She was my secretary and I was very fond of her. But she had a drug problem at the time, and Randy tempted her to bring him information in exchange for payoffs. I asked Michael to help me trace the company leak and he, of course immediately discovered Damaris meeting Randy."

"So, Michael's ex-wife was bad. Really bad."

"She was bad," William smiled. "But she's been completely reformed for years."

"Michael is drawn to bad women," Patricia mused.

"Who isn't?"

"Well, what happened then?"

"Well, we were able to spoil Randy's last attempt on my company's job bids, to which he retaliated by seducing my wife."

"My friend Laura has had sex with Randy?" now Patricia was astonished.

"It's a soap opera, isn't it? At any rate, the next time Randy and I met, we commemorated the reunion with a fistfight. So you can see why he wasn't crazy about the idea of publicizing my lighthouse renovation in his magazine."

When Patricia intimated that she could lose her job over this, William was all concern, which charmed Patricia, who had a definite need to postpone paying the rent.

Hugo was far less compassionate as she tumbled the whole sordid mess out before him in his shop at closing time. Seeing she'd had a horrible day, he took her into his office and gave her a whiskey. She gulped it and gasped, then subsided on a leather sofa to await his reaction.

"So unless you get a check from me for the ad, Randy will know that you were lying and on the take."

"Yes," she replied and hung her head, then lifted it to promise, "But if you save me this once, I swear I'll pay you the money back immediately!"

"How do you propose to do that?"

"I'll sell my car."

"You mean the Mercedes is actually yours to sell?"

"Well, more or less. I can get some dealer to pick up the notes and still clear five grand."

"That sounds a bit drastic. Don't you know anyone who can cover you?"

"No."

Hugo couldn't resist lecturing her. "Don't you see Patricia that this has been coming a long time? Luxury is an addiction. You're living above your means. Take a lesson from Emma Bovary. You've very nearly come to ruin today."

"Yes, sir," she agreed.

"I want every stick of furniture returned to my shop."

"I thought you would," she sighed.

"But I don't expect you to sell your car," he told her.

"I can't think of any other way to raise that much money."

"Why don't you try to persuade me to pay for the ad?" he dared her, with a certain tone to his voice that suddenly introduced sex into the equation of Patricia's professional disgrace.

"Could I?" she looked at him with sudden hope.

"Yes. You could agree to be my slave every Sunday for a month."

"Your slave, Hugo? What does that entail?"

"Oh, I have lots of things for you to do. I have a stock room that needs cleaning. Letters and articles to enter for my next issue. A mailing to stuff. A little writing. That should work off about half the debt."

"What about the other half?"

"For the other half you will serve dinner to a select party as my well behaved parlor maid. Then you will be given to my most awesome male dominant guest for his private use. Need I add that you will be severely whipped? Accept my terms and I'll give you the check for the ad and call it a good bargain."

"I accept," Patricia said before thinking.

As it turned out, Patricia had ample time to fulfill Hugo's requirement of the payment of the debt and didn't have to wait until Sundays. As soon as she came in with the check and the spread, Randy Price, who considered Patricia's relations with William Random as consorting with the enemy, summarily fired her.

This was the second time she had driven back to Random Point from Boston with tears in her eyes. Now she was off the hook with Randy. He wasn't about to put a contract out on her because the ad had been duly paid for. And things were pretty square with her and Hugo ever since she had agreed to his terms of reimbursement.

The fact that Hugo Sands had a heart did not escape her, and she would be grateful to him for the rest of her days for not exposing her to Randy's vengeance. An ad in Cape Cod Style was not worth five thousand dollars. But he was taking it and paying for it anyway and that was why she owed him a forfeit.

William Random would wait a reasonable amount of time before throwing her out of the lighthouse since she would tell him she had lost her job as soon as she got back. Michael was bound to be completely unsympathetic, but at the very least, he'd feed her until she got another job or lined up free lance.

Michael was on the night shift for a few days and Patricia didn't bother to wake him with news like this. The next morning she awoke feeling wretchedly guilty and utterly at a loss as to what to do first.

What she really needed was a thrashing, she thought, while having her morning bath, just to take her mind off the reality of what had happened and expiate her guilt. Since she was in a funk and had no focus, Patricia dressed in jeans, a flannel shirt and work boots and went directly to Hugo to report for work.

Hugo was fairly astonished to see Patricia first thing on a Friday morning in his shop and dressed like this. He'd never seen her in any outfit other than a smart business suit or cocktail dress and was charmed.

"I didn't have to wait until Sunday. Where's the stock room?"

As Hugo led her to the back, she confessed to him all that had happened since he'd given her the check. Hugo had seen her dismissal coming and said nothing. Instead he explained to her that some of the pieces got polish, while others needed only a rub with a rag. The floor, wall hangings and suspended pieces had to be thoroughly dusted. He expected every inch of the place to be gone over. He left her supplies and told her he'd come and get her when it was time for lunch.

Patricia began by sweeping the floor and there was a lot of it. She pushed all of the furniture to one side of the room first, and then back again to get both sides properly swept. This took about an hour and Patricia was nearly done when Hugo came back with coffee and saw her pushing the last piece, an enormous credenza, back into place.

"Patricia, what the hell are you doing?"

"I had to move everything to sweep."

"Don't tell me you've been dragging all this stuff around the floor?"

She stared at him.

"You didn't tell me not to move things," she protested helplessly as he took her by the wrist, found a convenient seat and turned her over his knee with exasperation.

"These items are delicate," he told her, warming the seat of her jeans with the palm of his hand. "You could have damaged something."

A hard spanking on the seat of her jeans was enough to make her tingle and think of nothing but sex until lunch.

The following day Michael brought back the furniture from the lighthouse in Hugo's truck. The youthful detective was not happy about spending his day off moving furniture, nor was he pleased at any of the recent developments in his girlfriend's career. Hugo was quick to notice the coolness in Michael's demeanor as he carted in merchandise.

"What's with Michael?" Hugo found Patricia in the small flagstone garden behind the shop having a smoke.

"Oh, he isn't talking to me," Patricia admitted unhappily. Hugo sat down beside her on the stone bench. "He says that my profligate lifestyle has led me to the brink of disaster."

"I could have told you that."

"You did. But you said it with a great deal more civility," Patricia squeezed Hugo's hand.

"What else?"

"Oh, I got a pretty good lecture on a wide range of topics. For example, were you aware that influence peddling is a crime?"

"Is he upset with you for losing your job?"

"Yes," she hung her head.

"Don't worry, you'll get more freelance than you can handle. And in the meantime, you've got enough friends around here to see you through. The important thing is that you're with us."

"Hugo, what a nice thing to say!" Patricia felt a glow suffuse her entire body at his warmth. She hugged him briefly then ran back out front to help unload the rest of the furniture. Now she felt much better. Michael continued to glower, but she stopped noticing. Presently he finished the unloading and was about to walk home, when he decided to take Patricia aside and talk to her. They went back into the stock room.

"Patricia, I've been thinking," he said, making her heart strain for fear in her bosom. "Am I getting fired from the girlfriend job as well?" she wondered.

"Yes, Michael? What have you been thinking?"

"That you'd better give up the lighthouse and come live with me to save expenses."

At length she replied, "That's vastly obliging of you, but considering what a perfect brute you've been today, the idea of being thrown on your charity is somewhat less than appealing. Excuse me!" She stepped past him, picked up her rubbing rags and oil and attacked a hope chest zealously.

"You know Patricia, it was pride that brought you to this pass. Isn't it time you showed a little humility?"

Patricia merely continued to polish furniture.

"Anyway, I'm not offering you charity. Just move in now and share expenses when you're able to."

"I would move in with you as a last resort only," she reflected bluntly.

"I see. Well don't do me any favors," he fumed, ready to leave.

"Okay," she returned pleasantly.

Michael left in a black mood. He'd been worrying about her alone in the lighthouse with her mattress on the floor, but now he told himself he didn't give a damn. Fancy her calling him a brute when he hadn't even laid a finger on her. When he really should have gotten out his razor strop and tanned her backside for so stupidly losing her very good job. He decided to teach her a lesson by not calling her for at least a week, or as long as he could hold out.

Meanwhile, Patricia, who rather enjoyed her mattress on the floor with the full view of the stars above her, had made a similar resolve. Besides, she was much too busy doing the editorial work, which Hugo had given her to think about Michael. Happily, the few pieces of furniture she had brought with her still supported her computer system, and she was able to work undisturbed with the ocean before her.

The erotic material Hugo gave her to work on was a welcome change from dry, architectural writing and kept her in heat the entire week. As with the stock room reorganization, Patricia gave the editorial work her full attention and did an exemplary job for Hugo.

In the middle of the week, when she was halfway through her task, Anthony Newton stopped by and was shocked to note the absence of her furniture. He had walked in at about one in the afternoon on a chilly, rainy day, which called for the largest fire Patricia could build.

She had just finished transcribing a crude but effective spanking story and eagerly related the high points to Anthony, who found it impossible not to become infected with her enthusiasm immediately. Especially when Patricia confessed that she not only needed but also deserved to be chastised severely for losing her job. No one had yet taken the time to do this properly, and she felt quite amazed that such a momentous error could go unpunished, considering that she was all but surrounded by dominants.

Never one to shirk a responsibility, Anthony hastened to occupy one of her two remaining straight-backed chairs to administer a very sharp correction to Patricia, dwelling with particular warmth on the ramifications of losing one's job in today's economy. Patricia took as long and hard a spanking as he could give and afterwards thanked him for his trouble in characteristic style. Now she felt Michael's absence even less and returned to her work with renewed energy.

Once the editorial work was turned in Patricia began to plan the final phase of her payment to Hugo, which was the execution of the dinner party. A glance at the guest list was enough to convince Patricia that the hardest task was before her, for Hugo had assembled to observe and enjoy her humiliation: Laura Random, Anthony Newton, Susan Ross, Marguerite Alexander and finally, the mystery dominant, Victor Kesselring.

Laura understood that even though Hugo was thoroughly disenchanted with Victor, he was still determined to sell the sadistic Swiss collector that set of furniture he'd obtained for him and was now going to use Patricia as bait. Since Laura had jinxed the sale the first time, she warned Patricia about Victor with much less trepidation than she felt for her friend. But she discovered to her relief that Patricia cared nothing for the whipping, her main concern was in the degradation of having to wait on Marguerite and Susan, both of whom she considered rivals for Michael's affections.

Patricia went to Anthony and asked to borrow Dennis for the night to help her cook and serve at Hugo's party. This favor was readily granted and Dennis was sent the day before the dinner to assist Patricia in the marketing.

Determined to make this an occasion of personal achievement rather than shame, Patricia bought the Chez Panisse cookbook and set out to prepare the ultimate meal.

Victor had been surprised to receive the message from Hugo promising a special treat the next time he passed through Random Point and made it his first stop on returning to the states. When he was told, over his first drink upon arrival, of the slim blonde with the high pain tolerance who was working off a penance to Hugo, Victor almost smiled with anticipation.

Patricia looked completely delectable in her formal maid's outfit, black seamed stockings and high-heeled pumps. She met no one's eyes but kept her eye on every dish, every glass of wine and water, expertly assisted by Dennis at every turn.

The dishes were very well received. So much so that no one thought of anything other than doing honor to them one by one. Patricia watched from the doorway with tension. The guest of honor, Victor, seemed to be enjoying his meal. Dennis knew what wines to fetch from Hugo's cellar to complement each course.

Marguerite chatted gaily the whole time to Victor, pausing at the outset to look at Patricia and pronounce the word, "Charming," as she took in every dainty aspect of her costume and demeanor.

Susan stared at Patricia and blushed for her as she took away the dishes of the first course. Hugo had taken Susan and Laura aside before Victor's arrival and warned them about what they might see that evening.

"Now, I don't want any nonsense out of you two about Patricia," he warned them sternly. "She's doing this to pay off a large debt to me and she's fine with the whole thing. I know you two delight in obstructing justice, but tonight your intervention will not be necessary." He eyed both sisters with gravity.

"Yes, sir," said Susan. Hugo looked at Laura. "I won't interfere," Laura promised solemnly.

"And you, young lady," Hugo looked at Susan, "don't go falling in love with Patricia and offering to take her place or anything noble like that. As Laura can tell you, Victor is a martinet and Patricia is a lot better suited to his methods than either of you are."

"I won't say or do a thing," Susan swore meekly.

"So, what are we supposed to do, Hugo?" Laura ventured to ask.

"I know I'm asking the impossible, but just behave yourselves."

Between dessert and brandy Susan and Laura snuck out to the kitchen to congratulate Patricia on the splendid job Dennis and she had done.

"It was this darling boy," Patricia said candidly, locking her arms around the trim, aproned waist of the English boy and placing her fair head on his snowy collar. "He did 90% of the work."

Dennis reddened deeply but looked quite pleased at the affectionate praise from this beautiful, poised lady who was for some lark playing the role of servant girl that evening.

Susan smiled at Dennis too, but for that moment he was only aware of Patricia. Susan and Laura exchanged a look. Meanwhile Patricia downed a glass of wine and took a good look at Susan Ross, wondering whether she knew that Anthony had been her lover as recently as three days before. Patricia had hardly eaten all day and the wine hit her fast.

"So," she asked Susan, "why are you involved with all these older men?"

Susan was not expecting this type of address and looked at Laura in surprise.

"All?" said Susan.

"I mean Anthony and ... Michael."

Marguerite Alexander had entered the room in time to hear this last exchange and the statuesque redhead was less than pleased by it.

"Yes, Susan, do tell us why you must have so many of our men,"

Marguerite accepted a glass of wine from Patricia as she joined the group.

"Come to think of it," said Laura to her sister, "you have had them all!"

"Who else besides Michael and Anthony?" Patricia demanded.

"Well, my ex-husband William, our lawyer Sherman, and of course, our host, Hugo," Laura supplied the names while counting off fingers. "That's five that we know of."

"Tell you what, cutie," Patricia proposed flippantly, "Since you're only lacking one for six of the best, I'll let you have Victor for nothing."

"No thank you," said Susan, having received a complete description of Laura's night with Victor from her sister. Besides, even if she had known nothing at all about Victor, she didn't like the look of him and the way he never smiled.

Patricia had been having these exact thoughts all through the dinner, for although she seemed to look at no one, she had looked long and hard at Victor Kesselring and had taken an instant dislike to him.

"Here," Laura handed Patricia something to smoke. "You'd better get your head straight before you go up."

"But don't drink too much more," said Marguerite, removing the wine bottle from Patricia's reach, as she was already on glass two. "If he puts you in bondage you'll be in trouble if you're drunk."

"Oh, have you played with him too?" Patricia looked at Marguerite with interest. Although the stunning, bespectacled bookseller was Patricia's principal competitor, being near her like this Patricia felt somehow more excited than jealous, for a curious attraction had begun to operate on Patricia for Marguerite.

Certainly it was difficult for anyone who loved beauty to remove their eyes from the heavenly contours of Marguerite's body under the midnight blue crepe sheath, least of all Dennis who had been virtually paralyzed with adoration ever since Marguerite strode into the room on her 5" heels. Dennis had met Marguerite on several occasions over the years and her presence never failed to overwhelm him with the ardent desire to serve women forever.

"Victor can be a very difficult man to please," said Marguerite tactfully. "Are you sure you have to do this?"

"Honor demands it," said Patricia, touched by Marguerite's concern. "I was a very bad girl and ran up a big debt with Hugo. This is the last thing I have to do to pay it off."

"I wish you didn't have to," said Laura compassionately. "He's the most horrid man in the universe."

Patricia stared at her girlfriend with some alarm and would have eagerly continued the discussion of Victor with the three girls, but Anthony came to find them and bring them back.

"Victor's brought back some hardcore B&D videos from Europe and Hugo's going to put them on." Anthony announced, taking Susan out of the room.

"I'd better get back too," said Laura, kissing Patricia and squeezing her waist. "Just remember you can say mercy if it gets too rough."

"Marguerite, I'm getting scared. What should I do?" Patricia asked sincerely, smoking hard.

"Just seduce him as soon as you can," counseled the redhead wisely, embracing Patricia. "And by the way, you cinch magnificently." Then she too left.

Patricia told Dennis to go in with the cognac while she freshened up.

"Oh god," she said, falling into a chair, "my feet hurt already! I hope he doesn't put me in stand-up bondage."

Dennis hesitated to leave her at these riveting words, but forced himself to do so. When he returned an eternity later, he was thrilled to see her still sitting and smoking and drinking another glass of wine. He immediately got to his knees before her and begged to be allowed to massage her poor, tired feet for a few minutes. Patricia was happy to allow him this liberty and watched with interest as he tenderly removed her shoes and began to massage her stockinged feet, which were narrow and elegant.

Patricia began to experience bliss under the English boy's skillful manipulations and decided to reward him by pulling up her skirt to mid-thigh and allowing him to admire her black stocking tops, lace suspenders and the milky white thighs, which surmounted them.

Dennis grew dizzy with excitement at this mark of the lady's favor and blushed to the roots. Patricia was charmed and impulsively raised her skirt even higher to allow him a glimpse of her sheer black panties as he continued to massage her feet. It was at this interesting juncture that Hugo walked in. Patricia immediately pulled down her skirt and Dennis busied himself in fitting her back into her shoes.

"Patricia, why don't you join us?"

"Like this, Hugo? Or should I change?"

"What have you got on under there?" Hugo asked, virtually ignoring Dennis, who swiftly completed his task, then busied himself at the sink.

"Why, a very sexy corset, of course," replied the slightly intoxicated blonde, who had been immensely cheered by the attentions of Anthony's young driver.

"Show me," said Hugo, folding his arms and waiting. Patricia pertly unbuttoned her uniform and let it drop to the floor, revealing a perfect black satin waist cinch that gave her a shape out of Sweet Gwendolyn. "My god, Patricia, have you been laced that tightly all night?" he walked up to her, turned her around and saw that she had her laces pulled to the utmost extreme.

Now that he mentioned it, mused Patricia, her back had begun to ache and she felt a bit faint, but all of the discomfort had been worth it when she remembered how no one could take their eyes from her swaying, wasp-waisted torso as she'd served.

Hugo quickly unlaced and slightly loosened her stays, then retied the laces. "There! That should feel a little better."

Patricia took a slightly deeper breath than she had taken all evening and thanked him profusely. "You can go in like that."

Patricia entered the room where they all were. The lights had been dimmed and the focus was on the hard S&M video Victor had brought back from Germany. Hugo had told her that Victor's submissives were always required to kneel in his presence, and she acknowledged that on entering the room, the scene had begun. So she went to her allotted place and knelt, aware of everyone's eyes on her exposed, corseted figure. Victor was pleased by the extreme slenderness of her frame, so greatly enhanced by the fully boned cinch. A sheer bra and scrap of panties revealed as much as they concealed and everyone could see that Patricia's cherry nipples were erect.

For a few moments Patricia became absorbed by the events being portrayed on the screen. She had never seen European videos before and was shocked. Patricia did not like the movies and wished she were back in the kitchen with Dennis. In fact, she had pretty much decided that she wanted to marry Dennis someday when Victor suddenly stood up and told her to go upstairs and wait for him in the room Hugo had set aside for his use.

After Victor and Patricia had gone upstairs, Susan and Laura volunteered to help Dennis clean up in the kitchen while Marguerite, Anthony and Hugo stayed to watch the videos with decadent enjoyment.

"On your knees, girl," said Victor when he caught Patricia lounging in a chair in Hugo's splendid guest bedroom.

"Sorry, master," she replied without true repentance, getting into the required position. For her pertness she had her face promptly slapped. Although the blow wasn't hard enough to make her ears ring, it was more than a tap and the gesture brought tears to her eyes.

"Don't be flip with me," he told her, going into a cupboard for equipment and coming out with leather cuffs and a thin lashed flogger. Patricia held her hand to her cheek and stared resentfully at the floor. "And don't whimper," he told her, disdainfully taking her hand away from her face.

Victor sat on a chair beside her and asked for her wrists, which he quickly cuffed. Patricia deliberately held her wrists taut to give herself some escape room. If Victor noticed he made no comment. She would hold her place with or without the cuffs. The bondage was merely a symbol of his control.

He unceremoniously pulled her up to a standing position by the cuffs and from there to the edge of the big, richly covered bed, where he bent her over with her arms in front of her and her feet on the floor. Passing a rope through a loop in the wristlets, Victor pulled her arms taut and attached the end of the rope to a hook under the bedstead. Now she lay face down with her bottom thrust up over the edge of the bed. Going behind her, Victor roughly pulled her little panties down and off, separated her legs as far apart as they would go with a leg spreader bar and cuffed her ankles to it. Now she was bent over the bed with her bottom and pussy fully spread and exposed.

Victor took up the flogger and began to whip her bare bottom with slow, hard, deliberate strokes, stinging her with the lash tips each time. Patricia was prepared for the initial onslaught of whipping to be severe and refrained from screaming as best she could. But when she did not cry or sob, as he was used to girls doing, Victor increased the intensity of the whipping, swinging harder and faster and scoring her delicate skin with dark red lash marks each time his weapon descended to wrap her vulnerable hips.

"Mercy, master, that's too hard!" she cried, within moments of his beginning.

"Nonsense," he scowled, stopping momentarily to examine her already marked bottom and give it a slight rub.

"I swear it is!" she looked at him with trembling lips.

"Are you telling me how to discipline you?"

Patricia turned away from him and bit back the response that naturally sprang to her lips. He proceeded to whip her again, every bit as hard as before. She concentrated on submitting, trying to make sense of the pain by remembering how many errors she had committed to deserve this punishment.

She thought about what Randy might have done to her if Hugo hadn't bailed her out with the check and that helped for a second or two. But surely Hugo never meant for her to be beaten this violently.

"Master, please! I can't take it this hard!" she cried, turning her upper torso as much as she could to look at him. He paused to return her glance scornfully.

"I thought you'd agreed to submit to discipline tonight."

"Discipline yes, torture no!" she protested, still in shock from the white-hot pain of the whip on her bottom.

"Very well, if you can't take a proper whipping, we'll switch to something milder," he unbuckled his belt as he said this, drawing it out of his trouser loops, then doubling it and holding the buckle end in his hand. Patricia could only imagine his definition of the word mild, but subsided on the bed.

The moment he started to strap her Patricia realized that her disciplinarian was out of control. She remembered how much wine Dennis had poured for the guests during dinner and how the brandy had gone around twice in the den.

"Please sir, I beg for mercy!" she said again, after the first six strokes fell crosswise upon her well-whipped bottom. He seemed to be exerting the full strength of his arm and Patricia knew there was no need for this. Each stroke provoked a cry from her that was heard by all the company below.

Victor paused, as though to reward her with the mercy she sought. But the instant he saw the tension go from her shoulders, he treacherously stepped up behind her and gave her the end of the strap straight down the middle of her bottom, so that the very tip of it struck her spread sex. Now the scream that issued from Patricia was enough to cause the hair of everyone below to stand on end, especially that of Hugo's cat.

For Patricia it was all over. Without waiting to ask for permission she jerked her right wrist out of the leather cuff and then freed the other. Flipping over onto her back, with the leg spreader still attached to her ankles and a glare of bitter anger in her eyes, she trembled and sobbed her way into a sitting position and ripped off the ankle cuffs. Then she got to her feet, and dashing the tears from her eyes, first backhanded Victor across the face as hard as she could, then extended her hand for the strap.

"Give me that belt, you miserable coward," Patricia demanded, transfixing him with her gaze. He handed her the belt. "Take my position across the bed," she ordered, in a violent passion. "No! Pants down first, you despicable bully. I'm going to teach you a lesson you'll never forget!"

Victor got into position immediately, with a look of fascinated admiration on his cruel face that made Patricia angrier than before.

"How dare you strike me like that!" she asked and without waiting for an answer began to strap Victor's thighs and buttocks rapidly and with all of the strength in her arm. That the 46-year-old Genevan was toned and fairly well proportioned she noticed but hardly cared about. She didn't care how she aimed or what she hit either. Her only purpose was to hurt and humiliate him as much as he'd done her.

"You never strike a woman there, do you understand me, Victor?"

"Yes, Mistress," he moaned as the leather cut into his flesh.

"Spread your legs," she commanded and returned the favor he had done to her with the end of the belt. He could hardly remain stoic when she struck his balls like this, but the bedclothes in which he hid his face muffled his reaction.

Now she returned to his buttocks and legs and whipped him from his hipbones to his calves.

"I don't know or care how you treat your Eurotrash sluts, but you're in America now, and when you have the good fortune to be given a well-bred submissive to play with, you treat her with kid gloves! Do you understand me, you sad, pathetic excuse for a human being?" When she felt herself growing dizzy with the exertion she ordered him to get up.

"Unlace me. Now!" she snapped, turning her back on him with utter distain.

"Yes, Mistress," he replied, going to work with nimble fingers on her laces and finally freeing her from the corset. She meanwhile had undone the garters and was happy she had for once chosen modern, stay-up hose, for she had to lose the corset at once or faint.

Patricia did not let Victor know what a rapturous relief it was to be unlaced, but instead ordered him to hold her panties for her to step back into. Now garbed in her heels, sheer black hose, panties and bra, Patricia demanded the whip.

"Fold my corset properly and lay it on the dresser. Then I want you entirely naked with your arms around the bedpost. That shall serve as my whipping post and I shall whip you until exhaustion overtakes me!"

When Victor complied with these instructions, unable to refrain from drinking in every inch of her newly sprung dominant beauty with his eyes, she cuffed him to the bedpost and attached his ankles to the spreader bar in the same way he'd done to her. Then Patricia stuck her head out of the room and in a loud, clear voice called, "Someone send me Dennis!!!"

The three in the TV room, who were still watching B&D videos, did not hear Patricia's call, but the three in the kitchen did and Dennis looked at Laura and Susan for instructions.

"Go to Patricia if she wants you," Susan encouraged the handsome, blushing boy, who immediately ran up the stairs to the room where Patricia was. She met him in the hall and told him to go back downstairs and bring her the apron she had worn to serve dinner in and a tray of ice cubes.

"And when you come back, come directly in, my darling," Patricia told Dennis, briefly rumpling his neat brown hair. Dennis almost tumbled down the stairs to obey her strange commands, with the image of her remarkably beautiful body imprinted on his mind forever.

When he got back to the kitchen the girls were agog to hear what was going on. But Dennis couldn't stop to talk. He grabbed what she had asked for and ran back upstairs. Knocking discreetly at the door, then entering as he'd been bid, Dennis was completely unprepared for the sight meeting his gaze.

By now Victor had been blindfolded with his own handkerchief. Patricia stood by his side, holding the whip.

"Come in, Dennis. Oh, you brought the frilly apron. Good!" Patricia took the apron and tied it around Victor's waist, making a bow at the back. "I see you're shocked, young man. But never fear. You've only been brought up here for an object lesson. You see, our guest, Mr. K., is a very crude man. He entirely disrespects women and to prove it, he's abused three of the worthiest women you know."

Patricia allowed Dennis to watch in amazement as she flogged the aproned banker until his flesh was fully mottled purple, black and blue.

"And to think that he treated me so badly after we gave him such a wonderful dinner!" Patricia lamented, flashing Dennis an intimate smile. "Now that I think of it, Victor, you've yet to thank me for the beautiful dinner," Patricia said with some impatience.

"Thank you, Mistress!"

"Comes a bit late. But just to show I have no hard feelings for your neglect, I've decided to give you a special treat! Ices for dessert!" Patricia broke the ice cubes into a bowl and flashing the wondering Dennis a grin, approached her victim.

"I have an entire bowl of ice here, Victor," she slid a cube over the surface of his buttocks, "enough to cool your ardor for tormenting women who are your superiors." She then proceeded to insert the ice cubes into his rectum any which way she could. If her intent had been to arouse him, she might have supplied herself with some lubricant to ease the way and stopped at three or four. But her intent was to punish her persecutor, so she gave him the entire tray all at once while Dennis watched.

"That will be all, Dennis. Leave me alone with the ridiculous creature now."

Dennis was only too happy to be dismissed at the present moment, the situation becoming far too esoteric for an innocent instep worshipper like him.

Although the fact that Patricia had turned to him– Dennis– for assistance, in the very moment of her metamorphosis from submissive to dominant, was a delight to the sensitive boy.

As he went down to the kitchen Dennis reflected upon how much more exciting his life had become with the entrance of his mistress and her friends into his employer's life. Not that he ever imagined or expected to see anything like he'd seen tonight, a revelation he intended to share with no one.

"Hurt, Victor?" Patricia inquired, with a happy smile, as she swung a heavy wooden paddle against his bottom repeatedly. By now Victor was heavily marked and made distinctly uncomfortable by the ice she had forced into him. Patricia paused in the punishment to grab him by his very large, fully erect, uncut cock and squeeze it as though she were wringing out a sponge. "And to think I was actually prepared to let you put this in me!" she reflected with amazement. "I suppose that I should thank you for apprising me of your true nature before I made a fool of myself and treated you like a real man! Instead, I've made you my girl. Haven't I, darling?"

"Yes, Mistress."

"Haven't I taken you? And am I not still doing so?" Patricia took up the paddle again and whacked his bottom vigorously, until he moaned.

"Never have I been treated so roughly and rudely by a man in the scene," she continued to excoriate him, perspiring greatly with her exertions, yet still unsatisfied that he had sufficiently felt her wrath. "Do you find it enjoyable to frighten a woman out of her wits?"

"No, Ma'am," Victor lied.

"Answer honestly," she said, smacking him so hard that he made a deep, animal noise in response.

"Yes, Ma'am!" he croaked, his flesh now speckling.

"Your whipping is now concluded," she decided, throwing down the paddle and freeing his wrists. "Get down on your knees, take your cock in your hand and come for me. Yes, with your bottom still full."

Patricia gracefully disposed of her half nude body in an armchair and directed him to kneel at her feet and masturbate. She'd watched several mistresses do this while visiting the Vault with Michael and remembered the lesson well. This would not be a scene until Victor came and she had three more minutes of patience left. And so resting the tip of her shoe beneath his scrotum, she helped the process none too gently along.

"That's right, Victor. I'm not done hurting you yet," she murmured, leaning forward to twist his nipple as hard as she could. Now it was all up for Victor. Patricia lurched back in time to miss being sprayed with the sadomasochist's milky effusion.

"Good boy, Victor!" she congratulated him, "You finally managed to do something right!"

Patricia drove home with renewed energy and quite pleased with herself. But she also felt inexplicably excited and hoped that there would be a message from Michael when she got home. There was something better than that. Michael himself was awaiting her arrival, having fallen asleep in front of her fireside on a handsome chaise lounge that hadn't been there when she'd left that morning.

As Patricia walked into the room and Michael woke up, she noticed many charming pieces of furniture that hadn't been there before. And yet these were not the items Hugo had previously lent her, but different antique pieces from various periods, all complementary.

Michael looked at his watch and saw that it was midnight.

"I finished my shift and decided to come by and see if you were here. I guess I fell asleep."

She sat down beside him and felt the fabric of the couch with appreciation.

"Where did all this stuff come from?"

"Apparently Anthony had it sent down from his house."

"How amazingly nice of him!"

"Remarkably nice," Michael observed cynically, causing Patricia to blush but instead of replying, put her head on his shoulder.

"Would you be jealous if Anthony liked me?"

"Does he?"

"I'm sure he likes me more than the man who marked me so badly tonight," said Patricia, pulling up her skirt and her panties aside to show Michael her bottom, which was heavily bruised.

"Patricia, what in the world have you been up to?"

"I was paying off a debt of honor to Hugo which involved playing with a man who wasn't very considerate. But don't worry, I fixed him good. He looks worse than me." Patricia climbed into his lap and hugged him hard.

"And is the debt of honor paid?"

"As far as I'm concerned it is."

Suddenly Michael did not feel like cuddling her and put her off his lap.

"I hope you're proud of yourself," he scolded, "a woman like you reduced to accepting hard whippings from strangers to pay off her debts! And all of this stuff from Anthony. Let me guess how you paid for it. And what about the rental on the lighthouse? You can't possibly afford this place now that you're out of work. Or do you plan to fuck William into letting you stay for free? Patricia, what are you becoming?"

Patricia, who did not normally color at accusations, felt her face grow warm at this one.

"Michael, I've already been thoroughly punished tonight, so please don't add insult to injury," she said, with some heat.

"Oh, sweetheart," he sighed, pulling her back into his arms. "I'm sorry. That wasn't a nice thing to say; especially after all you've gone through tonight. But who was this person who marked you? I can't imagine anyone having to hit you so hard. Should I go and arrest him?"

"Yes! That would be outstanding!" She jumped up and down. "You could bust him on a technicality when he's leaving town tomorrow, then we could get him handcuffed and hog tied in your dankest cell and I could fuck him senseless with a Billy club!"

Michael raised an eyebrow at this, but soothed her with caresses.

"Actually, he would like that," she mused. Then she stretched out face down across his lap. "Oh Michael, won't you massage my bottom, please? It aches so! I heard it's better if you stimulate the circulation of blood to the injured area."

"I will but you realize I can't keep you in this position without spanking you a little, especially with you flaunting your infidelity the way you're doing."

"You can spank me a little. I want you to."

"I don't like the idea of you and Anthony Newton," Michael said, spanking her a little.

"You had his girlfriend. Why shouldn't he have yours?"

Michael said nothing as he stroked her bottom. Patricia wriggled and pressed against him. "I saw both your girlfriends tonight," Patricia told him, "Susan and Marguerite."

"Oh? They were there while you were being whipped?" Michael was still adjusting to her knowing about Susan.

"Not in the same room, but they knew what was going on. Marguerite had played with Victor before and gave me prudent advice before I went upstairs. She complimented me when I needed bolstering and never once took advantage of my humble position tonight as I cooked and served dinner as Hugo's maid. I really liked her!"

Michael could hardly believe that the most jealous woman he'd ever dated now seemed to admire Marguerite. Especially when Patricia admitted, "Michael, I was attracted to Marguerite. She and the other girls being there to witness my so-called shame was what made tonight fun."

Michael continued to pet her without comment, attempting to envision Patricia waiting table for Marguerite and Susan.

"I wish I'd been invited," he commented.

"For some reason Hugo spared me that, though I suspect it was only because we already had an even number of men."

"If you ever cook me dinner I promise not to whip you nearly as hard."

"On my newly reduced budget I expect to be cooking quite bit this winter," Patricia promised.

"That sounds like heaven," he told her, kissing her bruised bottom. Patricia wriggled at the ticklish attention and spread her smooth, slim thighs.

"Oh, Michael," she cried impulsively, "I've been so ill-used tonight! That bad man actually whipped my pussy!"

"Poor baby!" Michael examined the injured area with gentle fingers and concern."

"If only you would kiss it and make it better!" she cried boldly.

"Darling, I'd be happy to," he assured her, turning her over and sliding her up a little on the sofa before kneeling between her white thighs. Now he would prove to Patricia that he was anything but a brute and could indeed give her pleasure gently. Patricia let him cup her silky bottom in his hands and gave herself up to his tongue. "Poor, little, punished girl," he soothed her, before making her come in a very few minutes.

Hugo Sands called on Patricia the following afternoon, natty, immaculate and bearing ivory roses.

"Got some furniture, I see," he commented with a smile, recognizing pieces from Anthony Newton's house. "You are an enterprising girl!"

"Anthony is my friend," Patricia proudly announced, in the tone of a clever girl.

"I am too," Hugo said, handing her a check for a thousand dollars.

"For me? Why?"

"It's your commission on the sale to Victor. This morning he finally bought the suite of colonial furniture I've been trying to sell him forever."

"But, I said nothing to him about furniture last night," she regarded the check with disbelief.

"You put him in a buying mood."

"Do you often sell furniture like that?" she asked, folding up the check with a smile.

"Most of the time it's done more conventionally, but with Victor I take advantage of the fact that he's also in the scene."

"So, you're saying he had a good time last night?" Patricia grinned.

"Why? Does that surprise you?"

"Well, he was very hard to please," Patricia equivocated, unwilling to give Victor's secret away even though he did not deserve the courtesy of discretion.

"But you pleased him greatly and me too all this last week. You made your little blunder up to me with genius."

Patricia was shocked to realize that she was blushing and replied, "It was the least that I could do after you saved me from Randy."

"The least you could have done was much less than you did. I only hope that Victor didn't go too hard on you."

"Oh, I was able to call him to order after a while," Patricia smiled, for now her evening with Victor was but a strange memory. She had no desire to whip her own lover, but she was glad she had brutalized Victor.

After Hugo left her, Patricia sat down at her desk overlooking the cove and wrote a note in fountain pen on her monogrammed ecru paper.

Dear Marguerite,

I wanted to write and thank you for your kindness to me last night.

It never occurred to me when Hugo arranged for you to come to dinner, that your presence would lighten my ordeal.

The pleasant recollection of your elegant person and charming manners remains uppermost in my thoughts.

I hope that you will come and visit me soon. Let me know in advance and we'll get Dennis to come and serve us lunch.

> *Yours truly,*
> *Patricia*

Chapter Two

Carter's Plan

Carter Webster was impatient for Aurora Milne to stop moonlighting at The Keep. To the wildly imaginative scriptwriter, every aspect of his new lover's part time job was wrong, from the constant exposure to males off the street, to the danger of entrapment by undercover cops, to the insulting wages paid for the extraordinary services rendered by Aurora and her associates. And although it was true that his pocket Venus didn't sit around in her underwear, she did run around the club in a corset, which was almost as bad.

On the Tuesday following their first sexual encounter, morbid interest drew him once more to the discreet B&D establishment nestled on a shabbily respectable tree-lined side street of old Hollywood. He hadn't seen her since Sunday, though they had managed an awkward telephone conversation. He arrived just in time to see Aurora lead a gentleman upstairs for a session, and then trip down the stairs a half hour later with a pink bottom clearly visible to all beneath the hem of her blue brocade corset.

"Carter! What are you doing here?" she pulled him off to an alcove where they sat on a love seat together. She looked flushed, happy and surprised to see him.

"I was going to ask you the same thing," he replied stiffly.

"But you know I work on Tuesdays," she said softly.

"I told you how I feel about you working here."

"Carter, I don't know you well enough to let you decide where I work," she said calmly.

"Fine," he said without concealing his disappointment. "Do as you please."

A moment of uncomfortable silence ensued and Aurora was about to rise when he handed her some money and told her with determination to book an hour in Bishop. She took it away uneasily, in dread of a harsh scene.

A few minutes later she led him upstairs and presently they found themselves alone in the best-equipped dungeon in the house, hung with art by Bishop. Carter removed his jacket and hung it on a peg. Then he turned to see Aurora looking so frightened that it gave him a start.

"What's wrong?"

"Scared," she murmured.

"Of me?" He didn't know whether to be flattered or irritated. "Come over here," he took her in his arms. "I thought we had a nice time on Sunday. I didn't even spank you."

"But..."

"But what?" He made her sit beside him on the bondage bed.

"I just can't get that horrible scene in Hard Time out of my head," she declared, referring to one of the popular films he had scripted.

"What scene?"

"The one where the gangster whips his girlfriend with a coat hanger."

"Damn it, Aurora, the coat hanger whipping is practically a convention when you're writing about prostitutes and pimps. I certainly didn't originate it," he hastened to point out.

"And then there was that other scene in Lipstick and Mascara, where the kidnappers cut off the girl's finger and sent it to her brother in a box!"

"Sweetheart, do you have the slightest idea of how many kidnappings have involved fingers in boxes over the ages? It's almost a dramatic tradition. Even Shakespeare made use of mutilation to titillate his audience. Remember Titus Andronicus? Now, does that mean Shakespeare was personally into cuttings?"

Aurora bowed her head. "I stand corrected," she said.

"Good. Because I'll become quite exasperated if I have to explain to you one more time that I'm not a sadist."

"I never meant to offend you," she said with lowered eyes. Carter relaxed when he saw that reason had penetrated her prejudice.

"Why don't you instruct me on the use of the equipment in here?" he suggested, dismissing the previous subject.

"Well, this piece we're sitting on is called a bondage bed. It's padded and upholstered in leather, so it's pretty comfortable to lie on. It has d-rings on the sides placed at strategic points to attach cuffs or ropes. There are many different ways a girl can be bound to this piece of equipment. Or, it can be used as a simple spanking bench," Aurora explained with rising color, wondering whether she had offended him by attacking his art.

"How many different ways have you been tied to this bench?" he teased her.

"Five or six, at least."

"Show me the positions."

This request did not make Aurora altogether comfortable, but she complied and demonstrated the arms over head position, the spread-eagle, both face down and flat on her back, the all-fours, the knee to elbow and the classic hogtie.

"And what have you had done to you in some of these positions?" he demanded, when she stood up again.

"Cropping, whipping, tickling, teasing, hot wax..." she trailed off, unable to meet his unreadable gaze.

"No fucking? Not even in the all-fours position?" It was hard to decide from his insinuating tone whether he was amused or annoyed by his darling's accessibility to all who entered the club to purchase her time and take liberties with her young body.

"Carter, I told you that isn't allowed. Only pure B&D is permitted."

Carter sat down on the bondage bench and looked up at her. "Pure B&D, huh?" He took her little hand and gently drew her down his down across his lap. "You're either lying or kidding yourself and I don't think you have it in you to lie." Resting his hand on her bare bottom he asked, "When was the last time you let someone masturbate you in this room? Tell the truth."

"I can't remember," she replied, greatly embarrassed.

"Last week?"

"No."

"Last month?" he patted her bottom smartly, causing a flutter in her tummy.

"The week before last," she admitted, remembering that this was the dungeon in which she had first knelt before Victor Kesselring.

"Is that pure B&D, Aurora?"

"No, sir," she replied, her heart pounding faster.

"Well? What should I think about that?"

Carter sounded like her conscience and Aurora felt ashamed.

"I hope that you won't think too badly of me for being so weak," she appealed to him over one shoulder. Carter didn't answer but instead reached for a hairbrush which had been left on the table and, gripping her firmly by her trim, corseted waist, applied the solid oval wooden back to her bare cheeks a brisk dozen times. Aurora gave a little cry of shock each time the brush fell and whimpered in a gratifying manner afterwards. He then put her on her feet.

"That was for being such a little hypocrite! Now tell me about the X-frame," he said, surprising her by naming this fixture correctly. Aurora, blushing profusely and rubbing her bottom charmingly, stammered out an explanation about the fittings of the X-frame and demonstrated how it sat atop a wheel, which could spin a full 360 degrees, sending the fettered (and often hooded) passenger into a controlled orbit.

Since neither of them cared to try the X-frame, Aurora proceeded to the whipping post, the uses of which she described in eloquent detail. She demonstrated her favorite position of being lashed to the whipping post and encouraged him to take up a short flogger and feather her creamy white shoulders and back.

Carter had never used a whip before but he had watched Mistress Hildegarde artfully flagellate several of the other submissives the previous week and now imitated her subtle style of beginning with dozens of light, circular, fanning strokes to produce a briskly massaging effect with the multi-lashed whip.

Aurora closed her eyes and hugged the whipping post, feeling herself once more a captive on her favorite pirate ship.

"I've done worse things in this dungeon," she admitted to provoke him. She wanted a good flogging now that she was well warmed up.

"Did you say something, girl?"

"I said I've done much worse things in this room than permitting men to merely touch me."

"Oh?"

"Yes, sir," she said gravely, remembering the many liberties she had allowed Victor and one or two others.

"Tell me about every wicked thing you've ever done in this room."

When Aurora failed to respond he lashed her firmly across her bottom with the flogger.

"Did you hear me, young lady?"

"Yes. But, it's hard to know where to begin," she replied, hiding her smile at her own daring. Now that she was beginning to trust him, she felt as though she could be a little pert.

This answer earned her another smart stroke. A garland of pink lash marks momentarily decorated her voluptuous bottom, which was already suffused with a glow.

"Oh!" cried Aurora.

"Don't be insolent."

"I'm sorry."

"Tell me what's been done to you in this room."

"I've been... given head," she softly revealed.

"You let a client give you head?"

"Yes, sir."

"That seems very wicked to me, considering the strict prohibitions Mistress Hildegarde has put on such behavior in her house," Carter observed.

"It was wicked."

"Perhaps I should get Hildegarde up here and let her punish you herself for misbehaving like that."

This suggestion did not surprise Aurora, who did many double sessions with her best friend, the youthful mistress of the house.

"Oh, yes!" she encouraged this plan.

"Very well, then," he said, taking her down from the whipping post. "Go and get her."

Aurora hesitated slightly.

"Well?" he asked impatiently.

"I'll need a bit more allowance to fetch my mistress," she explained with some embarrassment. Carter pulled out some more money and dispatched her.

A minute later Aurora returned with Hildegarde, a tall, green-eyed, brunette, about 25 years old, in a lilac velvet Victorian evening gown, which exposed her white shoulders and deep bosom to perfection. Hildegarde was thrilled that Carter Webster had requested her company for the remainder of his session with Aurora, for she was both sensible of her guest's importance and susceptible to his personal charm.

The spanking horse was selected as the next piece of equipment and Mistress Hildegarde tied Aurora down over this trestle bench in seconds with a single piece of rope to bind her wrists and another to fasten her ankles. Then the mistress took up a stout wooden paddle and asked, in a seductive, dulcet tone, how her darling had given offense.

"I thought you should know that she's been breaking your house rules," Carter reported, taking a seat.

"Is this true, Belinda?" Hildegarde addressed her by her scene name.

"Yes, ma'am."

Carter sat back with some contentment and watched Hildegarde paddle Aurora. It was evident in the body language of the two young women that the submission of the one to the other was lovingly given and received. They looked quite romantic in their complimentary Victorian attire, with their tiny waists so becomingly corseted and their swelling hips so womanly.

As Hildegarde bent to administer the paddling, Carter could at least admire her round, velvet bottom, if not covet it. Aurora had told him that Hildegarde was strictly dominant and since Carter had no plans to go submissive, he forced himself to refrain from fantasizing about taking the soft and sensual mistress, deciding instead that they would be friends.

"Belinda, haven't you been liberally warned about spoiling the clients?" Hildegarde demanded.

"Yes, Ma'am."

"Then why do you persist?"

"For a variety of reasons."

"Such as? And hurry up, we're not patient!" Hildegarde whacked Aurora firmly with the paddle on either cheek.

"Sometimes I'm just curious," Aurora admitted.

"Such curiosity is both undignified and dangerous," Hildegarde scolded, smacking her hard two more times. "What else tempts you to break my rules?"

"I like to please people," the blonde girl replied.

"Except me," Carter couldn't resist adding, causing Aurora to blush with confusion.

Aurora didn't speak again until the paddle had connected with her now quite tender flesh many times.

"Please forgive me, Mistress!" she finally cried, coming to her limit for paddling. Hildegarde spanked and wielded a paddle harder than most men that she knew.

"Forgiveness may soon be forthcoming, but you must first confess all of your sins," Hildegarde paused to stroke Aurora's punished bottom. "Now what have you left out that may require an even more severe correction?"

"I've smothered a man with my bottom," Aurora admitted.

Carter raised his eyebrows and Hildegarde said, "That was naughty." Now the paddle fell many times across Aurora's prettily upturned bottom. Each time it connected she gave a little yelp, for she had already taken a good deal of spanking for one night.

"If she does that, I'll bet she does even worse things," Carter suggested.

"Have you done worse things?" Hildegarde exchanged her paddle for a square tipped riding crop.

"Yes, ma'am."

"You'd better tell me all at once," said her mistress, tapping the crop lightly against her bottom in the crosswise manner, as though it were a cane.

"I allowed Martin Ivan to insert vibrating eggs into me," Aurora confessed sensationally.

Hildegarde sighed with disappointment. Then she quite

deliberately spread Aurora's bottom and used the square spanker on the end of the crop to punish the offending areas.

"I didn't mean to be bad!" Aurora protested.

"You broke the rules," Hildegarde reminded her, finishing off the spanking with her very firm hand. Then she kept Aurora in this position for some time, spreading and teasing her and threatening to demonstrate to Carter how the vibrating eggs worked. With all the whipping and caressing and exhibiting and discussing of her naughtiness, it wasn't long before Aurora succumbed to an embarrassing climax under the hand of her mistress and the eyes of her lover.

Afterwards Aurora did not know how to comport herself. Hildegarde settled her confusion by dismissing her to go and change into her street clothes. For the mistress knew that Carter would want to take the young lady home directly.

"She's lovely, isn't she?" Hildegarde remarked fondly to Carter while setting the dungeon to rights.

"Yes. I'm crazy about her."

"I guessed."

"I hope you won't hold it against me, but I'm trying to get her to quit working here."

"Don't be silly, Carter. I want much better things for my best friend than working in a dungeon. But perhaps she doesn't understand how serious your interest in her is."

"Tell her."

"I'll be happy to. But actions speak louder than words."

"I'm sorry?"

"I don't know whether you're aware of it or not, Mr. Webster, but our young lady rides the bus to work."

As Carter drove Aurora home a short time later he remembered Hildegarde's parting remark.

"You're pretty impoverished, aren't you?" he demanded, making Aurora jump.

"No," she retorted with surprise. "I make good money."

"What do you make?"

"I do okay," she insisted.

Carter flashed her a skeptical look. Then suddenly they were home.

Carter liked to keep his house cold, which reminded her of Victor and the dungeon.

"What?" he asked, catching her smile.

"It's cold in here," she boldly said.

"Okay, don't get excited." He switched on the heat and started a fire. Aurora relaxed.

"Hildegarde thinks I should get you a car."

"Oh no! How impertinent of her!" Aurora was deeply shocked and embarrassed.

"Not at all."

"Carter, you hardly know me."

"That's ridiculous. I've spanked you, fucked you and we've discussed Diderot. And tonight I even watched your best girlfriend make you come. How much better do I have to know you before I get to care about your safety?"

Aurora flushed like a peach and turned her back on him in embarrassment.

"Aurora, stop being so damned humble or I really will thrash you," he threatened, sitting next to her by the fireside and taking her in his arms.

The next morning Carter stopped her from calling a cab and instead handed her the keys to his second car, an expensive new sports utility vehicle. He explained that he didn't want her riding the bus and warned her not to argue with him at the exact moment he was threading his belt through his trouser loops. Aurora flushed with pleasure and took the new car to work.

They began seeing each other and he began to spoil her. Within a few weeks her house was adorned, her closet filled and her outstanding bills paid. In short, he became her patron. Enchanted by these marks of favor, Aurora began to hope that she might soon quit her job at the law firm in order to resume her studies at UCLA and write her masters thesis while continuing to play at B&D in her spare time. But she didn't mention this self indulgent plan to Carter, for she was still uncertain as to whether she was a fad to him or the love of his life, as he now claimed.

When they talked about literature, she was convinced that love could exist between them, because Carter had been missing this sort of stimulation. But when she considered the films which he had authored, with their lean, inarticulate, trailer park goddess heroines, whose most meaningful relationships were invariably with their guns, she doubted that her own quiet academic appeal could sustain the sensational writer's interest.

There was one such a girl at the club. Her name was Mayo and she was a character straight out of a Carter Webster film. She was only 19, with short, bleached blonde hair and a full lipped, pouty mouth. Mayo was a tall, slim, Hollywood wild child, with a cracked, raspy voice from chain smoking and speed, and big, blue eyes. She took whippings, light bondage, and liked to stomp (not walk) on men. Mayo had an affinity for displaying her astonishingly beautiful body in fetish apparel but was indifferent to everyone at the club except Mistress Hildegarde, whom she would have killed for. Fortunately, Hildegarde was not bloodthirsty and generally used diplomacy in her dealings with the world.

Blind to her faults and charmed by her stunning street Amazon, Hildegarde tried to bring Mayo into as many double sessions as possible. They did look very well together and Hildegarde enjoyed whipping Mayo to the degree that it was a sex act. It was under these circumstances that Carter first met Mayo.

Carter had decided that rather than overtly pressuring Aurora to quit working at the club, which he was still intent upon her doing, he would try to find some subtler means of influencing her decision. But the simple idea of making her jealous did not occur to him until the aftermath of the first session he did with Hildegarde and Mayo. For when Aurora found out that Mayo had been one of the submissives Carter had seen the previous week, she reacted with a vehemence he had not thought her capable of.

"I don't think you should do any more sessions with Mayo, Carter," said she, a few nights later at the most expensive restaurant she had ever dined in. They sat in a private booth, with a glamorous view of the Pacific, but the thought of her beautiful man being exposed to Mayo ruined Aurora's enjoyment of the luxurious vista stretching out to sea.

"You what?" he affected astonishment but was inwardly gratified to have finally struck a nerve with this intriguingly calm young lady.

"Forgive me, Carter, but you don't know what she's like."

"I know all about her. I've been tape-recording her life story. It should take another 90-minute cassette to complete. We're up to juvie hall."

Aurora saw that he wasn't taking her seriously and immediately dropped the subject. But he brought it up again over dessert.

"Don't you think it was a bit presumptuous of you to tell me whom I can and can't play with?"

Aurora stared at him with wide eyes, astonished at her own temerity.

"I think we're going to have to have a little talk about that before bedtime, young lady," he mildly warned her, causing the most radiant of blushes to suffuse her face.

He worked for a few hours at his computer while she sat by the fireside and wondered whether he would remember to punish her before bed. He looked at her from time to time in such a way as to make her tummy clench. At last he stood and stretched and told her to get to bed.

She scampered into the bedroom and exchanged her street clothes for a sheer cotton nightgown, which he had bought her on their first shopping trip in Beverly Hills.

Carter made her lie face down across his bed for her strapping. Aurora was to learn that Carter was not one to overdo a scene. It was a dozen of the best with the strap and then she was free. Free to re-live the short, poignant licking all the while they made love, with the sharp sting of it to remind her of his control.

By this time Aurora was very much in love with Carter. She had never before had a lover in the scene and their mutual interest colored every encounter. She was much too shy to articulate her feelings to him face to face, but after the strapping she wrote him a letter, confessing all of her feelings in circumspect language. This joined her other letter in a green leather box, which Carter kept on his desk. The box would soon hold many emblems from Aurora.

And yet this was a letter which she deeply regretted sending when she returned to the club a few days later and discovered that he had been back in the interim to see Mayo again and finish the interview. Aurora felt her face burn with indignation while she was forced to listen to the crude but striking Mayo boast about the time she had spent with Carter.

They were perched on stools in front of the dressing room mirror and Hildegarde was giving Mayo a shoulder massage.

"He's like the coolest man in the world," Mayo exclaimed, having fetished Carter Webster's movies for years. Mayo normally resented men unless they brought her drugs, but Carter was different. It seemed to Mayo that he wrote her into every film he authored. He also tipped well.

"I was fuckin' honored to have that man whip me," Mayo intoned.

"He whipped you?" Aurora asked, in spite of her resolve to remain indifferent, as a painful twinge of jealousy fluttered her heart.

"Fuckin' A!" Mayo smiled at her mistress in the mirror. Whipping was the one disciplinary act that Mayo could actually respond to if it was from a sexy woman or a man who tipped well or brought good drugs.

"How was he?" Aurora asked.

"He was fuckin' great," Mayo condescended to declare.

Hildegarde was surprised to observe Aurora lay her lipstick down and stare into space. After Mayo lit a cigarette and flounced out, Hildegarde put her arms around Aurora from behind and pressed her lips to Aurora's throat.

"You couldn't possibly be worried," Hildegarde whispered.

"She's just his type, you know," said Aurora bleakly.

"No, honey," Hildegarde reassured her affectionately, "You're his type."

When Hildegarde and Aurora joined Mayo in the sitting room, the tall, corseted blonde was still pondering the phenomenon of Carter

Webster visiting their world.

"Do you think he'll come again? Carter Webster?" Mayo addressed herself to Hildegarde, for she made it a rule to ignore Aurora.

"Oh, I'm sure we can look forward to having Mr. Webster for a visitor as long as Belinda works here," said Hildegarde with a smile.

"Belinda?" Mayo stared at Aurora in astonishment. "You've played with Carter?"

"Darling," Hildegarde corrected Mayo gently, "Belinda brought Carter to us. He's her boyfriend."

Aurora didn't bother to be insulted by the look of utter incredulity with which Mayo received this statement, but instead went to answer the doorbell. The visitor proved to be Carter and Aurora blushed. He greeted her with a light embrace and a pleasant smile, then went directly to Hildegarde and Mayo to show them some photos he'd taken of them the last time he'd visited. Aurora sat down and tried to ignore them.

Hildegarde and Mayo were effusive about the color prints and Aurora was forced to admire every shot. The sight of Mayo's long, sleek, exposed thigh line depressed Aurora and she eagerly jumped for the phone every time it rang.

Presently Hildegarde, Mayo and Carter went up into a dungeon together while Aurora remained below to man the phones and greet new visitors. A few other girls finished their sessions and joined her. Gentlemen arrived and went upstairs with other girls. Aurora was forced to accept a tiresome tickling session, which was a torment to her preoccupied mind. Nor was she reassured to discover, on emerging from her session, that although Hildegarde had returned to the parlor, Carter and Mayo were still upstairs playing.

Dragging Hildegarde into the dressing room, Aurora poured her anxieties onto her friend's snowy bosom.

"He's just whipping her," Hildegarde calmed her friend.

"I can't take much more of this," Aurora claimed, getting into her street clothes with shaky hands. The tickling session had exhausted her and the thought of Carter whipping (her next favorite thing, after spanking!) a beautiful rival three years her junior and five inches taller than herself, made her want to go home and cry herself to sleep.

Yet when she remembered that instead of calling a cab she could drive home in the car he had given her, to the house he had freshly refurbished for her, with all her bills paid and many beautiful new corsets on order for her, she realized that she had become a spoiled brat overnight.

Was she the same young lady who had shivered in a dungeon at Victor's feet less than a month ago, ready to accept any order from a selfish, careless master?

If Carter chose to amuse himself with the likes of Mayo, it ought to be beneath her notice. Or she should rejoice in the added revenue his visits brought her friend, Mistress Hildegarde. As for Mayo, what did it matter if she chose to delude herself into thinking Carter liked her? The truth was that in spite of her startling beauty, Mayo was a not particularly original urchin, who would quickly bore the writer.

While these sensible observations soothed her troubled mind, they could not altogether eradicate the pang, which stabbed through her heart when Carter extended his private session with Mayo to an hour.

Aurora really did cry herself to sleep in the big easy chair by her bed. The next thing she knew, he was at her front door. She looked up at the clock and saw that he had come directly there after finishing his session.

"Why did you leave?" he marched into her house.

"Because I found it very upsetting to think about you upstairs playing with that awful girl."

"She's not awful. She's just a poor kid who didn't have the benefit of a good upbringing."

"Oh?"

"I should think you'd feel more compassion for her. She's had a rough life and things aren't so great for her right now either."

"That's just because she's a drug addict," Aurora said coolly.

"Damn it, quit being so self-righteous. While you were studying romantic poetry by rushing streams in Berkeley, Mayo was a 15-year-old hooker on the streets of Houston. Do you have any idea of what that must have been like?"

Aurora felt a lump prick her throat as the scolding continued, with Carter passionately recounting the trials of Mayo's sad, young life.

"You sound as though you're falling in love with Mayo," Aurora commented, as he paused for breath. "Perhaps you should have these back," she handed him the car keys. "Mayo doesn't have a car either."

Carter did not look pleased by her assumptions and proved it by taking her by the earlobe, pulling her over to the oaken chair, which graced the most perfect corner of her bedroom, and turning her over his knee.

"Me in love with Mayo, huh?" Carter smacked her full, round bottom through her ivory satin nightgown. "Did you say that to deliberately provoke me?"

"Well, you seem to enjoy whipping her!" she replied with spirit, though gravely humiliated by the indignity of being taken by the ear.

"How unworthy of you, to be jealous of Mayo," Carter scolded, spanking her vigorously with the palm of his hand.

"Why shouldn't I be? She's tall, lithe, ever so beautiful and still in her teens."

"Aurora, get me your hairbrush," he said sternly, pushing her off his lap. She stared at him with wide eyes, rubbing her bottom through her gown. "Now."

She brought him back the big, oval backed wooden hairbrush and allowed him to pull her back across his lap.

"I suppose you aren't beautiful?" he asked, baring her round, nicely pinkened bottom.

"I'm... acceptable," she replied judiciously.

"No, you're beautiful," he told her firmly. He slapped her bare bottom with the hairbrush numerous times, until it was flushed dark pink all over.

"Imagine my little Aurora jealous! That must mean you like me."

While she carefully framed her reply he continued to apply the back of the brush to her ample bottom.

"I like you!"

"Is that why you're jealous of Mayo?"

"I'm not jealous of her. I just don't trust her."

"Why? What do you suppose she's capable of doing?"

"Well, now that I realize how much she worships you, I suppose the worst she'd be likely to do is O.D. on your doorstep."

"Cynicism is not a becoming trait in a young lady," Carter told her and once again began to spank her hard with the hairbrush. The spanking had become painful, but such waves of sensation washed through her every time the brush fell that Aurora hardly minded.

"I'm sorry, Carter," she said at last, feeling the soreness begin to deeply penetrate into her muscles.

"Are you?" he laid aside the brush and pulled her up.

"Yes. And thank you for taking the time to correct me."

He didn't smile because she looked at him so seriously.

"You need a lot of correcting," he warned her, brushing her hair off her shoulders and kissing them.

"Carter, you were right about the club. It's no place for me and I won't be going back."

"Really?" The thrill of achieving a carefully planned victory exhilarated him. He pulled her down to sit on his lap and locked his arms around her waist. "And you've decided all on your own? I'm not forcing you?"

"Carter, am I right in supposing that if I leave the club you will refrain from returning there to play with Mayo?"

"You are a hundred percent right," he returned honestly.

"Then I will leave the club. There are bad elements there to which neither of us should be exposed."

"That's what I tried to tell you in the first place!" he cried.

"Well, you're smarter than I am," she admitted, enjoying the feel of his cashmere lapel against her cheek.

"You're plenty smart," he told her, patting her bottom as she snuggled on his lap. "You just don't have any common sense."

Aurora sat up and looked slightly offended.

"Well?" he demanded. "It's true isn't it? Think about the way you act. Hanging around unsavory places like the club. Traveling across county with total strangers who treat you like --" he stopped himself, realizing he was repeating information he had not heard directly from Aurora but secondhand through Susan and Laura. Aurora hung her head.

"I have made several mistakes," she admitted.

"Except if you didn't make that last mistake I would never have met you," he pondered. "I wonder what that means."

"Maybe it means that common sense is a fraud," suggested Aurora.

"Possibly just that once, but not from now on," Carter firmly declared.

"But Carter, what happens now? The Keep was my one interesting job. I can't just work at the law firm."

"What would you like to do?"

"Go to UCLA for my masters."

"Why don't you do just that and I'll take care of everything else."

"I can quit the law firm?" she bounced on his lap joyfully.

"Tomorrow if you like."

"And you'll take care of me?"

"I'll take care of you."

Aurora was overwhelmed.

"Carter, are you sure you want to invest this much money in my education?"

"Aurora, do you realize how relaxing it is for me to be with a girl who doesn't want me to get her a part? Besides, you're good for me. You've revived my interest in literature and I enjoy talking to you. I don't even have the desire to swear around you."

Aurora smiled, remembering Mayo's aggressively limited vocabulary.

"Thank you for that," Aurora answered fondly, "I couldn't have endured for you to talk the way the people do in your movies."

"But strangely, I can endure the thought of you kneeling naked in a dungeon," he teased her to a blush.

"I suppose I do have a dreadful double standard," Aurora realized thoughtfully. "My aversion to vulgarity seems incongruous, juxtaposed against my sexual availability."

"It's all right," he reassured her, patting her bottom. "A well bred girl seeking thrills in the underground is classic film noir. I will fulfill the role of the hard boiled dick who sets you straight."

"Carter?"

"Yes, dear?"

"If I'm to be your protégée, you must give me my rules for conduct," she told him seriously.

Carter was amused and replied, "Oh, you'll find out what they are when you break them."

It was Christmas week in Los Angeles when Carter came home one afternoon to find Susan Ross and Diana Stratton, the two brats he had met at the home of Anthony Newton in Random Point, having tea on his own sun bleached garden terrace, with Aurora once again serving.

Both Susan and Diana jumped to their feet, their faces flushed with pleasure and interest at Carter's entrance. Carter was about to kiss them in typical California style, but Susan initiated a handshaking ceremony instead. Then they all sat down to momentarily admire the green canyon wilderness, which canopied the swimming pool and terraced gardens.

"Well, I never thought I'd see you two troublemakers again," he remarked, a good deal more at ease with them on his home turf after three months of enjoying Aurora's company, than he had been as a spellbound beginner in the scene back in the early autumn when they had first met.

"And yet, Aurora's been writing to us all along," Susan explained, thrilled at the way Aurora's fortunes had changed since her sister Laura rescued her from an unwholesome master and brought her into their scene.

"I didn't know that," Carter observed, happy to see Aurora blush for keeping this important friendship a secret.

"We're having our winter vacation," Diana said, "so we decided to come out to Hollywood and check out the Scene."

Susan kicked Diana under the table and Carter noticed.

"Oh? And in what way?"

"Oh, you know, the clubs," Diana said hastily.

"What kind of clubs?"

"I don't know, Carter, you tell us," Diana returned innocently, realizing that Susan did not want her to mention anything more of their plans. "But, more importantly, do you have anything at all that we can smoke?"

This achieved the desired result of sending Carter momentarily into the house.

"Don't say a word to Carter about going to meet Mistress Hildegarde," Susan exhorted Diana.

"Why not?"

"Because he might tell Anthony."

"Carter noticed that you kicked me."

"I know," said Susan, "it's going to be hard to fool him for very long. I thought he'd be in meetings the whole time we were here, but instead, he seems disposed to notice us."

"How could he not notice us after the way we changed his life forever?" Diana pointed out haughtily.

"You girls aren't really going to work at The Keep all week?" Aurora demanded, thinking the idea both exciting and dangerous. Exciting because of the sensation the little blonde and brunette tag team would cause for that one glowing week, but dangerous because of the alarm it would give their dear loved ones back east when they found out about the girls' antics. And if Carter learned of their plan, he would surely betray them to Anthony at once.

Carter's return with the requested provisions precluded further discussion of Susan and Diana's plans.

"You're staying here with us, I hope?" he asked, looking at Aurora questioningly. She, of course, hadn't dared to invite anyone to stay at his house without permission.

"We're at a hotel at the moment," said Diana, "but we'd love to stay here."

"Yes, then you could keep an eye on us," said Susan, spreading marmalade on toast. She knew that Diana was looking forward to playing with Aurora again and she herself was not opposed to feeling the weight of Carter's hand on her own pert bottom.

The intoxications of an 85-degree day in the middle of winter were not lost on Susan Ross. Perhaps they would only play in a dungeon for two or three days, and spend the rest of the time at the beach. The point was that they were in California, spanking capitol of the country, they had ten days, and their host was a good looking young millionaire whose lover was a refined beauty they had all but given him.

"We want to go to Trashy Lingerie," said Susan, "and get fitted for Victorian corsets."

"And then we want to go to Dream Dresser for latex and leather," said Diana decisively.

Leather, latex and corsets, Carter mused. It almost sounded as though they were building a working wardrobe.

Susan and Diana spent two days assembling their kit. Then they spent the better part of an afternoon attempting to persuade Aurora to personally take them to The Keep and introduce them to the mistress.

"But Carter has asked me never to go back there, and I've given him my word that I wouldn't," Aurora explained, while driving them down Sunset in Carter's new convertible.

Diana explained, "But don't you realize that we long to experience the thrills and apprehensions, the stinging reprovals and stringent bondage – in short– the complete spectrum of fetish activity that plays out in the house of a brilliant young mistress?"

"It's for our information," said Susan to Aurora. "Remember, I'm still working on my graphic novel."

"But look at the trouble I almost got into," Aurora pointed out.

"Because you're too submissive," said Susan. "I don't think anyone could say that about us."

"But I promised Carter."

"All right then, just call and make an appointment for us and we'll go ourselves," suggested Diana at last, and Aurora agreed.

"When Carter finds out I've been concealing this from him, he may be angry with me," Aurora fretted.

"Are you afraid of Carter?" Diana teased.

"Of course I am."

"Oh, don't worry," Susan assured Aurora, "I'll take the blame for everything. Then maybe Carter will find it necessary to punish me."

Aurora looked at Susan with a sharp pang of unease, which was immediately noticed by the New York girl. Aurora felt that she owed Susan and her sister everything, but still she didn't like to think of anyone other than herself occupying Carter's lap, especially a precocious little hellion like Susan Ross.

"Would you really like that?" Aurora asked slowly.

"Only if you don't mind," Susan hastily amended her statement. "And I can see that you do, so let's forget I ever made such a forward suggestion."

"Oh, no!"

"You see why we have to go play at a club for a few days?" Susan explained. "It's only December and I already have spring fever."

Several hours later, while Aurora was chopping vegetables for dinner, Carter entered the well-appointed kitchen and asked about the girls. Aurora immediately colored.

"They've gone off on their own tonight," she replied. "I think they're headed for Sin-a-matic."

"On a Tuesday night?"

"I think so."

"Aurora, what are they up to?" he asked, over crossed arms.

"Carter, they're not up to anything," she replied, now floured to her elbows and deftly rolling out a piecrust. She had her fine, pale, blonde hair pinned up in a loose top knot and looked as creamy as an 18th century dairy maid.

"Are you actually making a piecrust from scratch?"

"It's going to be a Shepherd's pie," she explained, hoping to divert him from the subject of Susan and Diana in Hollywood.

"The kind of dish Tess D'arbyfield might have served her drunken father before she got a thrashing?"

"Oh, Carter, you know there isn't a single thrashing in all of Thomas Hardy," Aurora smiled.

"More's the pity. I'll tell you one thing though, there's going to be one here, pie crust or no pie crust, unless you start uttering some truth about what Susan and Diana are doing tonight."

Aurora looked stricken and felt tears prick the corners of her eyes as her guilty confession came tumbling out. As she had expected, Carter was very angry at the thought of Aurora steering two young women under Anthony Newton's protection to a place like The Keep.

"I couldn't stop them," Aurora protested.

"But you didn't have to help them," he snapped.

"They helped me."

"They helped you climb out of the gutter, you're helping them down into it," Carter snapped back, which immediately caused Aurora to dissolve into tears. Pressing her white apron to her eyes, she turned her back on him.

He turned her around and took her in his arms. "I didn't mean it like that." Aurora looked up at him with wet blue eyes. "But, you should have known better."

"I did, but they apparently planned this whole trip with the intention of playing at B&D in Hollywood."

"You must have glamorized your adventures when you talked to them."

"I'm not conscious of having done so."

Carter paced.

"Now I don't know what to do. Should I call Anthony? Go get them myself? Or pretend the whole thing isn't happening?"

"Please don't tell Anthony. Susan doesn't want him to know."

"Of course she doesn't, because she knows damn well that she's doing something he'd disapprove of."

"Why worry him unnecessarily when you know that it's perfectly safe to work in a club?"

"Sure, until the first deranged sadist walks in and flips out on someone."

"Oh, Carter, things like that may happen in the exploitative movie scripts authored by yourself and other Hollywood pulp meisters, but in real B&D, respect and consent are the keynotes of play."

"Oh? Then how do you account for the etiquette practiced by your previous master?"

Aurora laid the bottom crust carefully in the pan while trying to think of an answer that would calm his fears.

"Carter, Susan and Diana are savvy players. I'm certain they will know how to handle themselves at the club."

"I'm glad you're so confident, but my blood runs cold at the thought of Anthony Newton's girlfriend and her equally rare and precious sidekick being abused in a Hollywood dungeon."

"Carter, how can you talk so? Abuse? These women are in the scene. They're doing this for fun," Aurora exclaimed, beginning to be irritated.

"I still have to think about this," he brooded.

"You know, it's really none of your business what Susan and Diana are doing in Hollywood," she declared vehemently.

Carter gave her a long, steady look before replying, "Being as they're my house guests and the protégées of one of my most important associates, I happen to think it is my business." A moment later he added, "And you will bring me the hairbrush immediately for taking that insolent tone with me."

Aurora looked shocked.

"Right now, young lady."

Wiping her hands on her apron, she slowly exited the room and went upstairs to her bedroom.

Meanwhile, Carter paced, thinking, "If she doesn't come back with that hair brush, that's it!" Although he had no idea what "it" was, he knew that he was going to assert himself over this issue.

In a moment she returned, with glistening eyes and the hairbrush. Carter melted. However, this did not stop him from turning her over his knee, pulling up her skirt and applying the back of the hairbrush to her panties six times. She cried out loud as each indignant swat fell.

"You're getting twelve of the best for being so disrespectful," he told her on stroke six. She began to sob violently when he pulled her panties down to give her the second set of six on the bare bottom. Her satiny white skin was already tinged dark pink in six spots from where the brush had struck.

"Don't you ever take that tone with me again, young lady," he warned, between smacks of the heavy wooden hairbrush on her sensitive flesh. Aurora could only weep with shame and misery. He was right, so right! He was her dominant and she was his submissive. He was her rescuer and patron, she his spoiled darling. He was putting her through grad school, she lived in his beautiful house, had every possession she had ever wanted and they were taking their first trip to Europe together in the spring. How could she possibly have spoken so rudely to him?

Since she had been so unprepared for this spanking, every smack seared her. He had not bothered with a warm up. The dozen smacks were as hard as any she had ever taken from Carter and they made her cry bitterly.

Finally he lifted her off his lap. She stood weeping for some seconds.

"I haven't heard an apology yet," he said coolly.

"I'm sorry," she sobbed, too upset to even rub her bottom.

"Oh, never mind," he suddenly pulled her into his arms, deciding to forgive her. "At least I released some tension. I actually feel a lot better about the whole Susan and Diana escapade."

"You do?" Aurora sobs came to a halt.

"Yes, because I came up with the solution to my quandary while I was spanking you," Carter explained, mopping her face with the corner of her apron.

"You did?" she asked uncertainly.

"Yes. And it's a really elegant one. You're going to go back to work at the club this week. This action will serve the double purpose of allowing you to keep an eye on the brats while reminding you of what a hell I rescued you from."

"Me? Go back to the club?"

"Just while Susan and Diana are there."

"And do sessions?"

"You can do corporal punishment sessions," he decided, "but only if you think of them as coming from me for being the ungrateful, faux submissive that you are."

"I'm not a fake submissive."

"You're not even as submissive as the average Italian-American housewife I knew growing up."

"Carter, I am a true submissive. And I readily acknowledge that you are the world's most civilized dominant. I had no right to speak to you as I did. I can only think that those irreverent girls are having an undesirable effect on me."

"That's why you need to go back into a dungeon and get thrashed all week. I want to see you marked every night. That will teach you better than anything else how good you have it now, thanks to me. Oh, and don't forget to save up all your earnings and buy me some wonderful present," he added, on a whim.

"Oh, Carter," she smiled for the first time and lay her head against his chest.

It was the best week The Keep ever had. Every corporal punishment player in L.A. somehow managed to hear about the visiting girls from New York and popped in to do a session. While they were waiting, they played with Aurora, and she did go home marked every day.

Happily, this was the week that Mayo went AWOL from the club on the back of a bike bound for San Diego. This left Mistress Hildegarde free to entertain and instruct her two visiting imps throughout the days. A good deal of money was made and as rapidly spent, on shopping, sumptuous meals in Beverly Hills and other frivolous amusements.

Meanwhile, back at home, Carter glowered at them all.

"What's the matter, Carter?" Susan baited him on morning four. "You seem grumpy. Don't you feel sorry for us, having to return to the snow and ice in less than a week?"

"No, I do not."

"I actually have to go back to Poughkeepsie," said Diana, who was just on the verge of graduating college, while Susan was in her first year of post graduate design studies in Manhattan.

"Don't tell me you're enjoying working in a dungeon," Carter said incredulously.

"It's exciting," said Diana.

"And compelling," Susan added. "As a writer, surely you can understand the desire to penetrate a milieu and then incorporate your vision of it into your art."

"I suppose I can," he conceded, remembering his own compulsion to interview Mayo and spank every girl in the house that first week he discovered its existence.

"Skillful bondage enthusiasts have been coming in especially to tie me up," Diana revealed. "If they didn't pay me, I'd pay them."

"It's just playing, you know," Susan said, "like kids do."

"As in, playing 'doctor' and other naughty games," explained Diana. "Ever do that as a kid, Carter?"

"Frequently," he smiled.

"I think that people who do sessions are just trying to recapture that naughty playfulness in a simple, uncomplicated way," theorized Diana.

"I see, it's all completely innocent," Carter nodded.

"Perfectly so!" Diana declared.

"And you're saying that throughout your sessions yesterday, not one of the men who spanked or tied you up ever troubled to find out whether or not you were wet?"

Diana blinked at the audacity of this question, torn between the desire to slap his face and laugh in it.

"What?" she finally sputtered, unable to suppress a gale of laughter.

"You understand exactly what I mean. Do you or do you not allow yourself to be digitally penetrated during a session?"

Diana flushed, both at the raciness of the conversation and because it was focused on herself.

"Don't answer that question, Diana," said Susan mischievously. "If he wants find out how you behave in a dungeon he knows what he has to do."

"Oh? And what is that?" said Carter to Susan.

"Come to the club and play with her," said Susan, unwittingly alarming Aurora again.

"You know, Susan, it's lucky for you that you're Anthony's girlfriend and therefore off limits, because in my opinion, you're the one at this table who could benefit the most from a good paddling."

"I'm not off limits," Susan declared immediately.

"Yes, you are," he told her. "It's a male thing you wouldn't understand."

"Oh, Anthony couldn't care less about who I play with," Susan said, somewhat inaccurately.

"Oh? Then it's okay if I mention to him what you girls have been up to when I return his call later?"

"...I'd prefer it if you wouldn't," Susan replied at length, with as much dignity as she could muster.

"I understand. So you admit that Anthony would not approve of what you've been doing."

"I do admit that."

"And why do you think he wouldn't approve?"

"I suppose for the same reasons that you don't approve."

"But you don't respect our concern."

"I wouldn't put it that way."

"Here's how I'd put it: You're a spoiled brat who always has to get her own way, no matter what the risks."

As much fun as Susan was having with Carter, she couldn't fail to notice the effect their banter was having upon Aurora, who had been quietly refilling coffee cups and passing around plates of quiche throughout the exchange.

"I have to stop flirting with Carter!" thought Susan with a sudden rush of guilt, for Aurora was obviously anguished at the thought of Carter playing with anyone other than herself. "This isn't anything like my turf and I'm overstepping the bounds of hospitality." Out loud she said, with sudden humility, "I am a spoiled brat, but one whose master has a very hard hand from practicing piano from morning till night, so please don't tell on us!"

"Oh, all right," Carter grumbled, succumbing as predicted to Susan's appealing blue eyes.

The next day he rejoiced to hear that none of the girls intended to go to the club. Aurora told him this as he stood shaving. A few moments before he had pulled up the skirt of her sundress to pull aside her panties and inspect her bottom for the marking he expected to see that week. Aurora was still blushing from the examination, which had concluded with a couple of sharp smacks on her ravishing, only slightly marked, round, white bottom.

"So what will the little hellcats be doing to amuse themselves today?"

"I don't think I should tell you," said Aurora. He met her eyes in the mirror.

"Why not? It couldn't possibly be worse than what they've been doing," he remarked, rinsing his face.

"I don't think it is, but I'm not you," she handed him a towel.

"Thank you. So, tell me."

"They're making a movie."

"They're making a movie?" Since the girls were not actresses and had no connection with the film industry, this didn't make sense.

"A B&D video."

"Oh, no!"

"I had a feeling you'd object."

"Have they gone yet?"

"They left about an hour ago."

"Where did they go?"

"I don't think I should tell you."

"You'd better tell me."

"What will you do if I tell you?"

"Never mind that, where did they go?"

Aurora's brow became wrinkled as she shook her head. "I don't remember."

"Aurora, Susan is Anthony Newton's fiancée. Think of what the tabloids would make of her doing a B&D movie."

"But how would they ever find out?"

"How do they find out anything? They have their ways."

Aurora's mouth compressed into a thin line of resistance. Carter paced and thought. At one point he strode to the phone to call Anthony, but mid-way through dialing he put it down with a half smile. "I just thought of something," he said, turning to Aurora with relief.

"What?"

"It doesn't really matter if they do a video, so long as no one ever sees it."

Susan Ross returned to New York in a circumspect mood. The video had not turned out the way she expected and both she and Diana rued the experience, though Diana less than Susan. At least the brunette had enjoyed the excitement of being tied up by an expert at the bondage video studio, though the production values of the company had horrified them both.

Anthony was away when Susan arrived and did not return to the city until another week had elapsed and she had resumed her routine of going to class every day and working on her assignments at night. Then at last Anthony returned from his trip and the two were reunited after being apart for three weeks.

"I'm glad you didn't get a tan," Anthony observed, smiling at Susan over his desk. There was a large pile of mail to be looked over and Dennis had just brought in a pot of fresh ground coffee. Susan sat curled up on the green leather sofa contentedly watching her favorite man smile or frown as he leafed through his correspondence.

"Here's one from Carter Webster," he said suddenly, slitting open a padded envelope. "Probably a report on your behavior as a house guest," he observed astutely. Susan sat up with a pounding heart as she saw Anthony pull a videocassette out of the envelope along with a single sheet of writing paper. "Rather cryptic message," said Anthony reading the note aloud, "Dear Anthony, You owe me $10,000.00. Yours truly, Carter." Anthony looked at the cassette and read aloud, "Naughty Boarding School Girls."

"Damn him!" said Susan.

"You know something about this?"

"Don't bother putting it in the VCR. Just thrash me now and get it over with," she sighed.

"Susan, you didn't go and make a movie when you were out there?"

"I thought I did. But it looks like you're holding the master. Carter must have paid $10,000 for it."

"Whom did you make the movie for?"

"One of the B&D companies. Teresa's worked for them a million times."

Anthony dialed Carter's number and got through to the writer at once.

"I just got the tape," said Anthony, looking at Susan across his desk. "Thanks. No, I haven't watched it. I thought Susan and I could watch it together." Susan squirmed. "Is there anything else I should know? Really?" Anthony threw her a sharp look. After a moment he smiled reflectively and said, "I know, she can talk me into anything too. Well, thanks again, Carter. I'll get a check in the mail." Anthony hung up and shook his head at Susan.

"What did he say?"

"You've been a busy girl."

"It was sort of a research vacation," she explained. "I need to experience life. You know that."

"To think that you and Diana of all people would take off your clothes in a sleazy warehouse in Van Nuys," Anthony reflected. "Not to mention work all week at a club. It almost boggles the imagination." He strode across the room to the VCR and popped in the tape. Susan covered her eyes.

Carter had fast-forwarded to a juicy bit of action involving the bound, gagged, nearly nude, Susan and Diana. It was not a very dignified position with the two of them side by side over a padded horse. The background was quite stark and neither of the girls looked comfortable as a slim, cat-suited mistress cropped them.

"Please don't watch it!" she cried, after peeking through her fingers.

"Rather pornographic, isn't it?" he observed.

"It is not pornographic, Anthony. Nothing ever went in me."

"I know. I have lots of videos that have been shot in that same grey room. There's just something about the approach. I believe the word is objectification."

"Oh, Anthony!" she sighed, on the verge of tears. "You're right, of course."

"Susan, what in the world were you and Diana thinking?"

"We weren't happy with the script," she admitted. "But once we started, it didn't seem possible to back out."

Anthony turned away from the screen to spill the rest of the envelope's contents onto the desk. There was a roll of undeveloped film and two signed model's releases. Carter's damage control had been complete.

"These must be the publicity stills, huh?" he showed her the film can and she nodded.

"Well, I guess you had your experience, didn't you?"

"Yes," Susan replied unhappily.

"Good thing you decided to stay with Carter and Aurora."

"Yes, I guess it was."

"I'm glad I didn't find out about you working at the club until now. I would have worried."

Susan looked down with embarrassment.

"I hope that nothing awful happened to you girls there."

"No. It was okay," she said timidly.

"Susan?"

"Yes?" she looked up apprehensively.

Anthony smiled. "Relax. I'm not upset."

"You're not?" Susan's shoulders untensed.

"You and Diana wanted to give the scene a perfect movie. I understand that. But you can't achieve perfection in Van Nuys."

"No!" Susan couldn't believe he was taking this so well. He really did seem to understand.

"If you want to do something truly elegant, you're going to have to do it yourself, from start to finish."

"Myself?"

"I'll back you."

"I don't understand."

"Susan, if you and Diana want to do a movie or print a magazine, I can help you do it properly. You know I can."

"You'd do that?"

"Why not? It would be worth it just to drive Hugo Sands crazy," Anthony grinned.

"Compete with Hugo Sands?"

"Don't you think it's time his supremacy was challenged?"

Susan looked at Anthony with dawning comprehension. For the first time in their four-year relationship he was proposing a joint creative venture, and she was thrilled beyond measure. Then she looked momentarily doubtful.

"But, Hugo brought us together."

"And for that reason alone I love him like a brother. But what do you think about his chauvinistic attitudes?"

"He's getting better. Laura says he's almost entirely civilized now."

"But wouldn't your magazine be somehow different from his? Wouldn't it better represent the female point of view?"

"Yes."

"Think about that while you call Sherman and Diana to invite them over for dinner on Saturday night," said Anthony, rewinding the tape to the beginning.

"Anthony, you aren't going to show Sherman the tape!"

"Come on, Susan, you know someone is going to have to be punished for this mad escapade, and since we've just established that it isn't going to be you, that only leaves Diana."

Being Anthony, and decadent, the composer was determined to get the greatest entertainment value out of the adventure of Susan and Diana in Van Nuys; nor was Susan opposed to watching Sherman react to the tape, so long as she was safely lodged in the crook of Anthony's arm at the time.

Naturally, Diana was told nothing. Being Diana, she had experienced little or no guilt at taking part in the pandering video and had greatly enjoyed the portion that had involved her being tied both back-to-back and front-to-front with Susan.

"Sherman," said Anthony, after a very good dinner had been served and they enjoyed a second bottle of wine in his sitting room, "I have something shocking to show you. Brace yourself."

Diana looked at Susan questioningly, but Susan avoided her glance while Anthony turned on the VCR. Sherman appeared extremely puzzled. Nor did his brow clear when the image of his beloved Diana filled the screen, bound to a post, her mouth filled with a ball gag. A moment passed and Sherman still said nothing. It was then that Diana realized that due to the distortion caused by the gag as well as the new peach corset she wore on screen, he didn't even recognize her. But when Susan came into the picture in the next scene, ungagged and quite herself, except for being tied to an x-frame, Sherman suddenly understood why the gagged brunette had looked somehow familiar.

"Diana, you didn't!" Sherman exclaimed with horror, "And you, Susan? You, in a cheap, sleazy fetish video? I can't believe my eyes."

"Believe it," said Anthony, refilling Sherman's wine glass himself.

Diana, meanwhile, had gone rather pale at the sudden anger in Sherman's eyes.

"You told me you spent the whole time in L.A. sketching at the Getty Museum," Sherman accused her with a surprising amount of resentment.

"Oh, you don't know the half of it, Sherman," Anthony helpfully explained. "What you're watching here is but the noble culmination of an equally exalted week of frenetic sessions at one of Hollywood's most popular B&D salons."

"I beg your pardon?" Sherman wanted to not understand what he'd just heard, but the truth penetrated swiftly when explained by Anthony in a few more words.

"Yes," the composer concluded sadly, "Susan and Diana were for sale all week at a genuine bondage and whipping club, displayed for all and sundry to examine, handle, tie up, tickle, smack, even fondle, and I daresay at a price even a working man could afford."

Diana flashed Anthony an indignant look as he continued to inflame her already furious lover.

"Diana, how could you? I'm appalled," said Sherman, downing his wine with distraction.

"Sherman, Anthony's making it sound a lot worse than it was," Susan began to explain before Sherman cut her off.

"You, don't say a word," Sherman warned Susan, flashing her the kind of look that had originally caused her to form a crush on him several years before. "This was probably all your idea," Sherman accused Susan, who subsided in her chair and refrained from responding.

"This is what comes of letting them go to the Vault every week," Anthony observed, refilling Sherman's wine glass again. Diana kept her eyes demurely lowered, aroused by Sherman's indignation and determined not to break the spell by defending herself too logically.

"Sherman, Anthony took it pretty well. Why are you acting like such a stuffed shirt?" Susan asked him bluntly.

"Because I don't happen to enjoy the fact that my significant other has completely lost her innocence in the space of ten days."

"Sherman, Diana has been dreaming fetish all her life. It's not a question of innocence lost, but rather frustration vanquished," explained Susan. "You're in the scene just like us, surely you understand the need to experience one's desires."

"Susan, it's a shame you didn't decide to go into the law," Sherman acknowledged crossly. "All right. I see your point. It's all very reasonable. But I'm still not happy about it. And this ridiculous movie!" Sherman shot a contemptuous glance at the screen, where Susan was now being tickle-tortured. Susan hid behind a napkin.

"Don't worry, it will never be released," said Anthony. "Carter was nice enough to buy the master for us."

"You see the expense and unnecessary worry you've caused?" Sherman directed his scolding towards Diana, because she was his lover. Diana returned his gaze steadily and with all the passion in her romantic, 21-year-old soul, for Sherman was quite handsome and wonderful, in his reserved, intellectual way and she was coming to be violently in love with him. "Well? Have you nothing to say for yourself?" Sherman demanded, choosing to ignore the sensation of pleasure that pierced his own heart at the warmth of her expression.

"Yes, Diana, what do you have to say for yourself?" Anthony asked.

"Unlike Susan, I'm not writing a book," she replied. "My motives were purely decadent. I enjoyed being the center of attention."

Finally the wine took effect and extinguished what was left of Sherman's inhibitions. And even though he had never done anything like this before in mixed company, Sherman decided to spank Diana then and there.

"I'm sorry that you've felt neglected, Diana," Sherman said, taking her by the hand and leading her to the bottle green leather sofa, where he sat down and pulled her straight across his lap. "I promise not to neglect you again," he added, while smoothing down her cream wool skirt over her taut, oval bottom.

Anthony exchanged a wink with Susan that said, "Well, it took long enough, but the view was worth the wait." As the spanking began, firm and true, Anthony motioned Susan over to sit beside him on the loveseat by the fire. "See?" he whispered, "don't you wish you had a video camera now?"

"Yes, but Sherman would never agree to be in a video," Susan replied in a practical vein.

"Of course not, but you get the general idea."

Susan had watched Diana get spankings all week in the dungeons of The Keep, but this fully dressed, old movie-style spanking was the one that she liked the best. Even though there was almost twenty years between them, Susan and Anthony shared the identical experience of becoming obsessed with old movie spankings while still in junior high school and this affinity seemed to dissolve the generation that might have otherwise divided them.

Meanwhile, Diana lay sweetly across Sherman's lap, reacting with a whimper, a wriggle, a pant, and a sigh as his palm descended repeatedly on her upturned bottom. As always, her passivity bewitched him, dissipating his irritation to such a degree that he almost forgot that he was ever angry with her. But when he considered how many men must have enjoyed the small weight of Diana across their laps this last week at the L.A. club, his indignation surged and he brought his hand down hard.

"I'd better not ever catch you getting up to this kind of mischief again," he warned her, administering three dozen no-nonsense whacks that by the end had her kicking and squirming to escape his grasp in earnest. Finally he brought the spanking to a close with six of the best that nearly made her cry, then lifted her off his lap.

He looked at her and she gazed back at him wordlessly. Then, as though waking from a dream, Sherman suddenly remembered Anthony and Susan, who were watching them with the rapt attention of an opening night audience. Diana now turned to wink at them, without letting Sherman see.

"Now I suggest you take her home and start all over again with a hairbrush," said Anthony. Preparations were made to depart and within ten minutes a taxi arrived to take them uptown.

When they were alone in the back of the cab, Diana cuddled against him.

"As soon as I graduate college, can we get married, Sherman?"

"Certainly not," he answered emphatically, though his heart contracted with pleasure.

"Sherman, why?"

"Too old," he grumbled.

"Oh, Sherman, you're only in your 30's."

"Late 30's."

"Look at Anthony and Susan, she was only 19 when they met. Four years later, they're more in love than ever."

"That's because he's a glamorous, talented, celebrity. I'm just a boring estate lawyer."

"Oh, Sherman, I adore your modesty. It allows me to be the center of attention at all times."

Chapter Three

Marguerite and Malcolm

November 1,
Dear Ms. Alexander,

Thank you for responding to my ad in the New Rod Quarterly. You are certainly a seductive young woman. If Vargas ever drew a girl in glasses, she'd be you.

But your letter did not equally impress me. Frankly, you seem shallow, self-centered and vain. And for a submissive, highly demanding.

Your insistence on being "spoiled" also failed to charm me. Perhaps you should be advertising in the professionals' section if this is such an important criteria for dating in the scene.

I apologize if my comments seem unduly harsh, but the practiced ease of your heavily perfumed note rankled somehow. In a way I still want to meet you, because you do look delectably spankable, but I expect the encounter would be a severe disappointment to us both.

I wish you luck in your future choice of playmates.
  Sincerely,
  Malcolm Branwell
P.S. Do you wish me to return your photo?

November 4,
Dear Mr. Branwell,

I don't think we have to meet for you to spank me. I think that you have already spanked me. And perhaps a bit harder than even I deserve.

You may keep my photo if you wish, as I still have yours to look at in the magazine. It was what first made me write you. I thought it very handsome at the time. Now I simply regard it as the portrait of a very stern gentleman.

I am bound to agree with your several observations on my character. Yet with your final conclusion I am compelled to differ: I don't think that our playing in person would be at all disappointing and the fact that you do only betrays your inexperience at dealing with a woman of parts.

I trust that your ad will draw a great response. Among your correspondents you are sure to find the milksop creature you seek and with her soon enjoy the exquisite pleasures our scene has to offer. I wish you luck in your search.

Yours truly,
Marguerite Alexander

November 7,
Dear Marguerite,

I had been regretting my rude letter to you when your return note arrived.

I owe you an apology for presuming to analyze your character on the basis of a flirtatious note. Your perception of my inexperience was entirely accurate. Could the privilege of playing with a woman like you be anything less than the thrill of a lifetime? But blundering beginner that I am, how would I know that?

I will be in Random Point opening one of my new bookstores at the end of next week. Perhaps we could have lunch and I could attempt to convince you that I'm not as stupid as I seem. Please call me.

Malcolm

Marguerite handed her friend, Laura Random, Malcolm's letters with a sigh of irritation. "I appear to have developed a craving to play with a pompous, miserly prig who's about to put me out of business!"

"Branwell's Book Bag chain is his?" Laura considered Malcolm's photo in Hugo's magazine. She had studied it at length herself while laying the issue out for her lover and had been given several licks of the belt for fantasizing aloud about Malcolm B., who had posed stripped to baggy shorts on the deck of his boat looking young, rich and athletic. Malcolm was tall, with a lean physique and unlined skin. His ad said he was 31. Facially he reminded Marguerite of the 50's film star John Kerr, who once gave a spanking on an episode of Rawhide.

"What did you say in your letter to tame him so thoroughly?" Laura asked, comparing the language of his first letter with that of his second.

"Oh, I disarmed him by accepting his criticism with an air of humility then administered just enough of a scolding to let him know that for all his bluster he's a novice."

"Are you going to meet him?"

"I don't know." Marguerite sat down behind the polished wooden counter of her bookshop and put her chin on her hand. "He is very handsome, and apparently rich, but what good will it do me with his skinflintish attitude? I could bear to not be spoiled by a poor man. But for a wealthy lover to be close with his funds offends every instinct of chivalry."

"I completely agree," said Laura.

"And then again," mused Marguerite, "I've longed for a new lover for some time now and Malcolm does have the right look."

"He looks divinely virile," Laura commented.

"He's young, strong and barely used," Marguerite observed with a catlike grin. "And can't you see him in a well-cut suit and a grey fedora?"

"Perfectly," Laura agreed. "He's leaning on the rail of a cruise ship and you're beside him in a white sundress, picture hat and gloves."

"Oh, Laura, what should I do? He really is terribly good looking, with those corded legs and so on, but is he mature enough for me?" In spite of her smooth, fresh looks, Marguerite was 34 and very worldly.

"I don't like that crack about your not being submissive enough."

"That bothered me too. I'm not about to put up with another Victor!"

"On the other hand, even though he's snotty, he seems fairly cultivated. I like that he apologizes for being unduly harsh. That shows that he has some gentlemanly instincts, even though he chooses to suppress them. Does Hugo know anything about him?"

"No. He's a new subscriber. If I'm not mistaken, he probably only discovered there's a scene as recently as a few months ago."

"You mean he may not have even played with anyone yet?"

"As anal retentive as he is, he's probably been holding his lifelong desires in abeyance until now."

"Still, Marguerite, how could a man that firm looking not be able to give you a great scene? And for him to have gotten so far in business at his age surely indicates a streak of genius."

Marguerite agreed but decided that postponing it would increase the pleasure of their first encounter. So she wrote back promptly on her heavy book shop letterhead, inviting him to stop in at her bookstore on the day he came to town for a cup of tea by her fireside.

Malcolm Branwell was chagrined to realize that the woman he'd decided to pursue was the owner of a business whose business would greatly decrease when his business came to her town. But he was once again underestimating Marguerite, for there could be no chain store substitute for her enchanting shop with its gallery of rare erotica and all of the Edwardian ambiance with which she could infuse it. Marguerite's shop was the one the guidebooks mentioned. All of this Malcolm perceived in an instant on stepping into the fragrant and romantic bookshop, which filled most of the narrow, triple-decker house.

It was a Saturday morning the week before Thanksgiving and Marguerite, in a tailored grey wool skirt and vest over a white blouse, was busy with a half dozen customers at once. Malcolm browsed for some time, going up into the galleries and collecting expensive books.

Until he emerged from behind the large stack of books he had placed on the counter, Marguerite did not even recognize her correspondent in the shop. Her green eyes opened wide behind her becoming eyeglasses as she took Malcolm in appreciatively.

He was a broad shouldered and ruddy-complected young man, with crisp, short brown hair and the same color eyes. She liked his features and the cut of his clothes.

"Why, hello," she extended a beautifully manicured hand to shake his blunt one.

Bewitched by her mellifluous voice, it took a moment for Malcolm to recollect what he had been about to say.

"I've been all over your shop and I'm very impressed," he finally managed to blurt out, unwilling to relinquish her hand. "And even more ashamed of that horrible letter I wrote you."

"Yes," she smiled, "you should be."

"I'd like these books," he told her, throwing a credit card on top of the stack.

"Are you saying you don't stock these titles at Branwell's?" she teased.

"You know that we don't."

Marguerite began to write up the sale. The total exceeded five hundred dollars, but this seemed an inadequate consolation for having her business assailed by the corporate battering ram of Branwell's Book Bag. After the sale had been concluded he demanded the promised cup of tea and Marguerite obliged him by leading him over to the fireside where she always kept a pot on the grate. They sat at a small table enjoying the convenient lull in customer traffic.

"I suppose you can never forgive me for writing that first letter, can you?" he bluntly began. She inclined her head with an uninterpretable smile. "Well?"

"Well," she condescended to reply at last, "you were rather dreadful at first, but as you seem to regret your unkindness to me, I don't see why my eventual forgiveness should not be forthcoming."

"Oh, I do deeply regret it!" he swore, placing his hand lightly atop hers across the table. But she pulled it free at once and arched a slender eyebrow at him.

"I said forgiveness might be forthcoming, not hand holding, Mr. Branwell." Malcolm reddened. He had never felt so clumsy with a woman, and knew neither what to say or do to win her respect.

"May I take you to dinner?" he asked.

"I don't think so," she told him, not unkindly. "At least, not yet."

"Not yet? When then?"

"Frankly, Mr. Branwell, you're not ready to appreciate a woman like me yet. I suggest you let your ad run its course, play for a couple of months with a variety of young ladies, and if you still don't meet that perfect someone, call me again," she recommended with a degree of poise that unnerved him.

At this point a customer approached the counter and Marguerite jumped up to wait on him, leaving Malcolm in a state of acute frustration. Seeing Marguerite in person, hearing her voice and inhaling her perfume, was sufficient to convince him that he need never look any further for a playmate. But now she had imposed an intolerable penance on him for his initial rashness of address. He would be exiled for some months, during which time he had to force himself to play with women who were far her inferior.

He sat and drank tea, watching her conduct her business pleasantly and finding it impossible to leave, though it was evident that he had been dismissed. Finally when it became so busy in the shop that there was no further opportunity of attracting Marguerite's attention, Malcolm gathered up his books and left.

Resolved to accept and benefit from the practical lesson she had outlined, Malcolm refrained from attempting to contact Marguerite Alexander again for a period of six weeks. During this time he met every eligible woman in New England who had either answered his ad or ran one of her own in Hugo Sands' magazine. By Christmas week Malcolm had made contact with six different women and had played with them all.

They were nice girls, and thrilling to play with each in their way. But none of them possessed the polished womanliness of Marguerite. She seemed to tower above them all, not only in physical stature, but also in wit, beauty and accomplishment. And she had been completely right in her assessment that playing with others would increase his longing to obtain her special favors.

Meanwhile Marguerite seriously wondered whether the sanctimonious young millionaire should be made to pay for those favors after the insults that she had sustained at his pen. She did not hesitate to consult her original mentor, Hugo Sands on this matter when Malcolm's Christmas card arrived with an invitation to meet him for dinner in Boston and then attend the opera. The prospect of seeing a performance of Mahagonny was almost impossible to resist and she represented her desire to finally play with Malcolm just as strongly to

Hugo.

"Make him pay, baby. It'll kill him to have to do it, but he wants you, so he will," the cynical publisher commented. "And if you were meant to fall in love with each other, he won't care about having started out as a session."

"I was thinking of making him get me a suite at the Copley Plaza for the night." Marguerite suggested modestly.

"Sweetheart, do you know how wealthy Malcolm Branwell is? At the very least you should have a Christmas present."

Marguerite pouted momentarily, then flashed Hugo a mischievous look. "He'll be livid."

"So? He's got a big hard-on and it's time he was punished for his impertinence," Hugo said, fondly taking Marguerite in his arms. Marguerite allowed herself to be squeezed, momentarily grinding against him before pulling back.

"But Hugo, then he'll think I'm as wantonly materialistic as he first suspected and write me off as a high priced call girl."

"Who cares what he thinks? He's an idiot," said Hugo with some feeling. Marguerite had all but forgiven Malcolm for his first letter, but Hugo would need years to get over the insult to his brilliant protégée. Some of what Malcolm had intimated was undoubtedly true, but Hugo had little respect for a wealthy man who would have let Marguerite slip through his fingers because she had a modest addiction to luxury.

"Should I tell him what I want or ask him to surprise me?"

"Ask him to surprise you and you'll wind up with a juicer." Hugo predicted.

"But Hugo, you saw his first letter. Malcolm's ethics are as rigid as my stiffest corset. If I ask him for something juicy he'll hate me."

"Marguerite, use your head. Haven't you already got one perfectly serviceable stud on tap who gives you no money?"

Marguerite smiled fondly at the thought of Michael Flagg, acknowledged Hugo's point and sent Malcolm an E-mail message that night.

December 28,
Dear Mr. Branwell,

If you would like me to come to Boston on New Year's Eve you may have to bribe me. There's an art deco jewelry shop on Newberry Street named Damson's. I'm a good customer and they know my taste. A charming present might cause me to look upon your invitation with favor.

Your self-centered, vain, shallow and demanding friend in the scene, M.

Marguerite had correctly predicted Malcolm's reaction to her note. He felt such indignation boiling upon receipt of it that he could only work it off by going for a run in 30-degree weather. "Greedy little slut!" he thought, orbiting the Boston College reservoir. "I should buy her off, just for the satisfaction of giving her the thrashing she deserves!"

He visited Damson's that afternoon and asked to speak to the manager about obtaining a present for his friend, Marguerite Alexander. Marguerite had called ahead that morning to ask if the emerald and diamond bracelet from 1924 that she had admired the previous week was still available. She was told that it was still available with an attractive price tag of only forty-three hundred in cash out the door. Marguerite suggested the bracelet be put aside in case a friend of hers decided to stop in later. When Malcolm mentioned Marguerite's name, this was what he was shown.

He called her within an hour of making the purchase and tersely said, "Well, I've got the ransom. Where should we meet?"

She replied steadily, but with an aching, pounding heart, "A suite at the Copley Plaza would put us right across the street from the opera house."

"I'll see you there at six o'clock on New Year's Eve."

Two days later Malcolm dressed in a state of excited resentment for his first real date with Marguerite. Of all the women he had played with so far, not one besides Marguerite had asked for a bribe. But neither had their integrity, accessibility or breathless innocence seemed particularly compelling when compared to the sophisticated charms of Marguerite. Perhaps her particular radiance required some sort of extraordinary maintenance fees and this accounted for her apparent avarice.

Her approach actually made things a lot easier. Now he didn't have to feel awkward about taking the insolent girl across his knee. They now had a financial arrangement. This was less than what he'd hoped for, but better than no relationship at all.

But he almost forgot how irritated he was when she arrived, punctually, in a peplum waisted, smoky blue silk suit under a full-length sable (which he deplored), and four-inch heels. They had to hurry to fit in dinner before the performance so there was little time to discuss the more important reason for their meeting.

During the overture he slipped the bracelet case into her hands and she momentarily opened it, then smiled and put it into her purse. He wanted to shake her then and there for the calm with which she accepted the bribe.

They were in a private box and as soon as the lights went down he took advantage of his presumed temporary ownership of Marguerite's person by placing his hand rather firmly on her thigh atop her skirt. Marguerite looked at him with some surprise and a flutter of her heart. This was sudden! As she didn't resist this liberty, he grew bolder and slipped his hand under her skirt to caress her leg from knee to stocking top.

Marguerite shifted on her seat. His hand went between her legs and his fingers probed the silken crotch of her panties. She was already damp! Now she pushed him away, shocked by this too rapid caress.

"Spread your legs and let me touch you," he ordered, pushing her thighs apart and attempting to reinsert his hand between them. Marguerite was appalled. Disengaging from him, she exited the box. He followed her out to the corridor and demanded an explanation.

Marguerite reached in her purse and retrieved the grey velvet jewel box.

"Here," she thrust it into his hand. "Did you think this meant you own me?"

"Well, what the hell does it mean?" he demanded, following her as she paced.

"Your hand on my thigh through the skirt was charming, but what is this spread-your-legs stuff? How dare you talk to me like that on such short acquaintance?"

Malcolm flushed so brightly that she thought he might overheat. But he forced himself to calmly consider the situation from every angle before replying. True, he may well have made a fool of himself just now, but if that was the case, why were her panties so damp? No, he suspected this gorgeous brat was almost as excited as he was by the prospect of playing for the first time.

With lowered eyes he apologized for taking a liberty with her and begged her forgiveness abjectly. After this she was easily persuaded to return to the box and the remainder of the opera was enjoyed by Marguerite without the slightest impropriety being visited on her luscious person.

Malcolm was grateful for the time the performance afforded him for deep reflection. It seemed as though he needed every moment of the succeeding two hours to plan his strategy for the rest of the evening. As he sat quietly reproaching himself for his ridiculously aggressive behavior, she covertly gazed at his cleanly chiseled profile and wondered whether she had managed to unman him completely or only temporarily destarch his collar.

Only once during the performance did she flash him a mischievous smile after catching him looking at her. But this was enough to banish his discouragement. In spite of all the set backs he had suffered in the Marguerite campaign, her rebuffs did not so much bruise his ego as make him reevaluate his approach.

Thus, as they strolled back to the hotel after the performance, Malcolm plunged in with a bold, "You know, I have read your stories. We actually carry your books. I just didn't realize Alma was you until I talked to Hugo Sands the other day."

"You talked to Hugo about me?" Marguerite gave him her full attention.

"I'd just called to cancel my ad and I happened to mention that I had a date with a Marguerite Alexander and asked whether he knew anything about you."

"Oh my! What did he say?" She couldn't keep from smiling.

"He was rather curt with me. But he did say that you were Alma and that was all I needed to know."

"And was it?"

Discovering the previous week that Marguerite was an elegant author whose erotic prose had aroused him for years had shocked and embarrassed Malcolm. How he had misjudged her! But he wasn't about to let the cocky girl know how much he admired her descriptive powers.

"You certainly construct some Byzantine plots," he sidestepped her question.

"Actually they're quite straightforward and logical."

"All those complex motivations and subtle emotions. Do you honestly think the readers have the patience for all that?"

"Some do," Marguerite murmured.

"And I suppose you expect ordinary men to be as clairvoyant as your characters are when it comes to handling horrible girls?"

Marguerite simply smiled.

When they reached The Copley Plaza Malcolm asked her bluntly, "Am I going upstairs with you?"

"Didn't you intend to?" she replied, with flirtatious good humor.

"Yes, originally, but you sort of changed the arrangement at the theatre."

"We can discuss that," said Marguerite, preceding him into the lobby. When they arrived at the suite she found it very much to her liking. "Shall we have champagne?" she asked, picking up the phone to call room service.

"Anything you like," he told her, encouraged by her gaiety. As she went about examining the rooms, he followed her and looked at her. It was nerve wracking not knowing exactly what to do and she wasn't helping him.

The champagne arrived and since a token sip was all Malcolm took, he soon had the advantage of her. Marguerite did love champagne and after two glasses became quite voluble.

"So you don't think that women ought to be spoiled," she opened her gambit lightly.

"It seems a sexist requirement."

"Well, really, Malcolm, what could be more sexist than turning a grown woman over your knee and spanking her as though she were a child?" she demanded.

"That would only be sexist if the woman wasn't into it," Malcolm pointed out.

"Look, I spoil men to death!" Marguerite attacked from a different angle.

"Oh. I see. I didn't realize that," he almost smiled.

"No and you still don't," she insisted. "And even though that darling bracelet would compliment my eyes, you'll hate me if I take it so I have to behave."

"Do you care what I think of you?" he sat next to her with sudden warmth.

"And not only that," she ignored his last remark, "but your wretched bookmarket thrashed my Christmas business."

"The fact that we're competitors is regrettable," he agreed cautiously.

"I should have known you'd be as circumspect as a lawyer," she declared disdainfully, pouring another glass of wine. "Do forgive me for whining."

"Maybe I can figure something out to help," he said, thinking hard. "I've got some influence with the distributors. Suppose I ask them to give you the same discounts we get? Would that enable you to match our prices?"

"Yes," she smiled ironically, mostly impressed at the speed with which he had thought of a way to help her at no cost to him. Malcolm noticed her expression and felt as though she were laughing at him.

Seeing him at a loss for words she asked him to tell her about some of the girls he had met since seeing her last.

"That's right," he flushed, "you did order me to get some experience, didn't you?"

"I believe I may have made a good suggestion," she gently corrected him.

"I did meet a number of women," he admitted.

"And managed to play with them all?"

"Yes," he said, with a smile.

"I was wondering when I'd get to see you smile," she murmured. "You should do it more often. It makes you much more handsome."

Malcolm stopped smiling. "Yes, well at any rate, I don't feel at liberty to discuss my meetings in detail."

"Oh? Are you sure you want to miss this opportunity to tell me how much more exciting it would be to play with me?" she deliberately taunted him.

"You know, you're a very arrogant young lady," said Malcolm with sudden decision. There was no use putting this off any longer. Marguerite tried to jump to her feet a moment too late and he succeeded in seizing her by the elbow and turning her over his knee.

"No!" she cried, for form's sake.

"Yes!" he told her, shrugging off his jacket without relinquishing his grip on her waist. A muscular man, with vitamin-fortified strength infused into every unpolluted cell of his 6'2" frame, he had no difficulty in restraining and nicely positioning the lithe redhead across his solid lap. He noted with some relief that she did not resist.

"What are you going to do?" she asked, somewhat impishly, with a full glance over her left shoulder at him.

"Give you a good spanking!" he declared, raising his right hand slightly and bringing it down briskly, once on either snugly skirted cheek of her bottom. He couldn't be sure, but he thought that Marguerite said, "Oooooh!" as she gave a little wriggle across his lap. Malcolm followed this with a series of six more smacks on either cheek. She caught her breath and ground against his thighs.

"You do deserve this," he told her, repeating the twelve count, but harder this time. She reacted with growing excitement. "You're not arguing," he commented, slowly smoothing out her skirt. "That must mean that you agree with me."

He continued to spank her, quite firmly now, for several minutes uninterrupted. Marguerite knew a good spanker when she met one. He spanked her hard and pressed her to his lap so firmly that she could feel his desire to possess her. His choice of spanking her over her skirt, rather than greedily baring her all at once, gained back for Malcolm points that he had lost in the opera box.

Malcolm continued spanking her until she could feel the heat radiating between her panties and lined skirt. She indicated that her ordeal across his lap was better extended than abbreviated, by arching to his hand.

"You've got a lot to answer for," he told her, "playing hard to get for two months!"

"I beg your pardon, but it's only been six weeks," she replied, reaching back to rub for the first time.

"But it felt like two months," he told her, removing her hand and continuing to spank her.

"Ouch!" she cried, the heat beginning to fully penetrate now. "You're lucky it wasn't six months," she boldly asserted.

"Oh, am I?" He did not find her impertinence amusing and applied the next six swats more vigorously. Now for the first time she kicked her legs and tried to break the position.

"Ow! That's too hard!" she objected.

"Where do you think you're going?" he pushed her back down and renewed his grip on her waist.

"But –" she twisted on his lap to force him to meet her big, green eyes, "please don't spank me any harder!"

"Then don't say such naughty things," he admonished her, smoothing down her skirt again. Marguerite settled down across his lap again. "And say you're sorry," he added. She cordially ignored him. "Marguerite?" he patted her through her skirt ominously.

"Yes, sir?"

"Say you're sorry for being such a stuck up little brat!" he punctuated this command with six of the best. Marguerite cried out at each one but stubbornly refrained from answering him.

"Very well, I didn't want to have to have to humiliate you completely on our first date, but I'm finding your conceit intolerable. Lift up!"

"But, why?" she coyly asked him, reaching back to rub her bottom again.

"You know damn well why," he said, unzipping the back of her skirt and pulling it down and off. "You're getting it on the bare bottom." Suddenly her long, stunning legs appeared, gartered and hosed to perfection.

"No!"

"Yes, and immediately!" he declared, fingering the waistband of her pearl grey silk briefs.

"No!" she protested vehemently, refusing to be deprived of a spanking on her panties first. "You mustn't pull them down yet. I forbid you to!" she cried imperiously, trying to slip out of his grasp.

"All right. Calm down," he ordered, stroking the panties. The silk was so papery thin that his calloused palm nearly snagged it.

"And anyway, I'm out of balance now," she protested.

"What does that mean?"

"My jacket should come off too," she suggested.

"If I let you up will you promise not to run away?"

"I promise," she said at once and slid off his lap. Kneeling gracefully on the carpet she unbuttoned her suit jacket and removed it to reveal a dainty bustier in the same color as the briefs. She sat on her heels and waited, looking up at him.

"Well? What are you waiting for?" he demanded.

"A kiss," she told him, removing her glasses and placing them on the coffee table. He leaned down with a fiercely pounding heart and taking her face between his hands, kissed her lips for the first time. Nor could he resist placing one chaste kiss on her ravishing bosom while cupping it for a moment through the lacy bustier. He grazed her exposed throat with his lips, causing her to sigh.

"Do you know that you're a wicked girl?" he asked.

She grabbed her champagne glass and downed its contents haughtily, forgetting for the moment that she was still on her knees to him.

He pulled her back across his lap.

"Hey, don't!"

"You're really going to get it now," he promised. Malcolm began to dust her panties vigorously with the palm of his hand, thinking of the frustrations he had suffered over the last six weeks. He principally remembered her request for the expensive present before agreeing to their New Year's Eve date and his indignation swelled. Malcolm held her fast and warmed her panties thoroughly.

"I don't know why you think you have to be spoiled. You're

already more spoiled than any woman I know."

"Ouch!" Marguerite kicked her legs at the last series of smacks. "I deserve to be spoiled!"

"You deserve to be spanked. Imagine demanding a ransom before going out with me. I never heard of anything so outrageous in my life."

"Oh? You must lead a sequestered life," she replied.

"If you can still be so fresh I must not be doing this right," he remarked, increasing the severity with which he was bringing his palm down across her lushly padded bottom.

"Besides," she said, stopping him to rub, "I gave the bracelet back."

"Yes, you certainly did," he remembered her reaction to his touch in the opera box. "Embarrassing me as much as you possibly could in the process," he declared, tucking his thumbs into the waistband of her briefs and tugging them down over her hips and then to her knees. "There! That's better," he remarked, admiring her flawless, freshly pinkened bottom.

"No it isn't!" She attempted to pull her panties back up.

"No, you don't," he told her, taking her by the wrist and smacking her on the back of the hand before pushing it away and beginning the spanking all over again.

"Ow!" It stung more on the bare. "That really hurts!"

"I haven't heard an apology yet," he told her, pausing to rub.

"Mmmm," she said, burying her face in her arms.

"First you intimate that I can't have you unless I bribe you. Then you throw my present back in my face. Why the schizophrenia?" he interrogated her with more spanking.

"I simply changed my mind," she looked back over one shoulder to check the deepening color in her bottom, then subsided across his lap.

"And suppose I tell you to spread your legs now? Are you going to resist me again? Run away?"

"No," she softly replied, hiding her face again. Malcolm heard this shy avowal with great relief.

"Why did you balk in the theatre box?" he asked softly, gently separating her milky thighs and teasingly caressing their inner surface.

"Because you were being disrespectful," she replied, arching up to give him greater access.

"You don't like being given orders?"

"Not on such short acquaintance."

"Short acquaintance, huh?" He stopped stroking and started spanking again. "It's only been short because you put me off for so long. We could have been going out together for months now if you hadn't been so fussy."

"The only way to discipline a dominant male is to deprive him of one's company," Marguerite informed him, "and if anyone needed to be disciplined it was you!"

"Hmmph!" was his response, followed by several dozen hard smacks, which she held still for prettily. "You did admit that some of what I said was true," he pointed out, pausing to caress her again.

"That doesn't mean it was right for you to scold me in your first letter."

"Maybe you need someone to scold you," Malcolm bent his head to press his lips momentarily to her warm bottom; "And make you behave like a normal person."

"And how does my behavior differ from that of a normal person?" she pillowed head on her arms and felt five or six more smacks before he stopped to answer and caress her again.

"Well, for one thing, a normal girl doesn't sell her favors."

"That really bothers you, doesn't it?" she wriggled on his lap, flaunting her bottom and legs.

"Shouldn't it?" he mused, once again returning to the satiny surface of her white inner thighs with his fingertips. How could anyone who looked so pure and virtually untouched be so worldly, he wondered, without letting it stop him from more widely dividing her thighs and slipping his palm in under her soft pubic curls. He pressed down on her bottom with his other hand, sandwiching her in a way that she found maddeningly sexy.

"I don't think so, Malcolm, seeing as I only play pure B&D," she replied, grinding against his hand, whose fingertips now pressed against her clit. At last, when her wetness was impossible to ignore an instant longer, he inserted one and then another finger up into her pussy.

"And what does that mean?"

"That means no sex."

"Oh? You didn't plan to give yourself to me tonight?"

"That would depend on how you handled me."

"And how do most men handle you?"

"Not nearly so well as you're doing now," she murmured, allowing him to masturbate her deeply as his other hand crept around to bare and fondle her breasts. Her body responded to his touch in a way that seemed to invite further liberties.

Malcolm released and rolled her over. "Look," he said, cradling her in his arms, "I'm not moralizing. Prostitution is a noble profession, I just don't like to think of my girlfriend as being a part of it."

Marguerite stiffened at the word he had used and decided he had enjoyed the weight of her body on his lap long enough.

"I'm sure you think you're very clever but I don't find you amusing," she icily replied, getting her panties back up, springing to her feet and looking down at him disdainfully.

"Marguerite, don't get offended, I'm just trying to understand you."

"Considering your lack of imagination, that would be impossible," she declared, marching into the bedroom and pulling a grey satin robe from the closet. In an instant all exposed flesh disappeared.

Malcolm paced the drawing room anxiously until she appeared in the doorway.

"Marguerite?" he appealed to her with eyes full of worried regret.

"Are you still here? I was hoping you would have gone," she aimed for coolness but her voice was full of emotion.

"You're dismissing me again?" Now he was equally agitated. "Because of one remark?"

Marguerite recklessly drained the last glass of champagne. "Do you think I had nothing better to do on New Year's Eve than be insulted by you? I might have been with my friends in Random Point tonight. It's time for you to leave."

"I really think you could forgive one comment, Marguerite, seeing as things were going so well."

"Yes, they were going well," she said, her eyes welling with tears. "But then you had to go and ruin the whole mood with your crudeness. And to think that I allowed you to touch me! I insist you wash your hands before you leave. I couldn't bear the thought of your taking any part of me away with you."

"Oh, Marguerite, I didn't mean to upset you like this. I didn't realize you were so sensitive about certain words."

"Well, why shouldn't I be, when they are patently untrue!" she had a high color by this time and without her glasses looked even more exciting.

He sighed, "I'm very sorry that I hurt your feelings and ruined your New Year's Eve." He picked up his hat and coat. "I hope you don't have a headache in the morning from all that champagne," he added. "I'll call you."

Marguerite made no reply and did not attempt to detain him. After he was gone she turned off all the lights and looked down on Copley Square, where it had just begun to snow. She saw him cross on foot and guessed that he lived in walking distance in Back Bay. Though walking distance to that man could be miles, she reflected.

How wrong she had been to give him a second chance! Marguerite blushed as she thought of the liberties she had allowed him. More than enough to pay for a hotel suite, she decided coolly.

How interesting it might have been to yield to that hard body in the moonlight! She felt a pang for the pleasures her pride had cost her. But no mere physical sensation was worth the degradation of being thought common by one's lover. Before he was through with her he would learn just how uncommon a woman she was.

She curled up on the bed and hugged a pillow to her bosom, disturbed by the memory of his very erect cock pressing through his trousers as he spanked her. And he had been such a splendid spanker too! But none of this signified if he remained so prejudiced. Victorian style worked wonderfully for corsetry and underground erotica, but with regard to her own sexuality, Marguerite was a child of the 60's with all the liberation that implied.

Even so, she began to regret that she had not let him stay, if only to give her pleasure. His skillful manipulations had been highly civilized. Marguerite brushed her wet curls with her hand under the robe. Sex might possibly be all that he would ever be good for. But was even the best sex in the world worth putting up with his unbearable attitudes? Now she gave a sob of frustration and rolled over on her tummy. Dreadful man!

For treating her like this on New Year's Eve he deserved the most stringent lesson any dominant had ever been taught by his lover. She resolved not to give herself to him until he pledged both his heart and his hand to her and she found him worthy to accept.

He came to call the next morning at eleven. Dressed in beige riding pants, cordovan boots and a fine white wool shirt, Marguerite was drinking her breakfast chocolate in the sitting room and reading A Sentimental Journey by Lawrence Sterne. He sat at her tea table in his overcoat, still red in the face from the biting cold outside and mightily embarrassed by the mess he had made of their evening. Marguerite looked composed as she turned down a page in her book and gave him her full attention.

"That looks old," he told her, eyeing the lean, courtly, 18th Century dandy taking the pulse of a beautiful lady on the cover.

"You're not familiar with the novel?" the bookseller asked her highly successful competitor, somewhat ironically.

"No, why? Should I be?"

Marguerite merely smiled.

"Generally I don't bother to read any author who isn't alive to do a book signing," he explained.

"You don't know what you're missing," she gently reproved.

"I don't want to miss anything good. Why don't you draw up a book list for me to help me improve myself?"

"Be careful what you wish for."

"I'm serious."

"Very well then," she tore a sheet from her small spiral writing tablet with the Raphael angel on the cover and unscrewed her Mont Blanc fountain pen. "I'll write down five books I want you to read before I see you next."

"Wait a minute, I didn't agree to that!"

"You have no choice," she told him diabolically, writing neatly in her firm, round script and handing him the list. He looked at it and read aloud, "The Brothers Karamazov, The Charterhouse of Parma, Pride and Prejudice, Camilla and Pamela. How long are these?"

"Oh, four to nine hundred pages each," she replied with a winsome smile. "And in them you'll meet some of the best female characters in literature."

"I see I'm being disciplined again," he noted, pocketing the list.

"You'll have two, maybe three out of the five at your store. You'll have to go to a better store for the others. I'll write down the authors as you're too ignorant to know them."

"You know, I didn't get to go to brat school like you," he defended himself with some resentment. "I went to a community college and worked in my father's print shop."

"That sounds horribly bleak. No wonder you're so dour."

"Look, since it's going to be a least a month till I see you again, would you like to take a little walk with me this morning and see my place?"

Marguerite was extremely curious about where and how Malcolm lived and agreed at once to accompany him to upscale Marlborough Street, where he owned the top floor of an elegant old apartment building. Commanding extensive views of Back Bay and the Charles River, the loft had been decorated in the Italianate style, with walls washed in voluptuous Tuscan hues.

Each room held but a few pieces of furniture, clearly chosen by a talented decorator. A striped divan here, a highly rubbed writing desk there, a pretty cabinet against a far wall, all caught Marguerite's eye as Malcolm led her through the rooms.

"Who decorated for you?" she finally asked as they came to a stop at one of the bay windows overlooking the river. It was a frigid New Year's Day, very clear and bright.

"My ex-wife. But she took half the furniture with her when she left. That's why it seems so empty in here."

"How long ago was that?"

"About six months."

"Oh!"

"We weren't married long. I have wall calendars that outlasted my marriage."

"Why did you marry her?"

"She was decorating my apartment and we were spending a lot of time together choosing fabrics and so forth. She was pretty and flirtatious and seemed so eager to please that I mistook her for a potential submissive. In reality she was quite the opposite. And even though she pretended to think it was cute when I playfully spanked her during the courtship, once we were married she didn't have the slightest problem telling me that I'm disturbed."

"Oh no!" Marguerite felt so profoundly uneasy at the thought of Malcolm belonging to another woman that she wondered whether she wasn't already in love with him. "Thank goodness you discovered the scene!"

"It's nice of you to say so, even though you're mad at me," he remarked wistfully, never wanting so much to make a woman like him and never knowing so little about how to accomplish this.

Having disobeyed her passionate command about washing his hands, he had indeed retained her essence on his fingertips the previous night and this had painfully inflamed his desire for Marguerite. Severely tempted by her contours in the body-molding outfit, Malcolm had to fight the urge to reach out and encircle her waist.

"I suppose you realize how badly I want you," he said with his chin on his hand.

Marguerite colored but replied rather daringly, "Lesser men than you have had me faster. You must be doing something wrong."

"Come over here, you brat," he grabbed her by the wrist as she walked past him and feeling the window seat behind his knees, sat down and pulled Marguerite across his lap. "I'll teach you to be so fresh."

"Malcolm, don't you dare!" she cried, attempting to wriggle out of his grasp. However, once her magnificent bottom was upturned in this position, she knew that there was no escaping another spanking.

"I love your riding pants," he told her, warming her up with a couple of dozen affectionate smacks. "You should never wear anything else."

"You can't do this," she protested, trying to cover her bottom with her hand. "I haven't agreed to play."

"But it's so pleasant having you like this," he told her passionately, holding her fast by the waist and squeezing her through the snug pants. She felt his large erection under her tummy again and wanted to grind against it, but forced herself to pull away from him and jump up from his lap. Her face was flushed and her heart pounding as she adjusted her glasses and walked away from him.

"Marguerite?" he jumped up and turned her around to face him. She let him kiss her once, then she pulled away, gazing at him thoughtfully. He seemed to be improving by the moment.

"You don't completely hate me, do you?"

"No, Malcolm. I don't hate you at all."

"But you won't let me make love to you."

Marguerite laughed at him. "Do you always wear your hard-on on your sleeve?"

"You were sopping wet last night and I'll bet you are now too," he accused coolly, causing her color to rise again.

"I suppose you've enjoyed the favors of all the women you've played with so far?" she deftly repelled his attack.

"All except the two married ones," he confessed candidly.

"Oh? You draw the line at adultery?"

"They did."

"And do you practice safe sex?"

"Of course."

Marguerite smiled and dismissed the entire matter, saying, "Now I'd better get back to the hotel and check out. I have a three o'clock train to catch."

"Let me drive you back to Random Point."

"Why?"

"I don't want our time together to end yet, since you're determined to exile me for who knows how long."

Marguerite compared the inconvenience of running for platforms to the comfort of leaning her head against Malcolm's sturdy shoulder all the way to the Cape and chose the cozier option.

They reached Random Point before dusk and Marguerite gave him tea before sending him away with the five required books from her shop.

He reluctantly returned to Boston. Once there he no longer had the heart to date others and amused himself solely by going to the gym and reading through his solitary meals.

Every night he would call Marguerite to talk about the books he had begun to read. After several weeks of this, Marguerite knew that Malcolm was in love with her and she with him, for her heart throbbed painfully each time the telephone rang.

Malcolm could not remember ever enjoying a more bracing romance. Of course he didn't mean to indulge Marguerite endlessly, but meanwhile he was finding her increasingly desirable as he learned about her tastes, ethics and passions though the books she had given him.

Pride and Prejudice made him feel the folly of giving vent to one's first impressions. How relevant this lesson seemed to him now, as he recalled how twelve careless sentences, composed in a frenzy of righteous indignation, had nearly lost him Marguerite.

Now they were in the third week of the new year. He happily read all of Camilla but threw Pamela against the wall, because there were limits to which even he, as besotted as he was, would not go to please the woman he loved.

"What about Pamela, Malcolm?" wondered Marguerite on the phone that night.

"Pamela can burn in hell for all I care. I'm coming to see you."

A dart pierced her tummy as she consented and they arranged to meet after the last working hour of her week.

It snowed all Saturday and traffic was light in the shop. But there was a sudden invasion of customers at five. Then Michael Flagg dropped in for a mug of hot mulled cider. This made Marguerite uneasy. She looked at the clock. It was twenty-five to six. Michael leaned against the counter to wait for her to finish with a customer who was writing a check. Time raced by as Michael chatted to several other customers. Everyone knew and liked Detective Flagg of the Random Point police department.

Now the last customer had departed and it was fifteen minutes to six. Marguerite looked at the clock with such desperation that Michael asked her whether something was wrong. She flushed and confessed, "I'm sorry, darling, but if a certain gentleman walks in within the next few minutes, I'm going to have to pretend that you're just an acquaintance of mine."

"Oh? And why is that?" Michael's heart contracted at these few simple words spoken so kindly to him by his occasional mistress.

"He's someone I've become serious about."

"Define serious."

"You know Michael, just because you never asked me to marry you, that doesn't mean no one ever will."

"I never thought you'd consider it for a minute," he admitted in great surprise.

"No?"

"This gentleman who's about to arrive, am I right in assuming he's some sort of rich genius?"

Marguerite smiled demurely. Michael smiled back at her.

"And handsome, no doubt?" he teased her. She again merely smiled.

"Enlightened?" he ventured hopefully.

"Decidedly not. He already thinks I'm a bad woman because I asked him for a bracelet."

"Though he could well afford it?"

"It's the principal of the thing."

"Self-righteous?"

"I'm smartening him up."

"I don't know whether to feel jealous or sorry for him."

"I hope you'll feel a little jealous," she declared, unable to resist it when he leaned over the counter to kiss her on the mouth.

"Can I stick around to check him out?"

"Certainly not. In fact, you should go at once."

Marguerite walked Michael to the door and looked up and down snowy, cobblestoned Shadow Lane. All the little shops were pulling down their shades for the night and Malcolm was nowhere to be seen.

"I won't kiss you good-bye just in case he's around," Michael told her, "but don't forget I love you."

Marguerite watched him drive off, feeling warmth without regret. Then she looked at her watch and found it was six. The last thing she expected as she returned to the front counter to empty the cash drawer was to see Malcolm leaning against it, with folded arms and a cool expression.

"Malcolm!" she cried, "how long have you been here?"

"So you want to get married, do you?" he said, deliberately removing his jacket and rolling up his sleeves.

"Malcolm, what are you doing?" she backed away from him.

"Getting ready to teach my fiancée a good lesson!"

"But, why?" she felt the gallery steps behind her and ran up to the first level.

"Nice how you were planning to begin our relationship with a lie!" he ran up the stairs behind her as she ascended the second circular flight.

"What lie?"

"You were going to pretend you hardly knew that man, yet he's obviously your lover."

"I only wanted to avoid an awkward situation," she explained, still rapidly climbing the narrow staircase.

"Come back down here and take what you've got coming!" he advised as she scampered up to the third gallery in her impossibly high ankle straps. The view of her shapely bottom so snugly wrapped in a taupe wool pencil skirt was spectacular from behind and he appreciated it as much as any man could.

"No, I don't dare!" she confessed, seeking refuge among the most extensive collection of B&D erotica in New England. Malcolm joined her momentarily, pulled her out of the corner with an iron grip and looked around for something to sit on.

"So you're smartening me up, are you?" he demanded, dragging a straight-backed chair into the middle of the floor. Then grasping her by the elbow of her white cotton blouse, he pulled her straight across his lap. "I'll smarten you up, young lady!" He brought his palm down hard on either cheek through the skirt. Several dozen emphatic whacks descended on Marguerite's taut, upturned backside before she began to whimper.

Marguerite desperately tried to remember her entire conversation with Michael for damning remarks. Suddenly the balance of power between them had been reversed and Marguerite no longer felt either sophisticated or in control. She darted a glance at him over her shoulder and was not surprised by the air of authority with which he stared her down.

"Tell me the truth about you and that man," he stopped spanking her to pull up her skirt. Finding it too tight, he stood her on her feet and looking straight into her eyes, deliberately unbuckled her chunky belt, unzipped the skirt and made her step out of it.

"He's someone I've been seeing on and off for a couple of years, but it's not serious," Marguerite replied, reaching back to examine her already rosy bottom through her ivory silk panties.

"Not serious, huh?" He pulled her back across his lap, dazzled once again by her long, stunning legs. "What's his name?" he smacked her hard.

"Ow! Michael Flagg."

"He sounds as though he's already planning to cuckold me."

"Malcolm, you've misunderstood."

"You called him darling and let him kiss you."

"Oh, I let everyone kiss me!" she cried in some exasperation.

"Not like that I hope."

"Where were you to see so much?" she wondered indignantly.

"Hidden in the tiny alcove you've reserved for sensible books on money management. What did he mean by enlightened?"

"You know, Malcolm, cool."

"That's a pretty inarticulate answer coming from you. What the hell does that mean?"

Marguerite could not be compelled to answer until he spanked her repeatedly and much harder.

"I forgot the question," she finally cried.

"What did your friend mean when he wondered whether I was enlightened?"

"Not jealous and Victorian," she explained at last, reaching back to rub.

"I don't like him," Malcolm brooded, rolling her panties down to expose her completely.

"Malcolm, let me go. I haven't even locked the door downstairs."

"Oh, stop whining. I've been waiting for months to do this properly and I've even got a reason to this time."

Marguerite, who was fair and not frequently spanked, reddened deeply from his hand. The quick coloration might have restrained him had she not reacted to each smack in the prettiest possible way.

Had he really scolded her for not being submissive enough? Her little pants and whimpers as she took a very hard spanking excited him beyond compare. Everything about her was completely adorable to him now that he was certain she'd decided to be his.

"Why didn't you tell me about your boyfriend?" he stopped to stroke her bottom, which he'd spanked to a deep magenta and was radiant. He spread her creamy thighs and found her wet.

"You never asked me," she murmured, opening herself to his exploring fingers while grinding her muff against his thigh. "And besides, we haven't even started dating properly yet," she pointed out.

"Oh? And what is it we have been doing?"

"Flirting," she suggested mischievously. This got her twelve of the best from his very hard hand.

"When I undertake to read three thousand pages of literature to please a girl, I'm not flirting. Did you think that I was?"

"No, sir," she gratified him by saying meekly.

"And besides, you wouldn't be planning to marry someone you were only flirting with. So I've caught you in another lie." Another twelve of the best followed, making Marguerite cry out loud and begin to twist on his lap.

"I was simply considering possibilities," she explained.

"Well consider the possibility of being stood in the corner with your skirt up to your waist like a naughty school girl."

"Oh, please, don't make me do that," she appealed to him with her big, green eyes behind their attractive eyeglasses.

"There is an alternative," he told her firmly, stroking the sting from her bottom again.

"What is it?"

"Agree to begin our honeymoon here and now, with you bent over the little wooden desk."

"Only if you go and lock the door!"

When he raced back up the stairs, Marguerite was still rubbing her bottom with her light red hair down on her shoulders and her proper white blouse unbuttoned to her cleavage. He turned her to face him, unbuttoned the blouse all the way and pulled it off, and after this, her lacy bra. He then looked at her, as much as to say, have I really known you for almost three months without ever once seeing your bosom?

He took her large, luscious breasts in his hands and deeply sucked each nipple until Marguerite almost fainted from enjoyment in his arms. Then he bent her over the reading desk, and pressed her down until her tummy touched the blotter. She leaned up on her elbows to give him access to her breasts.

"You look irresistible in that position, Marguerite," he told her, pulling his belt out of his trouser loops. She flashed him a look over one shoulder as he shook out the strap and gave her lick with the end.

"Ow!" she cried and pouted.

"Take off your glasses," he commanded.

"No!" she resisted pertly. He gave her two hard swats with the belt that made her catch her breath and she took off her glasses and laid them on the desk beside her.

"So you want to get married," he repeated.

"No!" she replied, still vexed that he had overheard her dreadful remark. He gave her a hard whack with the strap.

"Don't lie to me when I have you in this position," he scolded, laying on the belt five more times, and scoring her pink bottom with light marks. "This is too exhilarating!" he thought to himself, while maintaining a serious demeanor.

Marguerite thrilled to the sight of her handsome persecutor shaking out the strap, raising his arm and bringing it down. When he threw her a glance she felt her tummy contract. "He is too handsome!" she thought to herself.

"How do you think I felt listening to myself discussed as though I were a cheap trick!" he demanded.

"That's your interpretation!" she cried, starting up, but he pressed her back down with a hand in the small of her back.

"Where do you think you're going?"

"You're saying vile things again!" Marguerite cried passionately, instantly ready to burst into tears.

"Now, you listen to me young lady," he threw the belt down and smacked her hard with his hand, "I'm not going to put up with any more of your hyper-sensitive histrionics. Understand?" Smack!

"Yes!" she replied, breathlessly, her tummy fluttering again.

"I'm still getting over the fact that you interrupted our last session right in the middle just because I said something that offended you. Then I got my winter reading list. That was what I had to go through before I could claim the privilege of doing this to you again."

"A small enough price," she commented, reaching back to rub.

"No rubbing till I say so," he said, capturing both her wrists in his hand and pinning them to her waist. "You're right though, I did like the books. And now we have something to talk about besides your checkered past."

"Then why are you still spanking me?"

"Because I don't like my lady to discuss me with other men."

"But I haven't agreed to be your lady."

"Fine, I'll just keep doing this until you do," he promised, delivering a series of heavy, satisfying smacks to her glowing bottom. She reclaimed her wrists to bury her head in her arms as he warmed her thoroughly with the palm of his hand, then returned to the strap for twelve more.

"Well?"

Marguerite felt very sore when he stopped, but still wanted him to go on.

"I'm just surprised that you found it so difficult to conquer Pamela," she baited him, reminding him of the nine hundred pages he had finally plowed through to satisfy the letter of their agreement.

"Oh, I conquered Pamela, all right, and now I'm going to... capture you," he decided, drawing back his arm to really make her feel the next twelve. "This is exactly the sort of whipping Pamela should have been given for being so willful."

"I'm a good deal more willful than Pamela," Marguerite warned.

"Oh, really?" he brought the strap down hard now. Marguerite gripped the desk and gasped her way through many more strokes. On another day, or in another mood, one-fourth the strapping would have dissolved her in tears and cries for mercy, but this afternoon, being vigorously whipped felt somehow perfectly romantic.

When one final volley of six was all that flesh could bear, Marguerite cried out at last. Malcolm was relieved when she did, afraid that they were both becoming carried away with the passion of their first real session. He saw as he threw down the strap and unzipped his trousers that she had become shockingly marked with broad swatches of rose standing out against the paler pink that stained both cheeks.

He pushed her back down over the desk. "I don't think I've ever had a woman put me off as long as you have." Malcolm had a condom out of its package and on his fully erect penis in seconds. Then he spread her legs, pulled her up by the hips and guided his cock into her slick sex.

"Slowly, darling, please," she urged, looking prettily back at him over one soft shoulder. She gave a little shiver as he gripped her by the waist and began to penetrate her deeply. As he drove his large cock into her one insistent inch at a time, he leaned over to fondle her breasts, pinch her nipples and then her velvety ear lobes.

"You're damned right I'm unenlightened," he told her emphatically, driving into her pussy like an oiled piston. "So you're going to have to behave yourself from now on."

"I will never do that!" she cried.

"Oh yes you will, if we get married," he warned, smacking her on her thighs several times. She gave a little pant of excitement at this treatment, causing him to repeat it more firmly. Every time he did, a pre-climactic shiver rippled through her, bathing the deeply sheathed shaft of his cock with her affection. Malcolm was amused that she still seemed more than ready to endure additional smacks. She, who had the tenderest, whitest skin he had ever seen.

"You're being deliberately naughty," he told her, "and I can't in all good conscience spank you any more. You should see how marked you are."

These words of love were well received.

"I don't mind being marked by my fiancé," she murmured, succumbing at that moment to a rapturous climax. Immensely gratified, Malcolm then allowed himself to release the pent up emotion not only of the last three months, but of his entire life.

Their first sex act was complete. And Marguerite felt very glad that she had taken the time to choose the little desk and straight-backed chair for her favorite gallery.

Chapter Four

Frances and Sloan

Marguerite's new husband disagreed about the manner in which she had determined to restaff her bookshop prior to embarking on their honeymoon. It was still only February; the dreariest month in New England, and all Malcolm Branwell could think of was how little his adorable wife would elect to wear in the desert. Yet here she was deliberately postponing their Jacuzzi soaked pleasures in order to play Cupid to two strangers!

"Why you can't just put an ad in the Boston Globe?" Malcolm looked up from his Wall Street Journal to complain as Marguerite worked on the ad that was to appear in the upcoming issue of Hugo Sands' magazine, The New Rod Quarterly.

"I told you, Malcolm, I want to give two worthy spanking people the positions."

"But Marguerite, surely you must know that business and romance don't mix."

"Malcolm, do wake up. Sexually excited employees are happy employees."

"Distracted employees," he grumbled, wondering if this sheer silliness about hiring scene people was enough of an excuse to turn the leggy redhead over his knee. "You know you're not a puppeteer, Marguerite," he told her disapprovingly. "What if your plan backfires and they loathe each other? What if he tries something with her and she brings a law suit against you?"

"But Malcolm, whoever responds to ads in Hugo Sands' magazine must necessarily be into it. Now listen to the ad," she said, and began to read off the screen of her laptop, "Sales person sought for charming

104

Cape Cod village book shop. Must be presentable and literate. Managerial skills preferred. Modest salary, nice living quarters included. Send resume and salary requirement."

"I thought you needed two people."

"Well darling, many people will answer the ad. I'll pick one of the boys with the bookkeeping skills to be the store manager and the wittiest girl to be the clerk."

"What if she's better qualified to be the manager?"

"That would create a different dynamic than the one I had envisioned, but I'll consider it."

"That's a relief at least."

"I sense you don't approve."

"I think you're being extremely silly about this whole thing."

"Malcolm, didn't you realize that my hobby is promoting romance in the scene?"

"Are they going to know that they've both been hired in response to the same ad?"

"I don't intend to tell them, but I expect they'll figure it out fairly quickly."

"Do I get to interview the girls?" he asked with an endearing grin.

"Would you like to?" Marguerite smiled at him with amusement, causing Malcolm to flush. "Darling, I think that would be delicious," she continued, shocking the young Bostonian. "You could pick the girl and I could pick the boy."

"Okay," he replied, in an uncertain voice. Marguerite smiled and printed the ad.

Two weeks later resumes began to arrive. The only candidate Marguerite ever seriously considered for the position of manager was Sloan Taylor, a tall, reedy, disarmingly attractive intellectual, the sound of whose cultivated voice instantly captivated her. He was currently managing a Branwell's Book Bag in Brookline, but openly repudiated the supermarket mentality of her husband's corporation and longed for a more rarified venue in which to exercise his bibliophilic talents.

Sloan possessed bookkeeping experience and could lift heavy

boxes. Moreover, he had a light, engaging manner and as far as Marguerite was concerned, divine taste in literature. He was fussy, compulsive and impeccable. Finally, he was single and eager to relocate to sequestered Random Point. Marguerite was enchanted and immediately installed Sloan in the shop.

Malcolm interviewed the only female applicant he felt likely to fulfill the romantic expectations of his wife. Frances Wu was a mischievous looking 23-year-old Radcliffe grad who had one year of work experience teaching remedial English at a Boston high school.

Frances was shy, cynical, death metal-friendly and contemplating her first piercing, although she did have the presence of mind to appear for her interview with Malcolm in a well behaved checked suit and perfect pumps.

This was the last time anyone would see Frankie in a skirt for some time, her favorite uniform for work consisting of black leggings, Doc Martens, rolled white sox, and an oversized wool shirt. She was small and very shapely, with long, straight black hair and big brown eyes.

"The store you'll be working at is my wife's shop in Random Point," Malcolm explained, "not a store in the regular Branwell's Book Bag chain. I'm just helping her restaff it so we can go on our honeymoon."

"I was hoping that the shop would be in Random Point," said Frankie, with delight. Frankie had been electrified to find the ad in Hugo Sands' magazine, and one of the thrills she anticipated on being considered for the job was the possibility of running into Mr. Sands while working on Cape Cod. She wondered whether the owners of the bookstore were also in the scene, including the handsome Mr. Branwell. It would be unbearably sexy if this were true.

"I was wondering why the ad turned up in the magazine where I found it," Frankie said conversationally, causing Malcolm to color with confusion and inwardly damn Marguerite for this perverse joke.

"I think my wife ran the ad in all the local literary journals," he replied a beat later, quelling further grilling and puzzling Frankie greatly.

"I'm very bossy," Sloan informed Frankie, over their first cup of coffee. "I hope you'll be able to get used to it."

"I'm pretty compliant," she readily admitted.

"You'd be the first girl I ever met who was."

Frankie smiled then looked at him seriously.

"Sloan, may I ask you a question?" she spoke with some hesitation.

"You may."

"Have you worked here long?"

"Just ten days," he replied.

She did a mental calculation and decided to press on. "May I ask how you found out about the position?"

"How did I find out about the position?" Sloan looked at her sharply. "I answered an ad. Didn't you?"

"Yes. But what ad did you answer?"

"Why? What ad did you answer?"

"I answered an ad in a magazine."

"Me too."

"A literary journal."

"I guess you could call it that," he smiled.

"Did we answer the same ad, I wonder?"

"My ad came from the New Rod magazine," Sloan admitted boldly.

"Mine too," Frankie said faintly.

"And how did you come by the ad?"

"I subscribe to the magazine."

"Me too."

"Is it okay if I smoke in the garden?" she asked with sudden embarrassment.

"Feel free," he told her. In a minute or two he followed her out. She was sitting on the stone bench opposite the sundial and shivering with her cigarette, for it was sunny but bitingly cold.

"What a dangerous piece of data you've given me, Frances," he handed her another cup of steaming coffee.

"Why?" she blushed.

"Because now I'll know what to do with you if you ignore any of my rules."

No one in Random Point had yet discovered Frances, so she had no friends in town. However, Sloan was an amusing companion with enough strange opinions, moods and ideas to challenge her on a daily basis.

Sloan did not deliberately try to find fault with Frankie, but his perfectionism led to continuous nitpicking.

"Frances, dear," he might gently begin, "you're the fastest shelver I've ever seen when you concentrate, but you simply can't continue to skim through all the books the way you're doing." Or, "While the ability to discuss Beckett and Stoppard is an admirable quality in a bookseller, three customers were lined up while you were bothering to impress one browser."

Their first real conflict arose out of her inability to follow his regimen on greeting the customers. Frankie was of the opinion that browsers ought not to be pestered. But Sloan had been taught differently.

"When a customer walks in," he firmly told her, "you should immediately approach him or her and say, 'Good morning, Sir or Madam, how are you today? May I be of some assistance?'"

"Okay," Frankie promised, inwardly recoiling at the thought of performing this awkward ritual sixty times a day.

"I can't make you dress like a grown up," he admonished her, "but at least I can insist you speak like one."

Frankie sensed a certain amount of bitterness in this statement, as though he had perhaps argued with his employers for the right to enforce a dress code in the shop and had been refused.

The next time she forgot to approach a customer in the prescribed manner he spoke to her with some warmth.

"Now Frances, I've told you how I want you to greet the customers, haven't I?"

"Yes," she stubbornly refused to meet his eyes and continued shelving books.

"Why is that so hard to do?"

"It isn't hard but I forgot."

"Well, please don't forget next time."

"I won't."

After this admonishment Frankie forced herself to address every new visitor to the shop in the proper manner and Sloan was pleased. But the next day she returned to her original style of looking up vaguely and smiling "Hi," when a customer walked in before returning to whatever book in which she had been immersed.

Sloan witnessed this behavior with displeasure and remonstrated with her at once. The son of a meticulous woman who had managed the bridal department of Bonwit Teller's for twenty-five years, Sloan's confidence in his mastery of proper business etiquette was unshakable.

"My dear Frances, do you think I instructed you yesterday in the proper way to greet our clientele just to hear myself speak?"

"Did I forget again?" Now she was genuinely embarrassed. "I'm really sorry. It's just that I'm not accustomed to speaking like that."

"More's the pity. But it's never too late to establish good work habits. Now I want you to concentrate on remembering to greet the customers properly," he told her sternly, then returned to the front desk.

Forty minutes passed and Sloan had all but forgotten their conversation when Frankie presented herself before him, choosing a moment when there wasn't a customer in the shop.

He looked at her in his disconcertingly impatient way. "Yes, Frances?"

"I'm sorry I can't seem to remember how to greet the customers," she said meekly, though with a hint of mischief in her eyes.

"Oh, you'll catch on, honey," he reassured her, in his vaguely maternal way, distracted by a sloppy row of books on a shelf within his sight. When he began to straighten them she followed him.

"You should spank me next time I forget," she candidly suggested.

Sloan looked at her sharply. Suddenly she had his full attention. "Perhaps I should spank you now," he snapped over folded arms. "After all, I've already had to speak to you on this subject two or three times."

Frankie quailed at the look of irritation which had spread over his patrician face. She hung her head and waited for him to take her hand

and lead her into the stock room.

Before she even knew what he was about Sloan had a chair under him and Frankie across his lap. Her heart pounded as he adjusted her compact form across his thighs, gripped her firmly by the waist and began to spank her briskly over her nubby leggings.

Frankie gave a startled little gasp each time his palm came down, but the radiant sting that it left in its wake seemed far from unpleasant to her.

"My dear Frances," Sloan commented, "you fit across my lap perfectly!"

Frankie was gratified and whimpered in response, hot thrills rippling through her every second. She had fantasized about receiving a proper spanking since her childhood, but had never met a boyfriend with enough understanding to supply it. Now for the first time she was getting what she wanted.

After briskly administering one hundred smacks to the seat of her pants Sloan set her on her feet. This left Frankie gasping with emotion.

"Now you get back to the floor and think about what just happened," he ordered coolly, though his own heart was racing.

"Yes, sir," she whispered, blushing to the eyes and scurrying out with one hand pressed to her bottom.

When she had gone Sloan took a handkerchief out of his pocket and needlessly mopped his dry brow. Had it really happened? On returning to the floor he threw Frances a sharp look, which caused her to flush. It had happened.

At six p.m., when Sloan was closing out, Frances approached him to say good night. He looked up at her gravely.

"Well, Frances, I hope you don't think I was too harsh with you earlier."

"No, sir," she could barely repress a tiny smile but did not meet his eyes.

"And did I make an impression on you?"

"Oh, yes!" she flashed him one deep look that almost knocked him off his feet with the thrill of mastery.

Sloan felt a tremendous urge to kiss her but instead kindly bade her good night and returned to his cash register tapes. It was snowy and dark when Frankie walked the few blocks home without noticing the cold.

That night it snowed so copiously that when Frankie got to work the following morning she found Sloan digging a path to the front door of the shop through a two foot drift. This did not put him in the best mood and his disgruntlement was further enhanced by an incident that occurred just before noon.

Frankie was arranging a display of gothic novels in the front of the store when Hugo Sands walked in, natty as an Esquire ad in a mohair suit, and immediately inquired of Frankie whether she had a copy of The Vicar of Wakefield.

"Do you know the author?" Frankie politely replied, causing Sloan to grind his teeth in mortification at the ignorance of his sole salesperson.

"It's Goldsmith, Frances, aisle 3," Sloan called out from the front register, adding politely, "Good morning, Hugo."

Frankie gazed at Hugo for a moment in surprise before darting off to the next aisle to find the book.

"Good morning," Hugo joined Sloan. "I see your assistant's finally arrived," he added with a smile. Frankie stepped up and handed him the paperback with a deep blush.

"Thank you," said Hugo.

"Excuse me, but are you the same Hugo Sands who publishes the magazine?" she asked in a rush.

"Why, yes. And you are?"

"Frankie Wu."

"Frankie, huh? And where did Marguerite find you?"

"I answered the ad for the clerk position that Mrs. Branwell placed in your journal."

"I see." Hugo visualized his customer database and recalled that an F. Wu had been a subscriber for about a year.

"I just want to say how much I love your magazine, Mr. Sands."

"Do you?"

"Oh yes! It's the most exciting thing I've ever read in my life."

"If you're that passionate about the subject, why aren't you a contributor?"

"You mean, write something?"

"Why not?"

"I don't have any experiences to write about," she admitted wistfully.

"None?" Hugo raised an eyebrow at Sloan, who was also a subscriber.

"Almost none," she corrected herself, casting a quick look at her boss, who did not seem pleased by the turn of the conversation.

"I'm sure you have a good imagination, though." Hugo took the book and his change from Sloan.

"Maybe I'll try," she mused.

"You know, I own the antiques shop across the street. You should come and visit me sometime."

"Thank you, I will," she said with a fluttering pulse.

"I'm surprised at you, Frances," Sloan scolded the moment Hugo left, "not knowing who wrote The Vicar of Wakefield! What are they teaching English majors at Radcliffe these days? Steven King and Danielle Steele?"

"Mr. Sands is very handsome," said Frankie, still staring out the door. "I thought he'd be an older man."

"He's 48," said Sloan with cool precision. Frankie was shocked. That did seem very old.

"How old are you?" she boldly asked Sloan.

"Thirty," he replied, somewhat stiffly, feeling centuries older than Frankie.

"You're thirty?" she seemed genuinely amazed.

"How old did you think I was?" he asked with some trepidation.

"I didn't think you were much older than me," she admitted honestly. This fortuitous comment caused a smile to spread across his wide mouth and banished Sloan's anxiety at finding a rival so dangerously close.

"I was seven when you were born," he said, helpfully suggesting a new perspective. "And Mr. Sands was twenty-five." On this merciless note, Sloan returned to work, confident of having lost no ground with

Frances.

A few days later, over lunch with Hugo Sands, Frankie spoke at length about spanking. It was the first time in her life she had ever articulated her feelings on this subject to another. For even though Sloan had spanked her, they hadn't discussed the phenomenon afterwards in the slightest degree, both pretending that nothing out of the ordinary had happened between them. This fact and certain other aspects of Sloan's behavior now had Frankie convinced that her supervisor was gay.

Hugo was extremely surprised at this observation and asked her to explain.

Frankie began in earnest, "Sloan is into show tunes, fashions and ancient movie stars. Sloan dresses for work and laments the passing of the days during which women wore gloves. Sloan grinds his own coffee and makes his own potpourri. Apart from that, he thinks I need a make-over and keeps pressing me to go shopping with him."

Hugo laughed at her and lit her cigarette.

"I might give credence to your theory except for one thing."

"And what is that?"

"The look he gave me when he thought I might be flirting with you."

"He gave you a look?"

"It was anything but disinterested."

"Then I wonder why he hasn't brought it up again," Frankie mused.

"Brought what up?"

"That he spanked me."

"Oh, he has spanked you, has he?"

"Just once. For some minor breach of business etiquette. That was about four days ago."

"And did the experience meet your expectations?"

"Oh, it utterly surpassed them."

"Did you tell him you enjoyed it?"

"Oh no!"

"Well, maybe he thinks you're offended."

"I don't think he'd care much. I forfeited his respect when I asked you who wrote The Vicar of Wakefield."

"Frankie, I think that due to your professional relationship, Sloan will require further encouragement from you before laying hands on your adorable person again."

"But I'm not going to ask him each time."

"No, of course not, but you could let him know that you're attracted to him. Then, once you're dating..."

"Oh, I don't know that I want to date him!" Frankie surprised Hugo by saying. "He's so stuffy and old fashioned."

Nevertheless, Frankie decided to take Hugo's advice and let Sloan know that she liked him as soon she came back from lunch.

Sloan knew that she had gone out with Hugo and was brooding over the regional guidebooks when she returned.

"Sloan?" she planted herself uneasily before him. "May I ask you something?"

"Sure, what is it?" he replied with some anxiety, afraid that Hugo had already tempted her to work in his shop across the street.

"Would you like to have dinner with me tonight? I'll cook."

"Why, Frances, I'd love to," he replied somewhat breathlessly. And then she knew that Hugo had been right.

Sloan didn't trust Frankie to cook, and soon took over at the little stove in Marguerite's guest house and improved considerably on the dish she had begun by preparing an impromptu sauce. Frankie pouted as he put the food on the table.

"What's the matter, sweetie? Taste it before you make a face."

"Oh, it smells wonderful. Much better than I could have done. But it defeats the purpose of my having you over to dinner, doesn't it?"

"But I enjoy cooking. I used to cook for my ex-girlfriend constantly."

"Why did you break up?"

"Oh, because she was silly and she bored me," he revealed in an offhanded manner.

"Was she pretty?"

"Sufficiently," he replied disdainfully.

"Did you ever spank her?"

"Often," he replied, as though this were a trifle, "she was naturally passive."

Frankie pleased Sloan by cleaning her plate.

"Do I bore you?" she asked.

"Hardly."

"Well, what do you think of me?"

"I think you might be the most wonderful thing that's ever happened to me," he said, with his hand on his chin.

Frankie was surprised by the warmth of his declaration and refilled their wine glasses in confusion.

"That sounds like a lyric to one of those Tin Pan Alley torments you play all day long at the store."

"You don't like show tunes from the 20's and 30's?" Sloan was crestfallen.

"As much as you like Punk."

"Excuse me, Frances, but I was 13 the summer I first saw The Damned, with a blue Mohawk and four piercings in this ear," he turned his head toward her to display his left earlobe. "You can still see where the holes were."

Now Frankie was awestruck. Was there any way in which this man was not somehow original?

It had begun snowing heavily again and Frankie raised the blinds so they could watch it coming down on the woods behind the guesthouse.

After they were finished eating Sloan insisted on cleaning up while Frankie sat smoking in the window seat.

"Have you always been so compulsive?" she asked.

"I prefer to think of it as being well organized. And the answer is yes. You should have seen my toy chest at age five. What about you? Have you always been so scattered?"

"Excuse me?" Frankie bristled.

"Well, just look at this place. You haven't unpacked half your things yet and you've been here nearly a week."

"I'm just deciding where everything should go first," she defended herself. "Which makes more sense than putting everything away twice."

"So when you do think you'll decide?"

"I was going to finish putting things away on Sunday. If that's all right with you."

"Now Frances, don't be sullen."

She glared at him and exhaled furiously. "You know, you're very critical," she said suddenly. He shrugged this off and continued drying dishes and putting them away. "Of course," she added recklessly after draining her glass, "at your advanced age one must expect a certain amount of fussiness." Sloan raised an eyebrow at her over his shoulder but made no reply. "Sloan, did you ever think that maybe you should have been born a woman?" she continued to bait him.

"Now just a minute," he stiffened and turned.

"Well look at you, so at home in an apron. With a demeanor so proper and nice."

"Not always," he warned her, finally hanging the apron up and dimming the overhead light

"Oh?" she flashed him a mischievous look.

"I can behave as improperly as anyone, if I choose to," he firmly declared, sitting next to her on the window seat.

"Like you did in the back of the store on Tuesday?"

"Oh, you mean that little spanking I gave you?"

"It wasn't little. I felt it for an hour."

"Oh, that was nothing. I didn't even pull your pants down, did I?"

"You didn't have to. I felt it anyway."

"Tuesday was a long time ago. I'm sure you've been naughty since then," he said, gently taking her by both wrists and pulling her face down across his lap. Again she wore the nubby leggings that encased her firm bottom so prettily.

"So I should have been born a woman, should I?" He positioned her perfectly and smoothed her pants down. Smack! His hand came down hard.

"I was only kidding," she protested.

"You were impugning my masculinity," he accused, bringing his palm down on her bottom five or six times in a row. "I don't like that."

"Oh? Then don't ask Mr. Sands to recount the conversation we had about you this afternoon," Frankie advised.

"Why not?"

"Well, I couldn't help but wonder aloud to Mr. Sands whether or not you're gay."

"Oh my," said Sloan gravely, "you are a wicked girl." Then he deliberately rolled down her leggings to her knees and renewing his grip on her slender waist, began to bring his palm down smartly on the seat of her high cut white cotton briefs.

"Ow!" she cried. "That really hurts!"

"How dare you spread such an outrageous rumor about me, young lady?" he briskly lowered her panties and brought his hand down repeatedly on her small, well-rounded buttocks. "You've actually made me angry!" he decided, and began to spank her hard enough to make her kick and squeal. Frankie was totally unprepared for this type of pain, which quickly taught her the difference between discipline and punishment.

Frankie was too new to the scene to know about the word mercy and its powers, but her sobs soon served the same purpose and Sloan stopped spanking her as soon as they began. When he let her up he was shocked to see tears over spilling her eyes. He took a clean handkerchief out of his pocket and dried her face with a sigh. But she was much more interested in trying to examine her deeply reddened bottom over one shoulder.

"I was only teasing you. You didn't have to spank me that hard. Now I'm never going to let you spank me again!" she cried, like a petulant playmate, then burst into tears once more. This time Sloan took her in his arms and let her sob against his argyle vest.

"Don't be such a brat. You know you had that coming for slandering me to someone whose opinion I value," he scolded, kissing her for the first time. After which she stared up at him with glittering eyes.

"I wouldn't care if anyone thought I was a lesbian," she asserted politically, not yet in the mood for kisses.

"I'm sure you wouldn't. You already dress like a boy. I'm

surprised you don't crew cut your hair."

"I've thought of it, but then I couldn't wear a ponytail. And you like my ponytail, don't you?" Frankie flirted with Sloan for the first time, the wine heating her blood.

"I like everything about you," Sloan admitted.

"I never would have known it from the way you act at work," she accused.

"Just because I've been reserved, that doesn't mean I've been impervious to your charms."

"Does that mean you intend to do something with that big hard-on I felt under my tummy just now?"

Her frankness rendered him temporarily speechless, but he rallied quickly.

"As your supervisor, I'm not sure it would be ethical to do anything with it."

Frankie stared at him in disbelief.

"Surely you don't think Mrs. Branwell would object? She's the most romantic person I've ever met. In fact, I'm babysitting for her cats while she's on her honeymoon and she left me the keys to her dungeon."

"Her what?"

"She has the most darling attic playroom, with a whipping post and a spanking horse and a bondage bed and mirrors all around. Would you like to see it?" Sloan hesitated until Frankie said, "She gave me the key and urged me to explore."

"Isn't Mrs. Branwell the most provocative woman you've ever met?" Frankie asked Sloan as they entered the pretty attic playroom.

"No, Frances, you are."

"Oh, come on," she laughed.

"Your modesty is very endearing, but when am I going to see you in a dress?"

"Maybe when the weather gets warmer," said Frankie, blushing.

"I'll bet you don't even own a dress."

"That's not true. I have a whole closet full of Betsy Johnson dresses."

"Chosen by your mother, to prevent you from embarrassing her on holidays, no doubt," Sloan intuited.

"How did you know that?" Frankie marveled, throwing open the mirrored double doors of Marguerite's corsetry armoire to let Sloan examine its luxurious contents.

"I'd love to see you in this," he told her, pulling a cream satin waist cinch out of one of the drawers and holding it up to her front. "Take off your clothes and let's try it on you."

"Not without stockings, shoes and a bra," she firmly replied.

"Oh, very well," he yielded to her sensible response and began to examine the room's unique furnishings. "But I really want to see you in feminine clothes some time soon."

"I'm sorry but I don't do frills."

"Oh, you'll do frills before I'm done with you," Sloan promised, stopping at the leather padded spanking horse. "Come over here, Frances."

When she came to him he sat her up on the bench and unlaced her Doc Martens. They fell on the floor with a loud report. Frankie had very small feet in little white socks. Next he unbuttoned her coarse grey overshirt and removed it. Under this she had on a cream cotton thermal undershirt. "May I?" he asked politely, gripping the hem. She nodded and let him pull the shirt over her head. The way she shook her long, shiny, black hair back into place enchanted Sloan. A plain white cotton bra with a tiny pink rosette at the cleavage cradled her perfectly rounded little bosom. Sloan freed her exquisite breasts from the bra and gently fondled them.

"Now, young lady," he said authoritatively, lifting her off the bench, turning her to face it and bending her over it, "I want your tummy flat across the bench." He took her by the waist and positioned her so that her bottom was uppermost. "Frances, answer me honestly," said Sloan, stroking her bottom through the leggings, "do you really think you've been punished enough for the way you teased me earlier?"

She turned her head to see them both reflected in the mirrored wardrobe opposite as he found a large oval hairbrush on a nearby vanity table. He laid it against her bottom so she could feel the smooth, wooden back. "Well, Frances?"

"No, sir," she admitted, for the pain of the previous spanking had now faded to an exciting warmth, while her clitoris had begun to swell and ache.

"No, I didn't think so either," he told her, drawing back his arm only slightly to deliver six moderate swats with the back of the brush.

"Ow!" cried Frankie. "I'm very sorry!"

"Are you? Hold this," he handed her the brush and pulled her leggings down to just below her buttocks, exposing her white cotton panties. Now he took the brush again and placing a hand in the small of her back, administered six more whacks in rapid succession. These stung her deeply, but Frankie's pubic mound was pressed against the bench the whole time he was paddling her and this brought her to the edge of orgasm.

Next Sloan pulled her panties down to just below her bottom, baring her blushing cheeks entirely, which made her feel like a little girl waiting for an injection at the doctor's office. She gave a little sob of excitement. He stroked her gently then lifted her luxuriant hair to kiss the back of her neck, thrilled by her meekness.

"My little rebel," he said fondly, with the back of the brush pressed against her bare bottom. "You certainly look the picture of compliance now." He began to spank her as firmly as he dared. As she panted and whimpered he felt encouraged to bring the back of the brush down across her petite bottom many times, suffusing her cheeks with a deep rose glow in a couple of minutes.

Frankie squeezed her eyes shut and ground against the bench as the brush came down again and again on her prettily exposed bottom.

Bringing the spanking to a close, he told her sternly, "I've a good mind to make you stand in the corner now."

Frankie whimpered a tiny, "No!" in reply and attempted to rise, but Sloan pushed her back down across the bench.

"I didn't say you could get up," he told her, pulling off both her leggings and panties to reveal her shapely legs for the first time. "Forgive me, Mrs. Branwell," Sloan thought to himself, unzipping his trousers and freeing the rampant erection that they had imprisoned.

Soon he began to possess her and Frankie yielded everything to him. She'd made love to other boys, but had never felt taken before, a sensation she had fantasized about for years. And the knowledge that Sloan had evolved to his present state of elegant manhood from a disenfranchised urchin with blue hair and multiple piercings only added to his mystery and power.

Frankie had always dreamed that sex itself would be different with a masterful lover, not boring as it usually was. Now she learned that her instinct had been correct. None of her boyfriends had ever bent her over like this, with something smooth and hard under her tummy, to grind against. Nor could she ever recall a boy holding her so firmly by the waist, which reminded her each moment of his subtle control.

His thrust was deep and true. The position even permitted her to hide her face and simply luxuriate in the feeling of being taken and taken care of.

The recollection of the spanking he had given her sent shivers of excitement through Frankie, counter pointing the rapturous sensations received from his pistoning cock. If she was tentatively in love with Sloan before, the moment he gave her her first orgasm across the horse, the sentiment became officially engraved on her heart.

It was going on one a.m. and they were lying in bed in Frankie's room by the light of the moon when Sloan decided it was time to go home.

"But you can't go now, it's still snowing," she protested bouncing up in bed as he began to dress.

"Frances, tomorrow is Saturday. I have to get into the shop early and do a great many things before we open."

"So leave here early in the morning."

"Frances, I'm sure you're very charming in the morning, but instant coffee makes me want to kill myself," he declared, with deep contempt for the contents of her kitchen cupboard.

"Sloan, you can't mean to terminate our first night like this!"

"Sweetie, it's a work night. Tomorrow night you can stay with me, all night if you like, and I'll cook you breakfast on Sunday morning. Okay?"

"No, it's not okay," she brooded, hugging a pillow to her Chinese-style lilac silk pajamas. "I can't believe you're leaving me now."

"Frances, we'll see each other at nine a.m., provided you aren't as late as you were today," he reminded her.

"Sloan, can't you stop being my boss for two minutes?" she cried. Sloan finished tucking in his shirt, then sat down beside her on the bed again.

"Frances, do you realize you're behaving immaturely?"

"I just want you to stay with me tonight," she replied with a jot more circumspection.

"I explained to you why I have to leave, dear."

"I really don't understand. Do people your age get tired sooner?"

"Frances, do you want another spanking?"

"No," she subsided against the oaken headboard.

"Oh yes you do," he told her sharply, pulling her across his lap.

"No!" she cried, putting back one little hand to protect her satin trouser seat. This he removed and, gripping her firmly by the waist, smacked her hard with the palm of his hand ten times. He was rewarded with a separate and distinct little "Oh!" each time his hand connected with a juicy report. After just a few smacks she began to kick her feet.

"Incivility is a mark of disrespect," he told her.

She sobbed with vexation.

He gave her an additional ten hard smacks, then released her. Frankie rubbed her bottom with a mixture of resentment and lust. "Now, are you going to behave yourself?"

When Frankie lowered her eyes and refused to look at him, Sloan shook his head in disappointment. "Then you really are a wicked girl," he pronounced with puritanical severity. "Good night, my dear," he said after putting on his overcoat. The kiss he gave the indignant girl was a cool one and he saw himself out.

The next morning Frankie got her revenge for his indifference to her nocturnal charms by arriving for work two hours late. She walked in at the height of the Saturday morning rush while Sloan was trying to serve five patrons at once. He directed a marrow-chilling look at her when she slid in behind the counter at the other end of the store and Frankie immediately regretted her rash behavior. The customers were testy from being kept waiting and Sloan's mood was worse.

The entire day was busy in the shop without an unharried moment until closing time. By then Frankie was almost in tears of remorse, for Sloan's stony countenance had played havoc with her emotions all day.

"Sloan?" she came up behind him as he washed out coffee cups in the kitchenette. He looked at her briefly, then turned back to his chore, stiffening his shoulders as he did. "I'm sorry I was late this morning."

"Hmmph!" he snorted.

"Does that mean you don't like me anymore?" she asked tentatively.

"I still like you," he said, finally shutting off the water and turning around. "But I'm very angry with you."

Frankie looked down at her shoes, unable to meet his eyes. A lump had formed in her throat that was impossible to swallow.

"Under the circumstances I don't think we should see each other tonight," he told her coolly.

"I understand. Well, good night," she managed to say and then turned and fled the shop. She was sobbing before she hit the moist, slate grey, 35-degree evening air in which she began to run home, pulling on her overcoat. She was eager to hide in her pillow and forget this humiliating day.

Sloan was nearly as upset as Frankie, not knowing whether he had been too harsh. It was now apparent that Frances was accustomed to getting her own way. Her extremely late arrival that morning showed not only a want of respect for her position but also a disturbing streak of vindictiveness.

She needed to be taught basic manners, but was it his business to do it? And yet if he were too cautious and failed to attend to her instruction in a timely manner, were there not others in close proximity more than eager to civilize her? Sloan saw danger in the direction of Hugo Sands' shop. It was difficult to know what to do. Her outrageous behavior appeared to beg for some sort of dramatic punishment. But he was certain it would not be proper to react to a work related problem by spanking her. He didn't count the first spanking he had given her because she had suggested it herself.

Being Sloan, instead of making the wrong move, he decided to sleep on the problem of Frances and take some form of action the following day. Frankie, of course, cried herself to sleep after writing in her diary for two hours.

On Sunday an old classmate from Columbia called on Sloan to take him out for the day and most of the night, leaving Frankie disconsolate.

Mondays, like Saturdays, were busy days at the shop and a private conversation seemed unobtainable. Frankie noted a new reserve in Sloan's demeanor, though he smiled at her pleasantly enough when they said good morning.

She brooded all day, feeling hurt to the point of tears by his indifference. Apparently she did not have a new lover after all. She sighed as she rung up sales. At least she could look at him across the store, be around him and hear his wonderful voice as long as they worked together. Perhaps in time he would forgive her, if he didn't fire her first.

Because Sloan smiled at her with a spark of flirtation, telling her to be good as she left for the night, Frankie returned home in a slightly more comfortable mood than she had left it. She did, however, still feel deeply injured that Sloan could make love to her so passionately on one night and do without her so completely the next. Yet she had gotten the sense towards the close of the day that he was softening toward her again.

Tuesdays were traditionally the slowest days and Frankie knew they would have chances to be alone. Despising herself for the ultimate submission it represented, yet too desperate for the touch of his hand to remain passive for one more day, she wore her cream silk Betsy Johnson dress with the white lace petticoat and ribbon trim.

The moment she entered the shop Sloan melted. All morning, whenever she looked up, his eyes were on her. At noon he put up the Out To Lunch sign, took her by the hand and led her upstairs to his private apartment at the second floor rear of the shop. As soon as the door was closed behind them he drew her into his arms and hugged her.

"Thank you, Frances. I know you wore this dress for me," he told her, stroking her silken black hair down her back. Then he pulled back for a moment to regard her sternly. "But there is still the matter of Saturday to be dealt with." In so saying, he stood her to one side, placed a heavy, straight-backed chair in the center of the beamed room and sat down on it with decision. "Frances, come here," he commanded, holding out his hand to her. She approached him timidly and covered in blushes, but gave him her hand and allowed him to lightly pull her across his lap. Then, being Sloan, he took the time to lift her with one arm while slipping the other underneath her to smooth out the dainty dress before lowering her back down.

"I was too angry to do this the other day, but I'm now quite ready to administer the spanking you deserve," he told her, pulling up both her skirt and petticoat to reveal a pair of buttock-sculpting white crocheted tights, under which her sheer white nylon panties were clearly visible. "Charming unpinnings," he told her, stroking her bottom with appreciation. "I'd told you you'd do frills for me."

"I don't mind if I get punished, if you forgive me afterwards," she turned to look at him with liquid brown eyes.

"And yet aren't you ashamed?" Smack! "A girl of your age, still so irresponsible?" Smack! Smack! Now Sloan pulled both tights and panties down to expose her ivory bottom. "Is this what I've to look forward to from now on, Frances? Tantrums when you don't get your own way and a poor performance at work?" He kept his hand on her bottom while she framed a reply.

"I'll behave from now on," she promised quickly.

"How do I know that?" He spanked her soundly until she thought of an answer, but perhaps less severely than he might have done if she hadn't worn the beautiful dress.

"Because now I understand how things are going to be," she replied after twenty or thirty successively firmer smacks.

"And how is that?" he asked as she reached back to survey the pink impression that his palm had left behind.

"You'll make all the decisions."

Sloan was about to reply with indignation that he wasn't a despot, but instead stroked her bottom thoughtfully.

"Not all," he corrected her gently, letting her up and helping her to

set her clothes to rights, "Only those that have a bearing on the shop."
She was still blushing furiously when he drew her into his arms to kiss
and caress her.

"I'm sorry I was rude about you leaving the other night," she
admitted with some difficulty. "I don't have much experience with
men."

"No? You seem very sophisticated to me."

"Me? Sophisticated?"

"The way you let me take you the other night was enchanting," he
explained. "I've never felt so close to a girl before."

"But..." she hesitated.

"Yes?"

"Well, are we going to see each other from now on?"

"What do you think?"

"I'm not sure what to think, after this weekend."

"Because I didn't call you?"

"Yes."

"Well, Frances, I'm sorry to say that for a few hours I began to
think that you weren't a very nice girl."

"But what about now?"

"Now I realize it's my duty to civilize you."

"Do anything you think necessary," she suggested breathlessly, for
she had been up in the third gallery reading spanking erotica all
morning. "You could even whip me!"

"Oh, you want a flogging, do you?"

Frankie lowered her eyes. Sloan remembered Marguerite's carved
whipping post and large collection of implements.

"No," Frankie meekly shook her head and pointed at Sloan's
leather belt. "That kind of whipping, I mean."

"You call that a whipping?" Sloan looked at his watch and decided
they could linger a few more minutes before returning to the floor. "If
I used my belt on you, that would be called a strapping."

Frankie felt nearly overcome with excitement as she watched him
unbuckle his belt.

"Come with me, Frances," he took her by the hand and pulled her
into his bedroom. "Face down on the bed, young lady," he ordered and

she instantly obeyed. Sloan still sighed impatiently and arranged her more to his satisfaction, with her arms under her head and her skirt pulled up to her waist. Then he smoothly pulled her tights and panties down to expose her bottom once more.

He kept her in suspense for a few moments, walking around the oaken sleigh bed as he decided which angle to begin from. She watched him until he told her to put her head down and close her eyes. Sloan tested the doubled belt on his own hand a few times, which caused her to flinch.

"It's amazing to me that a Radcliffe English major could confuse the word strapping with the word whipping," Sloan declared before laying the first sharp stroke across the centermost portion of her bottom. She gave a little cry of surprise as the leather stung her. "However, I will be happy to teach you the distinction." Again the belt snapped across her bottom, a little lower now and perhaps a little harder.

"Ow!" she cried, but did not break her position.

"Since this is your first strapping, you'll only get six."

"Do the first two you gave me count?" she asked, peeking up at him and reaching back to rub.

"No, they were just for practice."

"I hope they'll be more like the first stroke and less like the second," she ventured softly.

"You asked that very nicely, Frances," he commented, taking careful aim and beginning the count of six with the moderation she had requested. These were received with such sighs and whimpers that Sloan gave Frankie six more. She arched her bottom to them so prettily that he decided to continue strapping her.

"Harder now!" she cried at length with great cost to her personal dignity. He had now struck her several dozen times with the belt and her bottom was stained a dark plum.

"Lie still then and stop thrashing around. You're going to get six of the best to finish with," Sloan declared firmly. Placing one hand in the small of her back to hold her in place, Sloan gave her the six final cuts with the belt hard and fast. Frankie wriggled and sobbed through this exciting ordeal, which left her dizzy and terribly in love.

Sloan helped Frankie put herself together when it was over and even took a few moments to brush out her hair with his own wooden hairbrush. The proximity of the hairbrush in his hand reawakened Frankie's lust and she impulsively threw herself into his arms.

Feeling his erection pressed against her through his trousers, she looked up at him with a flirtatious smile.

"Stop being naughty, Frankie," said Sloan, glancing at his watch. "Or you'll be subjected to the fastest act of penetration on record. We're supposed to open the store in four minutes."

"We can do it in two and a half!" she eagerly suggested.

"Or we can wait till a more appropriate moment," he decided sensibly. "One of us has to be an adult," he told her, disengaging her arms from around his waist, giving her one final kiss, then sending her back to the floor with a parting smack. Flooded with shame and delight, Frankie dizzily found her way back downstairs.

Chapter Five

The Cocktail Party

One cold and rainy Saturday afternoon in early March, Malcolm Branwell found himself with nothing to do until Marguerite returned from a round of post honeymoon visits she was making to all her friends in Random Point. A small reception party for them would take place that evening at the home of the composer Anthony Newton, a fact that impressed and worried Malcolm. Meanwhile he had little desire to hear the details of their recent trip repeated five times and decided, against his better judgment, to allow Marguerite to range through her home turf unchaperoned.

Exploring her house amused him. He could breathe her in the air and was at that stage of acute infatuation where burying his face in pillows that carried her scent was not out of the question.

Her library was the room he paused in. She had many beautiful, good, old things to pick up and touch, besides thousands of books. Her enormous roll top desk was unlocked and tempting. He slid the top up and was confronted with a larger number of pigeonholes than he'd ever seen together. But what drew his attention was a standing row of tall, leather bound volumes stamped Journal on each spine. There were nine books in all. He opened the first and saw that the date went back nine years.

A ripple of irrepressible curiosity ran through him as he considered reading Marguerite's diaries. "They're probably literary journals," he told himself and flipped one open in the middle to find a reference to a strapping in Mansfield Park by Jane Austen. Then he opened to a second page at random and discovered another such notation, this one dilating on the submissive nature of Jean Jacques Rousseau.

He sat down in the leather recliner under the rain spattered window pane and opened the first volume to page one, marveling that Marguerite could have filled nine volumes with references to corporal punishment in literature. But as soon as Malcolm started to read, his heart began to pound and he instantly shut the book. He stood up and paced. Literary references the journals might contain, but if the passage he'd just scanned was any indication of their general content, what he'd discovered was his bride's personal sex diaries from the last nine years. And the name of Hugo Sands appeared on page one.

"Do I want to know, or don't I?" Malcolm agonized, while a cat followed him around the room rubbing against his legs. "Know the enemy!" he decided and seized the book he'd just thrown down.

From the journal of Marguerite Alexander

January 1, 1990

Determined not to let another year of sexual frustration undermine my will to eventually rule the universe, I eschewed all the typical New Year's Eve invitations and last night attended my first Scene party instead.

Breathlessly squeezed into my first latex hobble skirt, with the laces up the back and tottering on my first pair of 5" fetish boots, I felt warm and flushed rather than cold when I exited the cab before an ancient warehouse in the neighborhood of Fanueil Hall.

Inside the low-lit dance club there was sawdust on the floor and everything was painted black. The Sex Pistols were playing on the jukebox and there were a least two whippings taking place, but until I put my glasses on, everything was a blur.

No one seemed to realize I was doing Sweet Gwen with my outfit and every man but one seemed to think I was a mistress!

I didn't notice him for the first fifteen minutes or so, though he'd been watching me all the while. He was very tall, (thank you, Goddess!) slim, immaculately groomed and as handsome as Leslie Howard, with the nicest manners I'd encountered in years. His name is Hugo Sands.

When I told him that this was my first scene party he seemed very surprised, citing my Sweet Gwendolyn costume as proof of my sophistication. He knew!

"I've dreamed fetish for years, but this is my first outfit. I bought it through a British catalog I saw advertised in Vogue," I told him.

"I can't believe you've never played," he accused me with a smile. I was already love.

"Only some spanking games with a roommate at Bennington."

Hugo studied art history at Harvard and now deals in antiques, (I write as I beam.)

"What do you think of all these submissive men hitting on you?"

"Why, I think they're very silly!" I retorted.

"My dear, you'll make a fine dominant some day," Hugo promised absurdly.

"But I don't want to be a dominant," I pouted.

"You will someday."

"But I haven't even found out what it's like to be submissive yet!" I cried, highly exhilarated by this wicked conversation.

"Would you like to find out tonight?"

Now I was surprised into confusion. Yes, he was cultured and dressed in a wool cashmere suit, but did I dare trust a stranger met under these circumstances to take me home?

"I would love to find out tonight," I said, after only a moment's hesitation.

We left the hall and drove out to his house in Cambridge in his Jaguar, the sight of which calmed more fears. This man had too many material concerns to doing anything to jeopardize his enjoyment of them. Besides, he seemed so truly nice, so much my kind of person that I was anything but afraid.

I chattered all the way about my lifelong interest in B&D, discussing many books that had influenced my fantasies and found that he had read them all. Since I'd never really met a dominant man before, outside of the Grove Press novels I'd read, I asked Hugo Sands what went on in his head about women. He said that question would require a fifty thousand-word treatise to answer, but with regard to what I probably meant, he told me he was drawn to women who enjoyed corporal punishment. I felt my face go hot to hear it put so simply.

Hugo then speculated that I could no doubt be a terrible brat when I chose to.

Now my heart beat very rapidly. We were entering his snug brick house, which was quite wonderfully appointed and I knew I was in the hands not only of my first dominant, but my first spanker.

I told Hugo that I *was* a thoroughly spoiled brat who bossed all my friends around. He made a fire. I longed to curl up in his leather wing chair, but the skirt would only allow me to perch on the edge of the seat. We had some brandy and a smoke (the good stuff), before he made his move.

Now that I was relaxed I managed not to die of mortification when he informed me it was time for my *spanking*. I resisted, however, until he took me by my gloved elbow and turned me over his knee.

"Did you think you could wear a tight latex skirt around me for more than an hour and not get a spanking, Marguerite?"

I don't know what I murmured in reply, for I was only aware of the dizzying sensation of getting my first real spanking from a dominant man. Merely being pulled across his lap set my tummy fluttering so wildly that I thought I would climax at the first touch of his hand on my bottom. No words are adequate to describe the satisfaction that first spanking brought me. Every time I think of it a dart of painful pleasure pierces my heart.

I do think it was a rather hard spanking for a first spanking, but I wanted that. The severity made it thrilling. I had several miniature climaxes before he even unlaced the skirt to expose my panties. Ah, the way he held me when I squirmed!

I know it was a very hard spanking, because I'm so very sore today, but last night I hardly felt it, or felt it pleasantly. Hugo scolded me for egotism and conceit as though he knew me well enough to do so. I didn't mind. Hugo scolds charmingly.

What a maddeningly exciting way to begin the new year. I'm finally playing!

The next several dozen entries were given over to literary ana, story ideas, complaints about her job as a proposal writer and extensive wish lists referring to future wardrobe acquisitions and projected trips abroad. But once spring came she returned to her chronicling of her relationship with Hugo Sands and the first entry of this nature filled Malcolm with an animosity for Hugo he would not overcome for some time.

April 4, 1990

Lunched with Hugo and a wealthy collector named Mr. Sackman, a flirtatious older man who couldn't seem to keep his hand off my knee under the table. When I admonished him not to be naughty he giggled and blushed, but I was not to realize the significance of this reaction until Hugo called me at work later in the afternoon to tell me that Mr. Sackman was so taken with me that he was prepared to pay me many hundreds of dollars to *dominate* him.

"But Hugo, I'm not a dominant. I wouldn't know what to do or even how to comport myself," I protested.

"He only wants a spanking, Marguerite. You can do that, can't you?"

"I don't know."

"I think you can."

"But, then what do I do with him?"

"Give him a hug and go home."

I thought of the beautiful beige crepe sheath I'd seen in the window of Bonwit Teller's yesterday and agreed to try my best to satisfy the nice man.

Mr. Sackman lives on Beacon Hill, one square away block from my parents' house! He had the straight-backed chair already positioned in the middle of his study, with a heavy wooden hairbrush placed on the seat.

"Well Norman," I began, "did you think you were going to get away with what you did at lunch so easily?"

"But what did I do?" he coyly asked, which did not charm me. Meanwhile he had taken down his trousers.

"You placed your hand on my leg," I accused angrily, taking my seat on the chair. Mr. Sackman wished me to pull up my skirt and allow him to lie across my stockinged thighs but I didn't feel he'd earned this privilege yet and merely pulled him down across my lap.

Hugo had advised me not to be afraid to spank him hard, which I did, first with my hand, and then with the hairbrush, over his shorts and then on the bare. I didn't really know what I was doing, but my victim didn't seem to care. He whimpered and yipped a good deal, but held his position for a full twenty minutes while I lambasted his bare backside with the hairbrush. At last he cried, "Mercy, mistress!"

I made him kneel before me and kiss the brush and then my hand. Then I told him that he could get dressed. When he begged to see my breasts I pretended to be angry and made him bend over with his palms on the chair for a strapping with his own belt. I may have gotten a bit carried away with the strap because he cried mercy again after just a few minutes.

Within moments he put himself back together and we had tea. Then he handed me an envelope and I went on my way. I think Mr. Sackman is in love. And now I get to buy my new dress. Bless Hugo!

Malcolm slammed the book down with contempt. So Hugo was the one he had to thank for turning Marguerite into a dom and a pro all at once. And for all he knew, this decadent man still had an influence on his wife.

Remembering where they were going that night and who was to be there, Malcolm suddenly got another unworthy idea and began rapidly flicking through the later volumes for mention of Anthony Newton.

Marguerite provided a helpful map beginning with volume six, indicating those passages that involved the popular composer with a musical note carat at the top of each relevant page.

Malcolm discovered, to his horror, that Newton had paid handsomely for Marguerite's favors on their first night together and that they had gone far beyond her so-called pure B&D. Again, the introduction had been made at a party of Hugo Sands.

"Great, my host tonight is one of my wife's tricks!" he brooded, flicking back to the beginning of the Halloween party described in Marguerite's journal. It seemed that she had suffered a great blow that night at hearing that Michael Flagg had just married someone named Damaris.

Subsequent entries revealed that his marriage notwithstanding, Flagg appeared on Marguerite's doorstep like a dog in heat at regular intervals up until as recently as weeks before Malcolm and Marguerite's wedding, which Malcolm found more upsetting than all her other antics put together.

The cocktail party took place in Anthony Newton's music room and included only a handful of Marguerite's close friends. Malcolm noticed that their host, who seldom got up from his piano, seemed to be the proprietor of a flirtatious imp named Susan Ross. As soon as Susan heard who Malcolm was she turned her highly mischievous attention to him.

"We were all amazed that Marguerite got married. You must be a fantastic player."

"Susan, don't be impertinent," Anthony warned her.

"Oh come on, everyone know that we're all in the scene. What's your exact orientation, Malcolm?"

Malcolm was so astonished at being addressed like this by a total stranger that he gazed at her as though she'd spoken to him in a foreign language. But the forward young lady did make him forget how violently he resented Anthony Newton for having had his wife.

The next shock was being introduced to Michael Flagg and another pretty blonde, this one around his own age and very smart in appearance. Malcolm wondered why Anthony had invited Michael and even looked at Marguerite questioningly when Flagg and Patricia walked in.

"You had to meet sometime, darling," Marguerite whispered. "It will be fine." Malcolm forced himself to shake hands with Flagg and accept his congratulations, but he couldn't make himself like it.

However, he wasn't allowed to dwell on his suspicions for long, for Patricia Fairservis, the ex-editor of *Cape Cod Style*, was looking for work and Malcolm owned a book store empire.

It was no use telling her he didn't publish. Patricia was unrelenting once she observed a willingness in Malcolm to listen to her ideas. She took him aside and pitched herself for twenty minutes.

When Malcolm was released, Patricia had talked herself into a public relations position with Branwell's Book Bag. Marguerite joined them towards the end of the discussion and heartily endorsed the idea, for she had come to consider Patricia a friend.

Having refocused his attention from Michael to Patricia, Malcolm no longer felt filled with distrust and animosity and was able to turn with pleasure to shake the hand of the one person he had already met, little Frances Wu, who had been invited to the party along with the new manager of Marguerite's book shop, Sloan Taylor.

"Well, Frances, how are you making out in your new job?" Malcolm asked her stuffily, attempting to inject some normalcy into the situation. *We're all in the scene, indeed!* He shot little Susan Ross a narrow glance, which she returned with a wave.

"Fine, Mr. Branwell," Frankie replied in a lackluster manner that did not seem like her. Sloan shook Malcolm's hand after throwing one exasperated glance in Frankie's direction. Malcolm smiled as he suddenly remembered that according to his wife's calculations, these two were supposed to be in love by now.

The next to arrive were Hugo Sands and Laura Random, which threw Malcolm into a fresh tailspin. Hugo looked younger than Malcolm had imagined him to be and had great style. His companion was a charming brunette who greeted Malcolm with a perfumed hug.

"Finally I get to meet you!" Laura seemed genuinely excited. "Did Marguerite tell you we've been best friends since college? And did you meet my sister, Susan?"

Susan joined them and the girls pulled Malcolm over to the fireside where they sat him down, brought him the mineral water he requested and began to barrage him with intimate questions, few of which he could bring himself to answer, though he enjoyed the attention.

Hugo Sands, who didn't like Malcolm any more than Malcolm liked him, felt annoyed with Laura for swarming all over Malcolm and thought, as usual, that Susan should be thrashed.

"I was the one who laid out your ad," Laura informed Malcolm proudly. "I knew you'd do well with it."

"How many girls answered it?" asked Susan. Malcolm opened his lips to reply then thought better of it. "

"Tell us about yourself, Malcolm," Laura urged.

"Yes, don't leave out a single detail," Susan persisted.

"Oh, I'm just a boring, old businessman," demurred Malcolm.

"Certainly not!" cried Laura.

"You're much younger than our boyfriends!" Susan chortled. If Hugo or Anthony overheard this compliment, they ignored it. Meanwhile Susan was well on her way to charming Malcolm.

While she flirted in this way with Malcolm, Susan Ross was conscious of another young man's eyes on her, for Sloan was now standing by the piano conversing with Anthony about her.

Sloan had gone up to Anthony to tell him of his admiration for his work, expecting to receive a vague celebrity thank you and possibly an autograph. Instead Anthony greeted him like an old friend, for Marguerite had told Anthony enough about her new employee to dispose him favorably towards Sloan. Ever the romantic, Anthony was especially charmed by the idea of Marguerite and Malcolm hiring a couple on the basis of their being in the scene and likely to fall in love.

Anthony played some of Sloan's favorite Harold Arlen songs while they talked, causing his fan to beam with pleasure.

"Why is your little Frances sulking so?" Anthony asked.

Sloan sighed and confided that they'd quarreled earlier in the day and that for all her outward beauty, she wasn't a very nice girl and that he was almost completely fed up with her. Anthony, who loved gossip, was intrigued and pressed for further details, but Sloan was too ashamed of his childish new playmate to reveal them.

"We should trade brats for a night," Anthony suggested, loudly enough for Susan to hear him. Susan smiled, winked at Sloan, tossed her now impossibly long, blonde hair and continued to cheerfully torment Malcolm.

Sloan looked at Anthony in surprise.

"Pardon me?"

"It was just a thought," Anthony casually replied.

Leaving Laura to continue entertaining Malcolm, Susan jumped up and joined Anthony and Sloan, extending her hand to shake that of the very tall, dark haired young man, who now regarded her with great interest.

"I just thought I heard something strange so I came over," Susan explained.

"I simply suggested that Sloan and I trade brats for a night," Anthony told her pleasantly.

"Should I get Frankie over to ask her?" Susan asked with ill-suppressed excitement, for one glance at Sloan was enough to convince her that Anthony's idea was a happy one.

"God, no!" Sloan hastened to cry.

"Oh?" Susan looked disappointed. "Why not?"

"Because even if I understood exactly what you mean, I'm not really speaking to her," Sloan replied, folding his arms and sending a withering stare across the room to Frankie, who pretended to ignore him and continued to converse with Hugo and Marguerite.

"Oh boy, this sounds juicy! What did she do?" Susan demanded.

"He can't tell us because it's too horrible."

"All the more reason to let an objective third party arbitrate," Susan brightly pointed out.

"Yes, whatever she did, I'm used to much worse from Susan," Anthony admitted. "She probably just needs a good paddling."

Across the room Frankie pretended not to hear Anthony's last remark but it was hard not to feel that it had been meant to describe herself. Frankie's face burned with embarrassment.

"I think it's time you were introduced to Anthony and Susan," Marguerite said and took Frances over to them. Sloan stiffened when she entered the circle.

"We feel we're being talked about," Marguerite explained, making the proper introduction.

"Not you, Marguerite. You're too recently married to figure into our decadent schemes," said Anthony.

"I suppose that's true," agreed Marguerite, deciding it was time to rescue Malcolm from her always-dangerous best friend Laura and abandoning them at once.

"What decadent schemes?" Frankie looked from Susan to Anthony, thinking them a handsome couple.

"I was telling Sloan that we should trade brats for a night."

"For what purpose?" Frankie smiled, realizing she was being flirted with.

"Your boyfriend's fed up with you and I'm fed up with Susan," Anthony told her for the sake of convenience, though Susan had done nothing to merit this declaration.

"He isn't my boyfriend," said Frankie haughtily. For an instant she and Sloan glared at each other, the color mounting quickly to her face.

"Sloan, shall I show you the house?" asked Susan, linking arms with the new young man and taking him away while throwing a wink in her lover's direction.

"Is Mr. Newton always this friendly to strangers?" Sloan asked as Susan took him though the picture gallery.

"Only ones who might seem compatible with us."

"And how could he tell that so quickly?"

"Well, in the first place, we all knew that you and Frankie answered the ad in Hugo's magazine. In the second place, you're both adorably cute. And of course it didn't hurt that you're an Anthony Newton fan."

"But what did he mean when he said trade brats?"

"Oh, it's something we've done a few times before. We pick an attractive couple and switch partners for a night. It's a way of playing with others without actually cheating on each other, yet you avoid the awkwardness of a group situation."

"So, what happens?"

"Spanking and anything that seems to go along with it."

"And am I right in understanding that you were the brat to whom Mr. Newton referred?"

"Yes."

"What a shame that Frances isn't mine to give," Sloan said with feeling, as Susan's warmth began to thrill him.

"Oh, I'm sure you'll patch up whatever little quarrel you've had and then some time in the future you can bring up the subject to Frankie and see how she feels about it."

"And how do you feel about it?"

"Oh, I like the idea."

"But you don't even know me."

"That's the exciting part."

"If you are a brat, you're a very nice one," Sloan told her.

"Oh, I have good days and bad ones," she assured him, pulling him from the hall into her own private suite of rooms and locking the door behind them. *"He did give me permission,"* thought Susan, getting out her notebooks of erotic drawings to show Sloan.

"So what did you quarrel about?" Anthony asked Frankie, after getting her to sit beside him on the piano bench.

"I'd rather not say," she stubbornly replied.

"It must have been something *you* did, or else you'd say," Anthony observed, causing Frankie to color again. "I'm sure it was something dreadful."

"It was no big deal," Frankie burst out at last. "He's just such a stickler for etiquette that it's blown his pristine doily of a mind."

"Mr. Taylor does appear to have very good manners," Anthony pointed out approvingly.

"That's certainly true," she replied judiciously.

"You should make a full confession to me."

"But, what would you do if you agreed with Sloan?"

"Agreed that you'd been naughty? Oh, I should think I'd turn you over my knee."

"Oh!" Frankie's heart began to pound hard.

"I'm sure you've been spanked before, Frankie."

"Only quite recently."

"Yes, I understand Mr. Taylor has been trying to improve you."

"There's always room for more improvement," she shyly said, eager to find out what a spanking from Anthony Newton would feel like.

"Would you like to see ocean view from the top floor of the house?"

"Yes, please."

Anthony took her up to a pretty apartment on the third floor, offering a panorama of rocks and surf from every window.

"Now then, Frances," Anthony said, seating her beside him on a sofa, "I want to hear all about what's come between you and Sloan."

"Oh, I just did something immature," Frankie replied; "But completely insignificant in the greater scheme of things," she added with spirit.

"Oh? You committed some annoying, childish prank?" Anthony guessed.

"It's a little bit worse than that, but not much."

"Frankie, tell me."

"Oh, I skunked a waitress."

"You what?"

"Okay, here's what happened. We were out to dinner last night at Basil's and I was broke, as usual, so Sloan covered the bill. He also left the waitress a five. But I thought she'd been an awful waitress and since I was broke, I...slipped the five into my pocket on the way out."

"H'm," said Anthony, with his chin on his hand, "that is bad. How'd he find out?"

"I was spending the night and when I took my junk out of my jeans pockets to get ready for bed he saw the five. He said he thought I was broke and instead of telling him a lie, which I ought to have done, I admitted taking the money off the table."

"Then what happened?"

"Then Sloan got very angry and told me that we were going to get dressed and take the money back to Basil's immediately."

"And did you?"

"No. I told him there was no way in hell I was going to do such a ridiculous thing because she'd been a bad waitress anyway."

"Then what happened?"

"Then I saw him go in the bathroom and take his razor strop down from the hook on the wall. At that point I pulled my pants and boots back on and ran out the door. I had to run all the way home because I forgot my coat in my haste to escape and it was very cold last night."

Anthony shook his head. "No wonder Sloan is mad at you. Not only were you a social embarrassment, but you denied him the satisfaction of punishing you for it."

"I panicked."

"And then you were summoned to a party together today," Anthony commiserated.

"Do you think what I did was that horrible?"

"Well, it was certainly mean-spirited. One would hope you're not normally like that."

Frances felt tears well in her eyes. "It was just an impulse," she explained shakily.

"A very naughty impulse. Waitresses work hard for their money. Whereas, you're a spoiled brat."

"I know," Frances hung her head.

"So you agree that what you did was wrong?"

"I suppose so," she sighed.

"So what do you think you should do?"

"Return the money?"

"And tell Sloan you regret what you did."

"I'm not speaking to him at the moment."

"Oh? And why is that?"

"Because he scared me."

"A razor strop isn't so bad."

"I'd rather not find out."

"I could use a razor strop on you to where you'd like it."

"You could?"

"I could do the same with a cane. It's all a matter of technique."

"But you're not as mad at me as Sloan is."

"Well, perhaps you know best. But at the very least I think you deserve a good spanking. Don't you, Frankie?"

Frankie dropped her eyes and looked embarrassed. The event was not to be postponed a second longer. Frankie was about to get her first spanking from someone other than Sloan.

Anthony shrugged out of his suit jacket, loosened his tie and rolled up his sleeves while she regarded him with a pounding heart.

"Give me your hands," he said, extending his. When she did he pulled her across his lap. Frankie's thick, straight, jet-black ponytail reached almost to the waist of her smoky blue party dress and aroused

Anthony profoundly. He gripped her firmly by her small waist and spanked her on the seat of her skirt a couple of dozen times, fairly hard. Frankie buried her face in her arms and lay passively across his lap, feeling the hot waves of excitement wash through her as his hand came down on her bottom.

"You've been a selfish, inconsiderate little girl," he scolded, pushing her skirt up to her waist to reveal a perfect bottom in cream panties under sheer pantyhose. "And what's more, you're wearing pantyhose." Smack! Smack! "No attire could be more improper when attending a party of mine."

"But, I didn't know that. And it's cold out!"

"You might have worn nubby tights."

"Oh."

"But stockings and a garter belt would have been the best choice. Remember that for the future, Frankie."

Frankie didn't realize how much a spanking could hurt through tight, mesh nylon. And yet she had no desire to move out of her position.

"I'm sorry!" she cried, "I'll never wear pantyhose again!"

"They're coming down now," he declared, deftly hooking his thumbs into the waistband and pulling them down to just below her bottom. "That's better," he said, stroking her through the sheer, nylon briefs that encased her round cheeks so ravishingly. He could see the pink through the panties already.

His hand came down with metronomic precision on either cheek for several minutes, while Frankie squirmed, whimpered and finally kicked up her little shoes. The pantyhose hobbled her thighs together, restricting her movements somewhat, but not entirely. She deeply regretted having worn them now, for she had a great impulse to spread her thighs for him and invite him to probe her damp recesses with his strong, pianist's fingers.

Now Anthony pulled her panties down and finished the sharp, stinging spanking on her bare bottom.

"I want you to think about what a bad girl you've been, Frankie," said Anthony sternly before administering two dozen of the best. When he was done her cheeks were stained dark rose from his hand

and she had begun to sob, if not actually cry. "Now, young lady, are you ever going to mistreat a waitress or anyone else who serves you again?"

"No Sir!"

"Good," he said, pleased by her enthusiastic response. Now he gently pulled her panties and pantyhose back up and let her up. Frankie didn't know where to look or what to do, so Anthony pulled her back down to sit on his lap, put his arms around her tiny waist. She shuddered with emotion and wriggled on his thighs. "I'm sure you know what I'd like to do with you right now, Frankie," he said, "but that wouldn't be proper on such short acquaintance and with your boyfriend downstairs. Even though he is with my girlfriend now."

"He's not my boyfriend."

"Your escort."

"Should I...tell him what happened, Mr. Newton?"

"Yes and you needn't be so formal while you're sitting on my lap."

"Anthony, whatever it is you'd like to do to me, please do it!" urged Frankie, becoming more animated by the moment.

"No, I'd better show some restraint for once," he said, putting her off his lap. "Let's get back the others before they come looking for us."

As Frankie picked up her little velvet bag which had fallen on the floor Anthony remembered that she was broke and pulled a wad of twenties out of his billfold. "Here, bad girl," he told her, stuffing them into her purse, "I'm sure it's a week till payday and if you were flat yesterday it's only going to get worse."

"Oh, no!" she said, trying to give the money back.

"Frankie, if you were ready to steal from a poor waitress you should be able to accept a present from a millionaire."

Frankie returned to the party with a flushed face and still tingling bottom. But her mood became deflated when she realized that Sloan and Susan were still absent.

Frankie had every reason to be anxious because Susan Ross had taken an instant and passionate liking to Sloan and had every intention of seducing him.

Showing Sloan the portfolio was a masterstroke, for her drawings served the primary purpose of erotica, which is to arouse. He admired page after page of spanking and bondage sketches, exclaiming about each one extravagantly. Then midway thorough the book the drawings became much more perverse and exciting. Sloan became stuck on the first enema illustration, which showed a young 18th century gentleman in breeches and an open shirt, with the ripped muscles of a modern body builder, administering a clyster pump enema to a submissive young lady with her empire dress raised to her waist and satin slippers on her stockinged legs. Her hair was in Grecian curls and she pouted aristocratically as the humiliating rite was performed. A riding crop lay close at hand and this was what she regarded as she knelt on all fours on an upholstered bench. The drawing was entitled, "The Temperance Lesson" and had been rendered in colored pencils.

"Sloan, you've been on this page for five minutes," Susan told him.

"This is the most exquisite drawing I've ever seen," he flashed her a brilliantly penetrating look. "You are going to be famous some day."

"But, does it arouse you?" she asked naughtily.

"I should say so," he admitted.

"You can have it if you like. I'll have it framed for you."

"You're not serious."

"I've got dozens just as detailed," she said, and to prove it began quickly flipping through the color pages for him, astonishing him with the skill and variety of her work, which combined the eroticism of The Fornicon with the idealism of Frazetta and good fashion sense.

"Why don't you publish these, Susan?"

"I'm going to. When I have enough to fill a hundred pages."

"Are you a commercial illustrator?"

"No, I'm currently at Pratt Institute learning graphic design."

"How wonderful!"

"Let's get back to you becoming aroused," she said, reaching under the portfolio.

"Susan!" Sloan colored as her hand brushed the freshly sprung bar of iron in his trousers.

"Just seeing if you're excited."

"Well of course I'm excited, you little minx!" he pushed the portfolio aside, took her by the wrist and slapped her hand. She subsided and blushed. "What a bad girl you are." He looked at her thoughtfully. "Showing me these extremely naughty drawings, then actually–I can't even bring myself to say it– groping me!"

"But, I didn't mean anything," she protested.

"Oh no? Young lady, you need a spanking!"

Sloan did not wait for her to agree but easily pulled her across his lap and smacked her hard across the seat of her grey tweed leggings a half dozen times. Then he let her up.

"Now, are you going to behave?"

"Yes." She rubbed her bottom through her trousers, her pulse racing.

"Good, because I wouldn't want to have to unbutton your leggings and take them down. I'm sure that would embarrass you."

"But..."

"Yes Susan?"

"I like being embarrassed."

"I wonder what Mr. Newton would think if he knew how you were behaving right now," Sloan scolded, trying not to look too deeply into her mocking blue eyes.

"He's the one who suggested we trade partners. Don't you think he's playing with Frankie right now?"

"Is he?" Sloan wasn't sure he liked that, though he didn't know whether he was being protective of Frances or Anthony.

"They're probably having sex right now," she told him with conviction.

"I refuse to believe that Frances would have sex with someone she hasn't known for above an a hour and in the middle of a party celebrating her employer's nuptials."

"Believe what you like but I think you should loosen up."

Sloan couldn't help but laugh at the absurd girl.

"When do you go back to New York?" he asked.

"Tomorrow."

"Oh."

"I come back to Random Point every weekend I can," Susan said temptingly.

"Lucky Random Point."

Marguerite asked Anthony to play *Dearly Beloved*, then she asked her new husband to dance, which she had taught him how to do on their honeymoon. They danced under the windows, away from the others.

"Have my friends been treating you well?" Marguerite asked.

"Pretty well, under the circumstances."

"Circumstances, Malcolm?"

"The fact that every man here, except for Sloan, has been your lover."

"And who told you that?"

"You did."

"I have no recollection of doing so."

"I found your journals today while you were out and read them."

"Do you think that was wise?" she asked mischievously.

"No."

"Darling, you're not upset, are you?"

"Only about the fact that I couldn't get to you before Hugo Sands corrupted you."

"I have not been corrupted by anyone. And what a vile thing to say!"

"He turned you out," Malcolm declared matter of factly.

"How dare you?" Marguerite would have slapped her handsome husband's face had they not been in company. Instead she broke from his embrace and strode towards the bar, which was manned by Dennis, the English boy who chauffeured and valeted for their host. Malcolm followed her and watched with disapproval as she filled a tumbler full of white wine and downed it in several agitated gulps.

"My sincere felicitations on your wedding, Mrs. Branwell," said Dennis, refilling her glass carefully.

"Thank you, Dennis," Marguerite said warmly to the attractive boy, who had adored her for several years.

"You shouldn't drink, Marguerite. You only get emotional and blow things out of proportion," Malcolm counseled, without bothering to lower his voice in front of Dennis, whom he regarded as a piece of furniture.

She ignored his recommendation and departed with a replenished glass to join an intimate grouping of Laura and Michael in front of the large brown and pink marble hearth. When she'd gained her objective she tossed her hair and turned her back on Malcolm.

"Quarreling, Marguerite? So soon? What a shame!" Michael commiserated gleefully.

"Was it that obvious?" Marguerite shot a glance back at Malcolm and saw him frowning at her from behind a Perrier.

"Shall I go and steam him up a little more?" Laura suggested. "He must be magnificent when he's mad."

"Oh, he doesn't get mad. He just gets cynical and you know I hate being teased."

Making sure that Patricia was well out of earshot, Michael said, "I never teased you."

"No darling, that's the one thing you didn't do. Bless you."

"Why is Dennis looking daggers at Malcolm?" Laura wondered.

"Oh, because my husband had the bad taste to criticize me in front of him."

"Your husband is critical, then?" Michael encouraged her to complain.

"Tediously so!" the redhead declared.

"How about strict?" pressed Laura. "Is he strict with you?"

"With me?" Marguerite stared at her haughtily.

"Is there a chance that he'll come over here and give you a spanking?" Laura hopefully persisted.

"Highly unlikely, unless he wants to have an extremely short second marriage."

"He'll wait till he gets her home," Michael explained to Laura. "That's standard procedure."

"You two can both go to hell!" said Marguerite.

"But darling, you make such a handsome couple," Laura soothed her friend.

"Excuse me, I think I'll go powder my nose and make him worry about me for awhile."

When Marguerite got to the favorite bad girl powder room on the first floor, which Anthony had decorated especially for them, she found Susan and Frankie on a divan smoking.

"Well young ladies," said Marguerite, "did I do well in choosing our new man?"

"Which one?" Susan asked.

"Why, Sloan of course," Marguerite smiled, for it was far too soon to include Malcolm in the rotation. "Didn't you play with him just now, Susan? And haven't you been doing so, Frankie?"

"Well, we're of differing opinions about Sloan at the moment," Susan explained, happily setting to work brushing Frankie's beautiful, black hair with a perfect brush she found on the marble vanity. "Have you ever seen such hair?" Susan asked Marguerite, while sifting it through her fingers then brushing it out.

"Oh? Did you have a falling out?" Marguerite asked Frankie.

"It's just that he's so rigidly principled and I'm so... casual."

"How amusing, that sounds exactly like my situation," Marguerite admitted.

"They are two gorgeous men, however," Susan observed temptingly, which quieted both Frankie and Marguerite for a few moments. "Anyway, in Frankie's case, she was the one at fault," said Susan, "even she admits it now, and I was trying to advise her on how to best make it up."

"If anyone can do that, Susan, it is you," Marguerite complimented her young friend.

"So what do you think I should do?" Frankie asked Susan.

"Just apologize."

"I hate apologizing," Frankie replied moodily.

"Who doesn't? But it works," Susan counseled.

Meanwhile, Malcolm forced himself to go up to Anthony Newton during one of the few moments when he was not at the piano and thank him for hosting the party.

"You're quite welcome," said Anthony, "I'm one of Marguerite's biggest fans." The complete lack of guile with which the declaration was made caused Malcolm's shoulders to untense visibly. In fact there was something so friendly in Anthony's expression that Malcolm found he had the urge to confide in him.

"Even after the way she treated you the first night you met?" Malcolm blurted the cryptic question out in a rush.

"I remember being treated rather nicely by Marguerite on the first night we met," Anthony replied without hesitation. "I played Rogers and Hart and she sang. Your wife has a lovely voice."

"Humph!" Malcolm snorted cynically.

"Why, what did you hear?"

"Unfortunately I opened Pandora's Box this afternoon and read Marguerite's journals."

Anthony did not like the sound of that.

"And you discovered something that made you think Marguerite behaved in some way badly towards me?" Anthony was still mystified by Malcolm's original statement.

"Let's just say we both appear to belong to Marguerite's exclusive five thousand club."

"Oh, that!" Anthony smiled, then frowned. "She put that in her journal?"

"Oh don't worry, it would take a master detective to figure out that the Anthony N. with a musical note beside every entry was you," Malcolm reassured him with heavy irony.

"I take it you don't approve of artistic patronage."

"Artistic patronage, huh?"

"It appears that in your case, the money was well spent."

"Anthony, be honest with me," Malcolm said, "tell me how you felt when you found out you had to pay for her time."

Anthony thought a moment and had to smile.

"Okay, Malcolm, I'll admit I was slightly... surprised for an instant, but that didn't stop me from jumping at the opportunity to spank her."

"Yes, that sounds familiar," Malcolm brooded.

Anthony could see that Malcolm was desperately in love.

"Malcolm, Marguerite's going to be a perfect wife."

"You know, I came here prepared to hate you," Malcolm admitted, "but you're okay. This Hugo Sands character on the other hand..."

"Hugo? He's a gentleman and a scholar. In fact he's the one who put me together with my little Susan."

"But he's also the one who taught Marguerite to sell her favors! In fact I shuddered when I saw him talking to Frankie just now. God knows how much money she would bring delivered up to a wealthy businessman!"

"Malcolm, get a grip."

"I'm sorry but I don't like the man," said Malcolm firmly. "And Marguerite still seems to regard him as some sort of mentor or something."

"Malcolm, you have to realize that until Hugo came along there wasn't any scene at all in this part of the country. And don't you also acknowledge that if it weren't for his magazine you never would have found your Marguerite?"

"I do," Malcolm admitted.

"Then if I were you I'd stop complaining and send him a bottle of Scotch," Anthony suggested before drifting back to the piano.

When Frankie returned from her talk with Marguerite and Susan she found that Sloan was ready to leave. As they left the house together and got into his car Frankie flushed with shame at the memory of their last heated exchange. Sloan was still cool and scarcely looked at her until he drove up to the little guesthouse where Frankie lived.

"Good-bye, Frances," he said distantly, as she got out of the car.

"Sloan?"

"Yes?"

"I'm very sorry that I was so bad yesterday," she said with an ending sob. His stern face softened.

"Are you really?"

"Yes. I know that what I did was wrong and I'm going to return the money right now."

"That's a good girl," he said, with a smile.

"And I'm sorry I ran away," she added, wistfully.

"Perhaps I'd better come in so we can talk about it," he reflected.

"Oh, yes! Please do."

"That dress becomes you," Sloan told her as he put the kettle on. "I'm not surprised that Mr. Newton found you irresistible."

Frankie protested this assumption with a blush. "He was just being a gracious host."

"Really? I thought he seemed eager to play with you."

"Susan seemed just as eager to play with you."

"Well, did you play with Mr. Newton?"

"Did you play with Susan?"

"She teased me into giving her a few swats on the seat of her pants," Sloan admitted with a clear conscience. "How about you?"

"Oh, I got a little spanking," she replied.

"Is that all?"

"Yes."

"Good," said Sloan emphatically.

"Why? Would it bother you if I'd done more?"

"I certainly would have considered it the height of bad taste."

Frankie couldn't help but laugh.

"That little Susan is very wild," Sloan observed. "I hope you won't start imitating her."

"I liked her," Frankie declared, remembering how wisely Susan counseled her on how to deal with Sloan. Now she saw him shudder. "Not to mention the fact that she's the only one in this group who's my age. She can give me valuable advice on how to deal with dinosaurs!"

Sloan ignored the baiting and heaved a sigh. With Susan advising her, Frances would soon lose her charming shyness and become the sort of sophisticated, unembarrassable brat that he perceived the New York girl to be.

Sloan was joyful at finally having found the scene, but events were moving so quickly that he saw his relationship with Frances undermined by outside forces. Would Frances ever submit to his much needed moral guidance while fascinating men like Anthony Newton, Hugo Sands and Malcolm Branwell were so close at hand to flatter and spoil her?

"Oh, Sloan," she cried suddenly throwing herself into his arms, "please don't be cross with me anymore!"

He folded her against his chest, pleased by her warmth. "How antagonistic you were," he reflected, "to declare that I wasn't your boyfriend in front of Mr. Newton and Susan."

"I'm sorry I said that, Sloan. I wish that you would be my boyfriend."

"If I were your boyfriend, I would spank you every day."

"Including today?" She looked up at him for an instant, then hid her blush against his shirt.

"Especially today, young lady!" he declared, taking her over to her bed, sitting down on the corner of it and turning her over his knee. "Why, you were insolence itself at the party!" Sloan's palm came down vigorously on the seat of her skirt several times, each of which caused her small feet to kick, but he soon grew impatient with the thick velvet dress and summarily pulled it up to her waist.

"I'm sorry that I'm wearing pantyhose," she suddenly exclaimed.

"I like pantyhose," he said, caressing her slim legs from ankle to hip. "They make your legs so sleek. And of course, when I pull them down just to here–" he pulled her pantyhose down to just below her panties, "–they bind you charmingly." Frankie gave a little whimper at this observation. "Now you just lie across my lap and take your spanking like a good girl," he advised her in a seductive tone.

"I will!" she promised fervently, waiting with excitement for the first smacks to fall across the seat of her panties.

As Sloan began to spank her rather firmly he wondered whether Frances could have possibly been as forward with Anthony Newton as Susan had been with him. Had she, for instance, ground against his lap the way she was doing now?

"Frances," he said, while pulling her panties down, "if you want me to be your boyfriend, you're going to have to be faithful to me."

"You mean not have sex with anyone else?" she turned to look at him.

"You have another definition of the word faithful?" he snapped with irritation.

"No, sir," said Frances and dropped her head.

He stroked her for a moment.

"You seem sad," he said, "don't you want me to be your only

lover, darling?"

"People don't own other people's bodies," she murmured on principal, keeping her eyes on the floor.

"That's your attitude, is it?" Sloan bristled and brought his hand down hard on her prettily exposed cheeks a couple of dozen times. For Mrs. Taylor's boy was nothing if not a romantic, whereas Frankie possessed little reverence for the traditional conventions of love and indeed scarcely understood them. She knew that she did find excessively annoying the rigid sexual morality portrayed in almost all the books that Sloan recommended she read.

"You know, this isn't the 18th Century," she protested, putting one small hand back to protect her bottom. He removed it and renewed his grip on her waist.

"Some things never change," he declared and began to spank her again. This hurt, but his indignation thrilled her.

"So I suppose it wouldn't bother you if I made love to Susan?" he suddenly asked her.

"I didn't say that," she quickly replied.

"Oh? Are you saying you'd prefer it if I didn't?"

"...Yes."

"Good. Now we're getting somewhere."

"Where are we getting?"

"We're getting to where we both agree that fidelity is preferable."

"It may be preferable, but what if it's not practical?" she argued, for which she got the hardest volley of smacks so far.

"What do you mean, not practical? Since when is saying no to someone's sexual advances not practical?" he paused to give her time to answer.

"Temptations could arise to weaken one's resolve."

"Well, you're just going to have to force yourself to resist them. I did," Sloan told her with some satisfaction. Now he brought the spanking to a close with a dozen solid smacks that she would still feel two days later. These left her breathless, whimpering and fiercely aroused. Then he lifted her off his lap and set her clothes to rights. But she immediately pulled her panties down again to examine her bottom in a mirror. Frankie was shocked to see how red it was.

He watched her over folded arms, trying to ignore his own mounting excitement. "You're a very naughty girl," he told her, not in the least bit satisfied with her attitude. "I should tie you down and whip you till you cry for uttering such sentiments to your lover," he threatened, causing Frankie's tummy to contract with exquisite pleasure.

She came to him and put her arms around his slim waist and laid her head against his chest. "I just know I love and adore you," she said.

"Finally you say something sensible!" he said, drawing her more tightly against him and tilting up her chin for a kiss.

"Well? You haven't given me your comments on the party yet," said Marguerite to Malcolm as they sat enjoying the rain on the skylight in her attic playroom. It was around midnight and she had exchanged her party dress for a rich, full-skirted hostess gown. Marguerite was enjoying spending her husband's money.

"It wasn't as bad as I thought it would be," he grudgingly admitted.

"Malcolm, if you'd read those journals of mine before we got married, would you still have asked me to marry you?" she asked bravely, trying to seem casual.

"Of course," he replied candidly.

"There's a good lad!" She came and bounced on his lap.

"But that doesn't mean I wasn't shocked to learn how bad you really are."

"Oh, Malcolm," Marguerite giggled.

"You know, you never even told me that you dominate men."

"Why? Would you like me to dominate you?"

"No more than you're already doing," he said with a smile, "But what's that all about?"

"It's about being spoiled rotten and doing whatever you like. Everything you don't approve of, darling," Marguerite murmured, biting him lightly on the neck.

"Oh, yes, speaking of doing whatever you like, I notice you didn't hesitate to practically sit in Michael Flagg's lap tonight!" Malcolm put her off his lap, took her by the wrist and led her to her own spanking horse.

"Malcolm no! What are you doing?" Marguerite resisted, with a pout that begged for a kiss. He did her kiss her, deeply.

"I don't care if you are a mistress," he said, turning her around and gently bending her over the bench. "You're not getting away with flirting in front of your husband," he told her, pulling up her skirt and a bunch of stiff petticoats. She turned to look at him.

"But I was good," she protested, keeping her long legs together in her high heeled brocade slippers.

"You call that good? The way you practically stamped your foot at me in front of everyone?" he said, looking around for an implement to correct her with. A small martinet came to his hand. It was made of six thin rawhide lashes mounted from a wooden handle.

"No, Malcolm, not the whip!" she protested, knowing he had never used it before.

"Oh, relax," he told her, pushing her back down and pulling her silk panties completely off.

"Have I ever hurt you yet?"

"No," she admitted, her smooth, voluptuous white bottom now upturned and framed by the frothy petticoats.

He tested the whip on his hand a few times, then trailed the lashes lightly across her plump cheeks, which produced a ticklish sensation and made her shiver with awakened interest.

For a few seconds he merely teased her with the lashes, then he very lightly began to feather her with the tips by fanning her bottom in a circular motion. She looked back at him in surprise for he seemed to know what he was doing.

"Don't be afraid, I won't wrap it," he assured her, now beginning to bring the lashes down smartly, but in such a way that they fell across only the centermost of portion of her buttocks, avoiding her hips and thighs.

As the whipping became firmer Marguerite gave herself up to it. The thin strips of leather stung her creamy cheeks in the sexiest way imaginable. In between the harder strokes he dragged the laces lightly across her pinkened flesh, clothing and unclothing her bottom with a flick of his wrist. The whip set Marguerite on fire.

He was accustomed enough to her responses by now to know that she wanted him to go harder. Capturing the tips in his left hand he took careful aim with his right and let them go against her right cheek with a snap. Then he did the same to the left and continued to lash her in this manner eight more times. Marguerite gave a little cry at each connection but did not shift her position an iota, particularly with respect to keeping her legs together.

She wriggled her bottom and sighed, encouraging him to continue whipping her. Marguerite closed her eyes to savor her first real whipping from her husband.

"Do you know what would be so cute right now?" he asked, pausing to stroke her rosy bottom, which had colored to magenta under the smart little lashing.

"What, darling?" she turned her head but didn't move, except to put one hand back and give herself a rub.

"Something in your bottom while I'm whipping it," he shocked her by stating.

Marguerite's face flushed as pink as her bottom as she considered the proposal.

"But that would be so...undignified," she equivocated.

"No one would ever have to know," he promised, going down on his knees behind her to separate her ankles about two feet. Now her lightly marked bottom looked even more provocative.

"I may not have anything for you to use," she hesitated. But he'd already begun looking through drawers and cabinets for Marguerite's toys.

"May not have anything for me to use, huh?" he remarked with predictable cynicism while regarding the contents of her pear wood hope chest, which was filled to the brim with every exotic sexual aid he had ever heard of or imagined. "Any preferences?" he asked.

"Little pink and big grey," she shyly replied, then hid her face. Malcolm came back with a pink rubber anal plug and a cordless grey disc top vibrator. "And lube," she added.

"You mean I have to make an extra trip just for that?" he asked, giving her a hard smack.

"Yes, please," she replied flirtatiously, pleased by the esoteric turn the evening had taken. He came back with the lube.

"Spread your legs," he told her.

"But they are spread."

Smack!

"Spread them wider."

"Ouch!"

"Now reach back and spread your bottom for me."

"No!"

"No?" He himself spread her cheeks with one hand and sternly smacked her in between them several times.

"I mean, okay!" she cried immediately, but placed her hands on her bottom so hesitantly that Malcolm took them impatiently and positioned them to his satisfaction on either cheek.

"Show me your bottom," he ordered, remembering that the sexiest examples of his wife's writing had to do with humiliation.

"Do you know what I thought to myself when I saw you flirting at the party, Marguerite?" he asked, slowly lubricating her bottom hole with his fingertip. "I thought, that girl is really asking for it. She must really want me to punish her."

When she didn't reply he carefully spread her cheeks and pushed the small dildo up into her bottom. She whimpered and wriggled in response.

"No doubt this will ruin you for regular sex..." he let his words trail off as he switched the vibrator on low and pressed the round flat top lightly against her pubic mound. With his left hand so engaged, his right was still free to apply the whip stingingly to her freshly plugged bottom. In three strokes she came with the most endearing shudder of pleasure he had ever witnessed. Then it was all she could do to sink to the floor in a heap of satin and crinoline and attempt to come to her senses.

He sat down beside her and took her in his arms. "You let me embarrass you," he reflected ingenuously.

"You did say that no one need ever know," she reminded him sleepily.

Chapter Six

The Indiscreet Charm of Marguerite

"Tell me something about Michael Flagg I don't know," Patricia Fairservis begged Marguerite Alexander Branwell over their first cappuccino together in the lighthouse.

Marguerite sat curled up in the window seat that raw March afternoon, a glorious new bride. They had already extensively discussed Malcolm, Marguerite's new mate, and were now on the topic of Michael Flagg, the good-looking detective whose favors had been shared between the girls for a time.

"Michael is a romantic at heart," Marguerite disclosed.

"Really? I haven't seen it," Patricia chortled, remembering the trip to the Combat Zone bookstore, plugged.

"I've always felt that Michael is just as disposed to worship women as to dominate them."

"He certainly isn't that way with me," Patricia confided, flipping back her straight blonde hair to light a cigarette.

"You know, I have whipped Michael, on several occasions," Marguerite let slip with something like a giggle. Patricia stared at her.

"Are you saying he's really submissive?" Patricia asked with sudden anxiety.

"Certainly not submissive, but perhaps a bit more of a sensualist than you thought," Marguerite explained. But Patricia was too new in the scene to understand such nuances and felt betrayed. Marguerite noted the change and was sorry she had spoken.

Marguerite was to regret her rash admission even more the following day when she was having lunch at the inn and Michael slid into the booth across from her with an expression that could not be described as cordial.

"Why Michael, how are you?"

"Not very well thanks to you, Marguerite."

"Me?"

"Thanks to you I no longer have a girlfriend," he reported gloomily, ordering coffee.

"Oh, my dear!" Marguerite remembered her conversation with Patricia the previous day. "You don't mean she minded what I told her?"

"She minded, Marguerite."

"But, how could she be so unenlightened?"

"How could you be so indiscreet?"

Marguerite couldn't meet his eyes and felt vexed enough to cry with self-recrimination.

"I'll talk to her and make her understand," Marguerite offered.

"It's no use, she's lost all respect for me now," Michael said matter of factly. "She told me so."

"Then she's a little idiot!" Marguerite cried passionately. Michael sighed and looked at her.

"First you had to break my heart by getting married. Now you make it so I can't have Patricia either. What am I going to do with you, Marguerite?"

Marguerite blushed, surprised that he was not too upset to flirt.

"If I have to thrash her myself, I'll make her understand," vowed Marguerite.

"Marguerite?"

"Yes, Michael?"

"When may I expect satisfaction?"

"What?"

"I'm talking about me giving you the punishment you deserve for destroying my relationship with the Princess."

"Oh, Michael, darling, I'm afraid that won't be possible. You see, I've promised Malcolm that I wouldn't play with anyone else besides him."

"Who said anything about playing?"

"Michael, stop being horrid."

"Are you saying you refuse to submit to the strapping you have coming for breaking the first rule of the scene?"

"I couldn't think of it. Malcolm would hate me if he found out."

"Like Patricia hates me?"

"Michael, please stop guilting me! It's not becoming in a man."

"I know. That's why I want to admonish you properly with my belt across your backside."

"No, it's out of the question. I'm very sorry about Patricia and I will intercede on your behalf. Now, if you'll excuse me..."

"You're getting that strapping, Marguerite, one way or another."

Much later that night, when Marguerite was driving home after a party at Anthony Newton's house on the cliff, she heard a siren behind her. Looking in her mirror she saw Michael put the portable light on top of his unmarked car. She pulled over and looked up at him when he came to the window.

"A siren, Michael?"

"Get out of the car," he told her tersely.

"What's the matter?"

Michael opened the door, pulled her out of the car, spun her around and cuffed her wrists behind her back.

"You're under arrest."

"But, why?"

"Speeding while under the influence."

"But Michael, really! It's four in the morning. There isn't a soul on the road and I've only had a couple of drinks."

"Shut up and get in the car," he snapped. Marguerite never remembered him taking this tone with her before and she felt a tear moisten the corner of her eye. He put her in the back seat of his car.

"Michael please don't take me to the station to do whatever it is you're planning. I couldn't bear it!"

"Afraid of it getting in the paper and Malcolm finding out?"

"Michael Flagg, if you go through with this insanity, I swear I'll never speak to you again!"

He looked at her in the rear view mirror as she curled up on the seat, cuffed and pouting, in her pearls, sable and evening dress, her russet hair rippling to her shoulders.

"There is an alternative to the station house," he suggested, "Come home with me and take what you've got coming like a woman."

Marguerite had never been black mailed into playing before, but Malcolm was out of town until the following evening and she felt excited by the fantasy. Although Michael didn't need to know that.

"Very well," she agreed, rather proudly and refused to meet his eyes in the mirror for the rest of the ride.

Michael did not uncuff her until he had bent her over his spanking horse in his own playroom some five minutes later.

"Don't move," he warned her, pulling off her fur and smoothing down the back of her pearl grey velvet gown. She turned her head to see him unbuckle his belt.

The horrible part was that for once she'd actually done something that really merited a spanking, which was too humiliating to contemplate.

"You don't really deserve a warm up," he told her, pushing her skirt up to her waist to reveal a pair of pearl grey silk briefs that wrapped her like a present. "But I still love you, so you'll get the first fifty on your panties." He brought the belt down across her bottom with a snap.

Marguerite clamped her lips together and refused to make a sound. The strap came down ten or a dozen more times with a crisp, determined report. They were fifty she might have almost enjoyed had her mind not been filled with anxiety that she would be marked.

"Oh, Michael, please don't mark me!" she cried suddenly, before they had advanced to stroke twenty-five.

"Are you afraid of your husband, Marguerite?" He pulled down her panties to check for marks. She had already become deeply pinkened.

"Malcolm isn't free-wheeling like you. He'd never forgive me," she appealed to him with a melting look.

"I still don't understand why you get to demolish my relationship but I have to protect yours," Michael observed with perplexity, pulling her panties back up to finish the first set of fifty strokes.

"If only I'd known Patricia was so conventional!" Marguerite lamented.

"It surprised me too," Michael reflected. "Are you ready?"

"Yes."

"Now you're going to feel the way I strap Patricia," Michael warned her, then lay on the remaining strokes in two sets of twelve, hard enough to make Marguerite cry out at each whack.

Marguerite thought, "This Patricia is a heavy submissive!" But she liked the strapping. And it was very good to be with Michael again. However, when he bared her, she panicked.

"If you do the next set that hard I'll be marked," she stood up to examine her bottom, which was now a deep magenta in coloration and stinging from the strap. She rubbed it and went to a mirror. Michael folded his arms and waited.

"We can make a deal," he said, grabbing her when she returned to him and bending her back over the bench. He pulled her skirt up, made her step out of the panties and spread her legs. The next thing she heard was his zipper coming down.

A light, flaky snow began to fall at dawn, when Michael put Marguerite back into her car.

"I'm going to talk to her, Michael," Marguerite promised. He bent to kiss her good-bye.

"She can go to hell as far as I'm concerned," he said pleasantly. "Bye, honey."

"Bye, darling," said Marguerite, praying to the goddess not to let Malcolm return home early.

That afternoon Michael was shoveling snow off his front walkway when Patricia drove up. He gave her a look and said, "Oh, it's my fair weather friend," then continued with his work.

"Michael, I've been thinking."

"I'll bet that was painful."

"I guess I over reacted about your being a switch."

"Look, Patricia, just because I let one woman whip me once a year– that doesn't make me a switch."

"Do you want me to whip you, Michael?"

Michael, who did not reply, was glad that snow shoveling required so much energy, otherwise he might have been tempted to wring her neck.

"Michael, I love you whatever you are," she assured him.

"You didn't seem to feel that way yesterday." He put the shovel away and they went inside. Patricia peeled off her coat. She was dressed in beige wool leggings and a white sweater and her hair was in a ponytail.

"I'm very sorry about the way I spoke to you yesterday," she said with some difficulty, for apologies did not come easily to her lips.

"Okay," he said, "we'll forget it ever happened."

"Entirely?" she asked.

"I have no desire to go submissive to you, if that's what you're wondering about," he told her firmly.

"Well, but, do you accept my apology?"

"Sure."

"I don't know how I could have been so insensitive."

"You specialize in that."

Patricia hung her head. Her heart beat quickly as she wondered what would happen next. He came and sat next to her on the sofa and made her look at him. However she could not meet his eyes.

"What's the matter Patricia? Are you embarrassed?"

"Yes."

"Because you know you deserve a good spanking?" He drew her across his lap. Gripping her firmly about the waist, he brought his hand down a couple of dozen times in rapid succession across the nubby woolen seat of her heavy winter leggings. "You've been a disloyal playmate, haven't you?"

"Yes," she replied as he took down her pants and her silk tights to completely bare her creamy bottom.

"It's a good thing you had the sense to come over here and apologize," he told her, bringing his large palm down hard on her tender cheeks, which caused her to kick and cry. "I was never going to call you again."

The tone of indignation in Michael's voice caused Patricia's stomach to contract, but his hand coming down hurt too much to enjoy.

"Imagine being so narrow minded and judgmental!" he continued to scold her. "My own feelings aside, I should spank you very hard just for that one thing," he declared, putting additional force behind his swing.

"Ow!" she cried. "I'm sorry!"

"You know, Patricia, every time I think you've grown up and become a human being, you manage to disappoint me. Why is that?" He paused to stroke her deeply colored bottom.

"I don't know," she whimpered, really feeling sorry for herself now.

Michael delivered a final two dozen swats vigorously enough to make her wail like the spoiled child she was, then pushed her off his lap. She sat on the floor, rubbed her bottom and pouted until he kissed her.

"I'm glad that you decided not to desert me," he told her.

Marguerite's first marital infidelity greatly weakened her resolve to be faithful, especially with regard to Sloan Taylor, the handsome young man she had recently hired to manage her bookshop.

Winter hung on tenaciously, lasting into the second week of April and depositing Frances in bed with the flu. This necessitated Marguerite returning to her shop to assist Sloan for eight days. Even before this convenient inconvenience occurred, Marguerite noticed that Wednesdays had become her favorite day of the week. This was Frances' day off and Marguerite customarily popped into the shop for the morning or afternoon to help.

It was during these long periods of being snowed or rained in with Sloan that Marguerite began to fully realize that her employee was uncommonly attractive and exquisitely sensitive.

It was not that Marguerite wanted to do anything like play with Sloan. Being his boss, she had no desire to go submissive to him and as he himself was apparently strictly dominant, there was no chance of her becoming his mistress. Marguerite's freshly sprung desire for her subordinate was straightforwardly sexual. She knew from looking at him that he was handsome. She knew from Frances that he had a large cock. She simply longed to feel it in her.

Marguerite desired Sloan. She had to fight the impulse to run her hands through his black hair and bite his white neck. The faint scent of his spicy aftershave drew her to him. 6' 2" and lean, he wore his good clothes well, and this entranced her. His thoughtfulness and warmth added affection to her desire.

She knew that what she was contemplating was not permissible. Even the fact that he shared her taste in literature to an uncanny degree could not excuse a blatant seduction.

And yet, with Marguerite, thinking was planning and planning was doing. She knew her own nature too well to try to resist her impulses for longer than two or three weeks. The only obstruction to her desire was the possibility of Malcolm finding out. Whether their marriage would weather her first deliberate infidelity was a question that preoccupied her.

Naturally she was more than fond of Malcolm. She had married him. But unfavorable comparisons between the aggressive businessman and the refined bibliophile were bound to arise while Marguerite worked side by side with Sloan.

Malcolm wanted to read more, but ultimately he preferred to fill his spare time with physical pursuits, some of which she happily participated in and some of which she left alone. A good example was the weekend he decided to enroll in a ski rescue school in Vermont. Marguerite applauded his noble endeavor, and packed a picnic basket for his drive, then happily spent Saturday in the shop with Sloan.

Malcolm was not due home till late Sunday night and she decided to use this weekend to accomplish her deed.

Sloan was not ignorant of the fact that something was about to happen between himself and Marguerite, he only hoped he had the patience and resolve to wait for her to initiate it. For when Marguerite liked someone as much as she did Sloan, she became as mischievously lovable as a kitten. No man in the commonwealth could have resisted her, least of all himself.

Yet Sloan wondered if the embarrassment and potential hurt to Frances and Malcolm would be justified in pursuit of a relationship which most certainly would not include spanking. He sensed this every time they flirted, during which she was always extremely careful to maintain her dignity, both as his boss and a goddess. It was very clear to Sloan that while he would most probably be permitted to make love to Aphrodite, he would not be permitted to chastise her. Considering the beauty, roundness and perfection of Marguerite's bottom and Sloan's secret desire to lavish every type of attention on it, this was a very sad state of affairs for the inflamed but well-mannered young man.

Sometimes the absurdity of the situation frustrated Sloan, however, common sense told him to cut his own throat before laying disciplinary hands on the precious person of his employer.

Spanking Marguerite was positively out of the question. So naturally, this was what obsessed him. Her bottom was so lusciously ample. As a redhead, she would color so quickly and prettily. The very thought of taking her across his knee made him shudder with a surge of excitement. It was really too awkward.

Sloan had, of course, lied to Frankie when he declared that he did not think Mrs. Branwell the most provocative woman he had ever met, for he certainly did. But unlike Marguerite, who regarded Sloan as provided by the goddess for her amusement, Sloan had real respect for Marguerite and found the idea of seducing his employer to be extremely problematical.

In the end it was Sloan and not Marguerite who broke every rule, probably because his nerves were torn to pieces by the entire situation. They had just closed the door on Saturday night. Marguerite was pulling shades and Sloan was using an adding machine in his small back office to close out the day.

She was going around the shop collecting coffee cups when she entered his office. He didn't look up because he was adding. But as she leaned across his desk to grab a cup, her 24" waist caused Sloan to forget every rule of proper business etiquette and simply reach out to pull her down on his lap.

Marguerite gave a little gasp and looked at him in great surprise but did not attempt to repulse him.

"I'm sorry!" he immediately said, "But you're so irresistibly charming."

"I'm finding it rather difficult to resist you too," she smiled, locking her arms around his neck and kissing him.

"We shouldn't," he said several minutes later.

"Why not?" Marguerite was working on loosening his tie.

"Because you're married," he said, capturing her hands to kiss them.

"Oh, that," she said, while wriggling on his lap and allowing him to feel her bottom grinding against him.

"I'm sure your husband is insanely in love with you," said Sloan compassionately.

Marguerite felt somewhat vexed at Sloan for mentioning the uncomfortable subject of her marriage. "He doesn't have to find out," she firmly replied. They then resumed kissing. At length he suggested they retire to his apartment upstairs and Marguerite agreed.

She spent a few moments admiring the decorative improvements he had made since moving in. The more she touched and smelled and moved among his masculine things, the more eager to surrender to him she became. The fact the he was her employee now seemed completely irrelevant and she felt no more superior to him than Bertie Wooster did to Jeeves.

Meanwhile, every shred of his usual circumspection deserted Sloan as he watched her traverse his rooms in her crisp, tailored work outfit, a navy pencil skirt and matching wool vest over a white blouse, and medium-high ankle strap heels. She paused to admire a large, carved, Victorian box sofa, which had been sumptuously upholstered in honey beige brocade. "Is this new?" she asked, sitting down on it.

"Newly restored. The frame is from 1860. Do you like it?" Sloan came to sit next to her, handing her a glass of wine. She sipped with approval.

"It's wonderful. And large enough to do anything on."

"That was my thought."

"What would you like to do on it, Sloan?" Marguerite asked, causing him to color in such a way as to answer her question.

"Anything that would please you," he finally replied.

Marguerite laughed at him, which made him smile at her. "Many things please me," she elected to torture him.

"Tell me some of them."

"You've read my books."

"But they're all about B&D."

"Yes. Aren't they?" said Marguerite, virtually changing her mind about the tone of her relations with Sloan.

"Are you saying you'd be willing to play?"

"Do two people in the scene ever make love without playing first?"

"That depends upon whether they can agree on a definition for playing."

"Why don't you try something and see how I react?" Marguerite teased, delighted by his confusion.

"And what if you react badly?"

"Then I guess you could try something else," she suggested, her heart pounding in anticipation of the dynamic suddenly changing between them.

"What about role playing?" he asked, his color receding and his enthusiasm returning with a surge.

"That sounds like fun. I haven't done that in years."

"Any ideas?" he asked her.

"You decide," she encouraged him.

"Are you sure?"

"Quite sure."

"In that case, let's pretend that I'm your husband and I've just come home to discover that you've been unfaithful to me."

"That works," she cheerfully replied.

"My character is not unreasonable;" Sloan rose in his animated way to paint the picture, "he understands that his wife is a free spirit. But there's also the issue of respect to be considered. Don't you agree?"

"Oh, undoubtedly. Cheating on one's husband is a sign of disrespect, if not to the man, at least to the institution of marriage," Marguerite helpfully replied.

"Naturally, he's distraught. He paces restlessly as he tries to decide how to deal with this startling revelation," Sloan continued, mesmerizing Marguerite with his pacing.

"Oh, he must forgive her!" cried Marguerite.

"Of course he must forgive her, dear girl, but not, I think, before administering a very sound spanking." Now that the word had been said it was her turn to blush. Her lips curved into a quiet, catlike smile though she could not bring herself to meet his eyes.

He sat down beside her and very gently pulled her across his lap, causing her to admit to herself for the first time, that this was exactly what she'd had in mind when she had hired Sloan.

Sloan smoothed down her skirt, raised his strong right arm and brought his hand down twice, smacking her once on each cheek through the tight, wool skirt.

Marguerite settled in and closed her eyes. "You have a hard hand," she murmured, as he continued spanking her as firmly as he dared.

"It's just what you need," he told her, vigorously spanking every inch of her lush bottom several dozen times before pausing to let her catch her breath.

"I need whatever I want," she suggested pertly.

"Because you're a spoiled brat!" Sloan declared, starting all over again, but using a harder, faster stroke.

"Ow! That really stings!" she cried at length, reaching back to rub her bottom. Sloan pushed her hand away and stroked her himself. Then he very slowly pushed her skirt up to her waist to reveal a bottom snugly wrapped in a sheer nylon garter belt and panties and long legs in seamed stockings. Her fair skin was already darkly pinkened under the fresh white lingerie.

"I'm sorry," he told her, "but it's the only way you'll learn to take me seriously."

"I'm taking you very seriously, darling," she replied, grinding hard enough against his lap to feel his erection. Sloan's satisfaction in the moment was great. To pretend that he was Marguerite's husband enjoying the privilege of disciplining her was exotic beyond dreams. Her bottom arched to meet his hand now, in spite of the sting, convincing him that she was feeling more pleasure than discomfort.

"Didn't you realize that you had a jealous husband?" he asked, carefully tugging her panties down to bare her bottom.

Marguerite knew very well that she had a jealous husband. And it was pleasant to imagine that this was all that he would do if he ever did catch her cheating on him.

Even as Sloan spanked her bottom to a deep magenta, he thought, "I can leave it at this and prevent us both from committing a terrible error." Then he remembered that he was the one who had made the first move. By the rules of romance, to leave it at just a spanking would be an insult to Marguerite, not to mention the frustration it would cause them both.

A moment later, as he touched her intimately for the first time, he thought, "Who am I kidding? Doing this is just as bad as doing everything." Marguerite was very wet and had a scent like jungle flowers. Inserting his long middle finger into her sex to the knuckle, he pulled it out glistening and tasted her on his hand. The savor of her creamy essence ignited his partially Italian blood and every grain of resolve melted. He plunged two fingers back into her pussy to the hilt and began to possess her, still holding her down across lap, with his other hand on her radiant cheeks.

Marguerite was surprised at how deftly he plied her. This she really liked. She could almost come with his long fingers giving her pleasure while she still lay across his knee. But now that he'd aroused her to this pitch, she craved more spanking.

"Darling?" she said softly.

"Yes, Marguerite?" Sloan gently slid his fingers free.

"I feel my misdeed was most grave."

Sloan took this as his cue to unleash a more believable degree of husbandly indignation when he resumed the paddling. What bliss to be married to Marguerite and actually enjoy doing this on a regular basis. She seemed thoroughly content to lie across his lap and allow him to spank her as hard as he liked.

"I think that's enough," Sloan said at last, noticing some dark rose speckling under the deep pink his hand had left on her very fair skin.

"Are you sure I've been punished enough?" she asked brightly, growing very fond of his hand.

"I'm sure you're going to mark if I keep this up," he said, gently pulling her up and taking her in his arms.

"Perhaps we should do something else for awhile," she suggested, unknotting his tie.

Malcolm Branwell was made aware of his wife's infidelity with Sloan in a hideously unexpected way. Women being the intuitive individuals they are, and every woman in Random Point being a sort of witch by dint of simply residing there, Frances Wu guessed the moment she returned to work and saw her employer and her supervisor together; Sloan and Marguerite had had knowledge of each other in her absence. This suspicion was validated by the scent of Marguerite's perfume, lingering on Sloan's favorite vest and tie. She had gone through his closet with a nose like a cat.

Frances was both jealous and angry, seeing Sloan as a hypocrite for professing indifference to Marguerite, then seizing the first opportunity to seduce her. Sloan had long known of Frances' vindictive streak, but never guessed how far into mischief it would take her.

A few days after Frances' discovery, Malcolm received an anonymous letter telling him about the affair between Marguerite and Sloan. It was signed: A concerned on-looker. The letter arrived at the corporate offices in Boston on a Monday. It was the middle of the afternoon, and Malcolm had just gotten off the phone with Marguerite who was planning dinner. He'd intended to drive out to Random Point in about an hour. He'd even made a shopping list of items to pick up on the way home. He crumpled it up and tossed it in the wastebasket then stared bleakly at the wall as he decided what to do. Dully he dialed the phone.

"Marguerite? Me. Look, uh, something's just come up and I'm going to have to stay in town tonight." He hung up before his voice could betray his emotion. On the other end Marguerite looked at the receiver and suddenly knew that something was very wrong. As soon as she hung up, the phone rang again.

"Hello?"

"Marguerite?" It was Sloan and he sounded agitated.

"Yes, dear, is everything all right?"

"Not exactly. Frances has just given her notice. Apparently she figured out what happened between us and she's furious."

"How in the world did she?"

"She smelled your perfume on my clothes."

"Oh, Sloan, I'm so sorry!" Marguerite almost sobbed with vexation. "But tell me, do you think that Frances would be capable of betraying us to Malcolm?"

"In a heart beat."

"In that case, I've had a short and happy marriage."

"Oh, Marguerite, no! Mr. Branwell would never give you up over someone as unimportant as me."

"Look, darling, we've got to work on getting them back."

"I doubt there's any hope with Frances," he sighed. "She's gone back to Boston to stay with her parents for awhile. She says she couldn't bear to live in your guesthouse another day."

Marguerite was silent with worry and guilt. She had brought Frankie out to Random Point on a romantic whim and now appeared to be driving her away for the same reason.

"Oh, Sloan, what have I done?"

"Marguerite, don't blame yourself. I did make the first move," he gently reminded her. "Besides, Frances and I were never really compatible. And she was thinking of going to Europe with a knapsack in a couple of months anyway."

"Is this so?"

"Yes, she's been trying to get me to drop everything and go with her."

"But you don't want to?"

"Not at the moment."

"I regret causing anyone pain, but I don't regret becoming close to you," said Marguerite, hanging up.

It was raining when she left her house with an umbrella and walked the three village blocks to Hugo Sands' antiques shop. There were no customers in the store. Hugo emerged from his back office at the tinkle of the bell.

"Marguerite, what's the matter?" Hugo saw trouble in her face. Marguerite compulsively picked up and examined small objects while confessing all that had happened to Hugo.

"That little brat!" he declared angrily at the end of her recitation.

"Someone ought to cane her senseless for doing that to you and Malcolm."

"Oh, Hugo, it isn't her fault. It's mine. You can't blame the girl for being jealous and bitter. Here I dragged her out to Random Point, made sure she fell in love with Sloan, then took him for a play toy myself. What I've done has been perfectly loathsome!"

"Oh, sweetie," Hugo took her in his arms and hugged her. "You can't help being attracted to good-looking men."

"Should I have not gotten married?"

"It was time you got a husband, Marguerite. Everyone knew that."

"He won't put up with this, Hugo. He's probably calling his divorce lawyer this very minute," she fretted, pacing up and down the narrow aisles of the shop.

"He's in the scene, Marguerite, you know what you have to do."

"What?" she looked up suspiciously.

"Why, prostrate yourself before him, of course, and humbly beg his forgiveness, preferable wearing something tight. If you're lucky you'll get off with a thrashing and probably have the best sex you've ever had afterwards."

"If only I could believe that."

"Trust me. Put on your grey jersey dress with the fringe tie scarf and four-inch heels. Get in the car and drive to Boston. Now."

As Marguerite walked back to her house she thought, "Hugo's never been wrong before." Before the dress went on she laced herself into her new pearl grey satin custom waist cinch and finished with a matching lace bra and g-string with seamed hose. Her new pumps were from Paris and the wool dress Hugo had suggested had a similar label.

Driving into Boston in the rain Marguerite made positive projections for the evening, envisioning a splendidly passionate scene and then forgiveness. Imagining the scene brought a radiance to her cheeks and she wondered whether she hadn't done what she had with Sloan partially to incite her husband.

"What's the fun of being married to a dominant male if you aren't going to try his patience now and then?" she wondered, finding it quite easy to rationalize her behavior from this point of view. This way what she did almost seemed innocent, a childish plea for attention. Would Malcolm go for that?

When she arrived at his rooftop duplex in Back Bay at around ten, Malcolm was not at home. She guessed he had gone to his gym, then to dinner and would be returning any moment.

Two minutes later she heard his key in the door and rushed out to the marbled and mirrored foyer to meet him. Malcolm was astonished to see her and flushed with a mixture of pain and excitement. He filled out his tee-shirt and jeans as only a gym-rat can, and Marguerite longed to wrap her arms around his 28" waist very badly, but had no way of knowing just how angry he was and didn't dare get so close so soon.

"Hi, Malcolm, I hope you don't mind that I came."

"But, I told you I had something going on," he protested.

"Now, darling?"

"That's right," he said, "I have a late meeting tonight."

"Malcolm, you know that isn't true," Marguerite said softly.

"I'm sorry, Marguerite, but I think we need to spend a few days apart," he said decisively, strolling down the hall towards his bedroom. Marguerite's face became very warm as she realized that she had been dismissed. Pensively she walked down the hall to her own room and removed her hat and gloves. Then she lay on the bed face down, with her head pillowed on her arms, wondering what she should do. Hugo had counseled humility, but Malcolm hadn't stood still long enough for her to practice any.

Then he suddenly appeared in the doorway of her room, causing her to start up.

"It's true, isn't it? About you and Sloan Taylor, I mean."

"It's true that I was just a little bit naughty while you were away skiing," Marguerite admitted lightly.

"Is that how you see it?" Malcolm snapped.

"Yes."

"Well that isn't how I see it. And I won't be made a fool of."

"Oh, darling –"

"Don't darling me. I want an explanation of why you're running around seducing your employees when you're supposed to be married to me."

"Sheer self-indulgence," she replied in a properly regretful tone.

"Oh, is that so? Well, how would you feel if I indulged myself with every pretty girl who works for me?"

"I don't know how I'd feel, but I would try to understand."

"You know, I seem to remember you giving me your word on our wedding day that there would be no other men in your life from now on."

"I'm sorry," she meekly replied.

"Is that all you have to say after doing something like this?"

"I was bad," she admitted. "But I adore you."

Malcolm felt the tension leave his shoulders as he gazed at her open face. Now that she was here, most of the pain of the anonymous letter receded. He noticed how she'd dressed for him and was momentarily riveted by her impossibly small waist.

"Do you know that you need a good spanking?" he suddenly demanded, sitting next to her on the bed and pulling her across his lap. An oval, ebony hairbrush came easily into his hand from the dresser and he used it to administer twelve hard smacks to her skirted bottom. Marguerite caught her breath at each one but didn't cry out. A first punishment from an adored husband is a wildly erotic moment to any woman in the scene.

"Imagine me having to do this," he scowled, "not three months into our marriage!" He smacked her hard with the brush ten more times, then put it down, pushed her soft jersey skirt up to her waist and renewed the spanking on her bare backside, now pink and luxuriantly framed by the hem of the corset and rosetted garter straps. Now he spanked her twenty times without pausing. She could no longer lie still or keep quiet and on stroke twenty attempted to break his hold on her waist. Each fair cheek was now brightly reddened and she twisted to avoid the brush with such urgency that Malcolm decided to toss it aside. "Calm down," he ordered.

Malcolm reached under the corset to grasp her g-string and pull it off. Then he separated her legs and slapped her bare inner thighs, just above her stocking tops, ten or twelve times each. Marguerite's soft skin was very sensitive in this area and Malcolm's hand was very hard. Tears sprung to her eyes immediately but she suppressed the accompanying sobs. She did, however, close her luscious thighs so tightly that he was compelled to pry them apart.

"I'm sorry," he told her firmly, "but you need this." This time he pulled her bottom cheeks apart and applied his palm sharply to her bottom hole. These smacks made her whimper, but she did not pull away or try to resist them, even when he spanked her hard.

The punishment was quickly becoming erotic, in spite Malcolm's resolve to simply teach her a lesson. However, it did seem to be working, both to relieve his lovesick anxiety and to make her wet. He had a throbbing erection and his anger was gone.

"Let's get this dress off," he told her, and quickly pulled it over her head while somehow managing to hold her in position. "And this can go as well," he said, unhooking her bra and tossing it aside. Now he adjusted her position so that she straddled one of his thighs with her slick, pink charms fully revealed.

"This is the naughtiest part of all," he told her, tapping her spread sex with his palm. Meanwhile, he reached under her bosom to lightly squeeze her breasts and pinch her nipples, which had grown stiff. But she refused to stay properly spread unless he held her that way, so he let go of her creamy bosom and devoted his full attention to her intoxicating pussy. He only patted her glistening labia, but each little spank went through her like a current of energy, swelling her dewy pink clit.

"Tell me that you're sorry," he ordered.

"I'm sorry!"

"Beg my forgiveness."

"Darling, please forgive me!" she appealed.

"Swear you'll never do it again."

"I swear I'll never do it again!"

He let her up. She pouted until he took her in his arms and buried his face in her hair. "But you're such a bad girl," he said sadly, pulling away from her, "and I'm so disappointed in you."

"Oh, Malcolm, please don't say that!" she pleaded, throwing her arms around his neck. He pulled them away and looked at her sternly.

"If you want me to love and respect you as a husband should, you'd better do some reforming– and fast. I won't have the patience to put up with too many incidents like this one," he told her firmly, then left her alone and returned to his bedroom.

Once there, he threw himself on his bed and stared at the ceiling, trying to decide how he felt. When all was said and done, he had no heart to punish her severely. But somehow she had to be made to feel that she had committed a very real error. And yet he lay there aching with love for Marguerite and knowing that nothing would be resolved until he possessed her again.

"I went to her once," he thought, "now she should come to me." He concentrated on willing her to come to him. Nothing happened. Then he sat up and strained his ears, wondering if she was crying herself to sleep. This notion renewed his hard-on and made it even more impossible to concentrate on anything but his beautiful wife. Suddenly the door opened and Marguerite entered in nothing but a peach silk dressing gown.

"Darling? May I come in?"

Malcolm nodded. She sat next to him and looked pensive.

"Well?" he growled.

"Don't I deserve to be comforted?" she asked.

"Do you?" His tone was cynical, but he took her in his arms immediately and dimmed the bedside lamp. "I suppose it's always going to be like this, isn't it?" he guessed.

"Darling, I went a long time before I decided to marry. I picked you because your rigidity made the perfect counterpoint to my fluidity. Does that tell you anything?'

"Yes, it tells me that you're going to make my life hell," he brooded.

"But, it doesn't change the way you feel about me, does it? What I mean is, if you don't like me now because of what I did, we should end it this moment." Marguerite sat up suddenly, as though considering this possibility for the first time.

"I like you all right," he conceded, pulling her back down. "I more than like you."

Chapter Seven

Portia and Monty

The first annual Ivy League B&D Ball was to be held at one of the city's most elegant small hotels. In order to attend the ball you had to have gone to an Ivy League college, come as the guest of someone who had or simply be well connected in the New York B&D scene. Posters had been up at The Vault for weeks.

Obviously the rules for attendance were flexible, nonetheless, when word of the party escaped onto the Internet, Monty Powell, the party organizer, received a quantity of hate mail for being an elitist pervert. Meanwhile, the hotel's two hundred rooms immediately booked.

"Who is this Monty Powell, anyway?" Susan Ross asked Anthony Newton while she waited for him to finish dressing in their suite.

"Some 30-year-old Yale firebrand who works at Chipper Knight," her well-informed lover named a well-known Manhattan advertising agency.

"How'd you find that out?"

"I just E-mailed him and we chatted. He's anxious to meet you."

"Does he have a girlfriend in the scene?"

"I think he's throwing the party to find one."

Malcolm Branwell wasn't happy about attending the ball. He didn't think it was worth an entire trip to New York when he had such pressing work back in Boston and Marguerite already appeared too excited for his comfort.

She had spent five hours at the beauty salon that day, only to come home with three or four extra threads of gold in her luxuriant russet hair. And why her gown cost two thousand dollars Malcolm still could not understand. It was enchanting, but now that they were married, whose attention was she trying to attract? He brooded as she took ninety minutes to dress.

They were currently lodged in one of the penthouse suites in the party hotel, which commanded a splendid view of Central Park eleven floors below. And Marguerite was happy. For her handsome new husband was jealous, her bustier gown was Dior, and many of her friends were expected to arrive before too much longer.

"I hope you don't think I'm letting you go off by yourself to play with other men," Malcolm warned her, his hand only inches from a hairbrush on the dresser. This was his first scene party and he had no conception of the casualness with which activity was normally initiated at such an event. He felt suspicious of every man Marguerite talked to.

"You can't be with me every minute," she calmly replied. But when she noticed him decisively reach for the hairbrush she forestalled the inevitable by immediately sitting on his lap and murmuring, "Only kidding, darling. You can stick to me like glue and I won't mind a bit. In fact, I'm sure I'll enjoy the attention." Malcolm eyed her skeptically but put down the brush.

Sherman Cooper was escorting Diana Stratton, of whom he was fonder than ever. However, he worried about taking her to the party. Especially when he heard what an expert rope man their host, Monty Powell was.

Sherman could have shaken Susan when she burst into their room to reveal this data to her friend. The fair-haired, 35-year-old attorney was already dressed and seated at the desk behind a laptop, making some critical notes to himself for a Monday meeting. Diana, his college senior lover, was in the window seat in a fairy princess gown, gazing out at the stars and down on the treetops. It was a balmy April night after one of the worst winters ever and every feeling New Yorker was enjoying it passionately.

"Anthony is down in the bar," said Susan encouragingly to Sherman, wanting to be alone with Diana and share the information she had about Monty Powell.

"I see I'm being thrown out," Sherman grumbled. The girls giggled at him and hugged each other since it had been days since they had last met. "Don't forget that this is a non-smoking room," he warned before departing.

"Okay, Sherman," Susan promised, closing the door behind him, locking it and wedging a towel along the bottom. Diana was already lighting up. Susan joined her in the window seat at once.

"What floor are you and Anthony on?" Diana asked.

"We're next door at the other hotel."

"The other hotel?"

"Uh huh. There's an even more exclusive hotel right next door with thirty luxury suites."

"Tell me more about our host, this Monty Powell."

"I've gotten a glimpse of him already. He's tall and fairly striking, with short, curly, brown hair and a hard body. He's dressed in a khaki shirt, riding pants and boots. He's got a flogger stuck in his belt and a crop under his arm. Oh, and I thought you'd be interested to hear - coils of white nylon rope wrapped around one shoulder."

"How about his face?"

"Arresting. Prominent nose, penetrating eyes, wide mouth," Susan reported.

"You were able to notice a good deal," Diana complimented her friend.

"I just peeked around the corner when Anthony first shook hands with him in the bar."

"Let's go down as soon as we finish this," said Diana eagerly. "I want to get tied up by this lion tamer."

"There's also a fabulous new woman we have to make our friend, her name is Portia Repton," said Susan, dumping her makeshift paper cup ashtray, "and she's just your type."

"Tell me!"

Susan whisked the towel out of the doorjamb and into a closet and opened the door for her friend. "Well, she's gorgeous, 25 years old, about 5'6", obscenely long brown hair in a ponytail, slim, and as poised as a mistress. She's wearing Donegal tweed trousers and a satin backed suit vest over a pure white blouse with stack heeled oxfords – and she's spanking girls, right downstairs in the main room."

Diana pondered this image as they entered the gilt elevator. "Think she's bi?"

"Oh, I know she is. We talked for about ten minutes."

"What else?"

"She bragged that she's the most spoiled rotten girl in New York. Her father wrote some computer program that made them multi-millionaires ten years ago and it's still in use today. Then, she herself started a business last year that's taken Manhattan by storm, a string of ultra upscale beauty salons for business women, with computer work stations, meal delivery, etcetera."

"Sounds like a wonderful idea."

"She's about to go nationwide."

"What an exciting woman!" Diana breathed respectfully.

Portia Repton was happy to make a cult of self-indulgence. The fact that this very human propensity had translated into a remarkably successful new business only proved its validity as a behavioral option. But Montgomery Powell did not agree. And as he studied her across the party room he brooded on her arrogance and beauty.

Twice he had approached her and twice she had rebuffed him, putting him off till later with a vague, non-committal smile.

After he found out who she really was, it seemed even more vital to talk to her. Sexual interest was now augmented by the equally powerful motivation of monetary gain. As an account executive at one of the city's leading agencies, it was his obligation to wrest the Repton account from the lackluster hacks that were currently in possession of it. Taming her could come later.

Now he looked down and was startled to see two youthful beauties looking up at him.

"Hello," the blonde stuck out her hand, "I'm Susan Ross. Anthony Newton said you wanted to meet me. This is my friend Diana Stratton. She wants to meet you."

"Hi, girls," Monty replied, momentarily forgetting Portia.

"If you don't mind my inquiring, Mr. Powell, are you just carrying the rope for effect or do you actually do things with it?" Diana asked.

"Come up to my suite and I'll show you," he dared her. "And you too," he tapped Susan lightly on the hip with his crop.

"We liked watching you whip," Susan confided as Monty ushered them out of the ballroom. They had not been the only ones to admire his flogging form. Even Portia had noticed, at last, out of the corner of her very sharp eye, that he was a masterful flogger. Not an hour had passed before women were coming up to Monty and actually asking for whippings after observing him in action. Having noted this, and being, by her own admission, the most spoiled rotten young woman in the city, Portia also wanted to feel his whip. This being the case, she felt vexed when Monty willfully disappeared.

A very pleasant fellow was Monty, with not a hint of the master about him, except in his expertise at tying and flogging. It was all a game to him. He didn't talk of punishment or naughtiness when he administered to the girls, but rather positions, implements and limits. He was interested in the technical aspects of corporal discipline more than the emotional ones and appeared to remain very much the detached, though serious practitioner while entertaining them.

Within minutes of entering the room, Diana found herself tied across an upholstered hassock, with her skirt pulled up and her panties down. The lash was administered with restrained enthusiasm for some fifteen minutes before she finally cried out for mercy. Even then, she hadn't truly wanted him to stop, but Diana was not a selfish girl and realized that there were many young ladies at the party who had never received such a perfect whipping, and therefore considered it improper to monopolize their host a moment longer.

Now that it was her turn, Susan tried to resist and in fact protested that it wouldn't be fair to keep him away from the party any longer. Ignoring her words and responding only to the mischief in her eyes, Monty pulled her over to the bench at the foot of the canopied four-poster and turned her over his knee, telling her that of course he had to spank her, otherwise she'd never know he cared.

Monty had the kind of lap a girl into spanking never wants to desert, but like Diana, Susan was reluctant to take too much of his time. Particularly when there were gentlemen like Michael Flagg in the vicinity, at sea in this unfamiliar environment and probably in need of the companionship of a friendly troublemaker. She did, however, take an even hundred swats on the bare bottom from his big, comfortable hand, that left her tingling for the next half hour. When he set her on her feet again she felt slightly dizzy and fell into his arms just to have somewhere to go.

"Thanks, now I know you care," she told him, finally breaking the embrace, which he had welcomed, and setting her clothes to rights.

"So you two little darlings both have boyfriends, do you?" Monty offered them each a glass of champagne.

"Yes, thank you," said Susan.

"Give me your phone numbers anyway," he said, tossing Diana a tiny address book he dug out of his shirt pocket.

"Oh, gladly!" said Diana, still bewitched by her perfect bondage experience.

"You talked to that awful girl, Portia Repton," Monty said to Susan abruptly, "what does a man have to do to get her attention?"

Susan thought a moment before replying. "She almost seemed to become interested in you as we all left together."

"I noticed that too," Diana added.

"Do you want us to talk to her?" Susan asked.

"What would you say?"

"We could ask her what really turns her on," Diana suggested, "then come back and tell you. That way you'd be prepared to devastate her once you got her alone."

"Wait a minute," said Susan, "that sounds like stacking the deck in Monty's favor."

"I don't mind doing that," Diana smiled at the first man who had ever properly tied her.

"I already know what she's into," Monty said.

"Oh really? And what is that?" Susan wondered.

"She's obviously into spanking."

"What makes you think so?"

"All she was doing downstairs was spanking girls."

"She seemed quite dominant to me," Diana observed. "Do you plan to go submissive to her?"

"Not unless I have to-- to get the Repton account."

Almost as soon as Monty re-emerged into the party he was confronted by Portia Repton, who marched up to him and proffered her hand.

"Hi," she said, "I'm available now," which somehow irritated him, then added, "what did you say your name was again?"

"Monty Powell," he said, firmly shaking her hand. "Your host."

"Oh! You mean little you thought up this party?" Portia regarded him with dawning respect. Monty nodded. "Well done!" she commended. "We need more like it. Making any money on the deal?"

"That would be telling," he smiled.

"I can keep a secret."

"I will say this, I'm realizing benefits, but they're not necessarily monetary," he replied, following Susan and Diana momentarily with his gaze as they traversed the room. Portia noticed this and frowned, for the girls appeared to be far too young and possibly too good for Monty.

"You seem to know how to whip," she changed the subject abruptly.

"Oh, I do okay," he said.

"I like a good whipping now and then," she admitted, as though she were discussing a game of golf.

"Really? I don't know if you're grown-up enough for a whipping."

"Pardon me?" Portia flushed with indignation.

"A spoiled brat like you needs a spanking."

"I don't allow myself to be spanked," she replied coolly, though with a deepening color.

"No exceptions?"

"Certainly not!"

"Well, think about it," he said, writing his room number on the back of his card and handing it to her. Portia deliberately tore the card into four pieces and let them fall to the floor. Now it was Monty's turn to take umbrage, but Portia merely turned on her heel and strode away.

The first thing she did to console herself was to find Diana

Stratton, take her by the hand and lead her out of the ballroom.

"Come with me, young lady," Portia told the petite brunette, "I understand you long to be put in a hogtie."

Diana was enchanted. First Mr. Powell and now this Venus in tweed trousers promising to tie her up! She willingly clung to Portia's hand as they migrated to the young businesswoman's suite in the more exclusive hotel next door.

Portia removed Diana's party dress but decided to leave the exquisite satin corset on when she put the younger girl on the bed and got out her rope bag. Only when Diana was securely hogtied, tummy down on the luxurious counterpane, did Portia begin to question her about Monty. She did this in the form of an interrogation, reaching into the bosom of the corset to lightly pinch Diana's nipples between questions. Then she pulled Diana's panties down to bare her bottom.

Diana willingly recounted every detail she could recall of their scene in Monty's suite.

"It sounds as though you girls spoiled him to death!" Portia accused, sharply slapping Diana's cheeks.

"We did, but he deserved it," the younger girl replied. Portia smacked her harder for that.

"Ow! I'm sorry, mistress," said Diana meekly.

"No wonder he's so proud of himself!" Portia observed, going around to pinch Diana's nipples a little harder now. The younger girl vibrated with pleasure.

"Mistress?"

"Yes?"

"He was thoughtful enough to throw this magnificent party," Diana pointed out.

"Don't defend him," Portia sharply replied, spanking Diana again. "But tell me..."

"Yes, mistress?"

"You said he spanked Susan."

"Yes, he certainly did."

"Assess his technique."

"Oh, he's competent mistress, and very tender."

"What do you mean by that? Are you saying that he touched you other than to administer corporal punishment?" Portia demanded severely, tapping her with a riding crop all over her exposed bottom.

"Oh, no!" declared Diana. "He was a perfect gentleman and a very nice one too."

"How about his attitude?"

"He didn't have one, mistress."

"Did he make you say 'yes sir' and 'no sir' and count the strokes?"

"No, mistress."

"Did he scold you?"

"No, mistress."

"Did he say anything about me?" Portia asked, finally untying Diana.

"Only that you were an awful girl."

"Oh, he did, did he?"

"Yes, but he said it with a hard-on."

"What do you know about him? What's his profession? Is he rich?"

"Susan said he works for a big ad agency. In fact, now that I think of it, he said he'd go submissive to you to get the Repton account," Diana blithely revealed, abruptly switching allegiance from Monty to Portia.

Portia smiled.

Portia next encountered Monty just before midnight in Anthony Newton's suite, where a private supper was being served for a group of friends. Monty had come searching for Susan and Diana, with a view towards continuing where they had left off, only to find the two girls surrounding Portia. Anthony was seated at the baby grand entertaining in his usual style while Marguerite turned pages for him and sang. Malcolm sat drinking a mineral water and keeping an eye on Marguerite.

As soon as the girls noticed Monty they looked at each other and with tacit agreement stood up and prepared to abandon Portia to him. Besides, Michael Flagg had just walked in and Susan was eager to introduce him to Diana.

"Looks as if your troops have deserted you," Monty observed, falling into a chair opposite her.

"Oh, they'd be back if I needed them," she replied confidently.

"Have you been thinking about what I said?" Monty tapped the riding crop against his jodhpured thigh. The party had deprived him of every accessory but this one.

"Oh, that and more."

"Tell me."

"I understand you work for an agency, Mr. Powell."

"Yes, Chipper Knight," he sat up with sudden attention, ready to switch to business mode immediately.

"Push a mouse?"

"Not anymore."

"Did you know I'm about to go nationwide with my chain of salons?"

"I did know that, Ms. Repton."

"I'll be needing radio and TV spots, print publication ads, in short, a big campaign."

"A product like yours sells itself," Monty complimented her earnestly.

"Yes, but I haven't been satisfied with the job our current agency has been doing for us."

"Nor would I be. With all due respect, no one has really heard about you yet."

"I wonder if you feel you could help me?" Portia asked with a smile.

"I could do amazing things for you," Monty vowed sincerely.

"It's a very interesting concept," she mused, "but I think I need more convincing."

"Let's have a meeting on Monday and I'll show you my portfolio."

"I've never had business dealings with a scene person before," she said almost flirtatiously.

"Oh, I have," Monty reassured her, "it's no different. Don't give it another thought."

"But I can't think of anything else when I look at you," she said, in a way that set off an alarm in Monty's head. He realized two or three sentences back that Portia was being too nice to him too quickly and now he began to suspect her of teasing him.

"Maybe a party isn't the best place to discuss business," he said pleasantly.

"I heard something about you and I was wondering whether it was true, Mr. Powell."

"What did you hear?"

"I heard that you'd go submissive to me to get the Repton account." Monty immediately colored and glared across the room at Susan and Diana, who were now engaged in conversation with Michael Flagg.

"Why? Don't tell me you like that idea?"

"I love it. It would teach you a lesson."

"You think I need a lesson?"

"A sharp one."

"And why is that?"

"I just find your kind of dominant maleness insufferable," she declared.

"Oh, this is silly. Portia, you know you like me," he stated with certainty.

"I'd expect you to think that."

"I only think that for one reason."

"And that is?"

"You're talking to me now."

"I'd still like to follow up on your proposal. Are you really willing to go submissive to me to get the Repton account?"

"Well, what do you mean by submissive?" he growled.

"A willingness to submit to B&D."

"Define D."

"Discipline, Mr. Powell, as in: Corporal Punishment. Me to you."

Monty did not reply for several minutes, during which time he fixed himself a drink, smoked a cigarette, looked at Portia, scowled at Susan and Diana, then returned with a decision.

"Come over here," he told her, pulling her by the hand to the writing desk. "Sit down and get some stationary out of the drawer." Portia obeyed and took up a pen. "Put it in writing; everything you plan to do and all I will receive in return."

"By hand? Here and now? Without my laptop?"

Monty folded his arms and said, "The sooner you start writing, the sooner you can teach me a lesson."

"Very well," she smiled.

Monty milled around the room for ten minutes while she completed her task. When she was finished she motioned him over and handed it to him. He read it and asked for the pen. They both signed the document, which he then folded up and buttoned into his breast pocket.

"Your room or mine?" he asked.

"Oh, mine, darling," Portia said, taking him by the hand. Along the way, she collected her troops, for she was far too cautious to attempt to restrain him alone. With the girls present, however, he would be honor-bound to keep to the letter of their agreement.

By the time they reached Portia's suite, Susan Ross had become aware of a palpable tension between Monty and their beautiful new friend. She understood that they were being called upon to assist Portia in topping Monty, however, it soon became apparent to Susan that Monty was not happy about it.

"Wait here, please," Portia told Monty, taking the girls into the bedroom for a conference. Monty paced and whacked the crop against his leg with increasing restlessness. Then he contemplated the glory that would cover him when he went into work on Monday with the Repton account and felt soothed. Finally the girls returned.

"Well?" he asked, "Got your nerve up?"

"Mr. Powell, you have agreed to submit to one half hour of hard whipping," Portia said, checking her watch, "therefore please remove your shirt without delay."

"Fine!" Monty stripped off his shirt and tossed it aside, revealing a gym sculpted torso that all three girls studied for several moments in respectful silence. Meanwhile, Monty fished the document out of his pocket and made both girls read and sign it as witnesses.

"It's going to be a shame to mark that smooth, white skin," said Portia regretfully. "Girls, get my leather cuffs out of the drawer by the bed and two of the tiny gold padlocks. I want him with his arms around the bedpost and that beautiful back exposed." Now that he was about to become her vulnerable victim, Portia felt a sudden tenderness for her handsome captive.

While Diana happily cuffed and locked him to the bedpost Susan felt troubled and whispered to Monty, "Are you sure you're all right with this?" Sensing that Susan was about to become upset with the game and possibly protest to Portia, Monty kissed her bare shoulder and winked at her. This had the desired effect of reassuring Susan and she said no more.

"Pants down too, Mistress?" Diana asked, leaning against Monty's back and circling his waist with her hands to find his belt buckle. Diana then felt him tense.

"Not yet," Portia purred, shaking out her big flogger and small martinet.

"Wait a minute, you said whipping," he protested, turning his gaze towards Portia.

"Strapping is a part of whipping, I'm afraid," the confident brunette replied, "and I only strap on the bare bottom."

She started feathering his back with the large, multi-thonged flogger, creating the effect of a circular massage that grew increasingly sharper as she continued. Susan sat on the bed to study his expression. Diana placed herself in a position to study Portia's style. Meanwhile Monty became quite agitated, not because of the whipping, which he barely felt, but because of the undignified strapping to come. Again he protested, "I didn't agree to any below the belt activity, Portia, and you know it. Now I demand you stick to our arrangement."

"It's all semantics, darling, and infinitely open to interpretation. Still, you needn't act like such a baby just because you're getting your breeches taken down. After all, you were ready to do it to me!"

Portia now began to whip him more purposefully, so that he did feel it.

"If you're really determined to do this, I insist you send Susan and Diana away."

"You're doing a lot of ordering around for someone I have in my power," Portia observed, lashing him so hard that he gasped.

"I'll see you later, Monty," said Susan, kissing him full on the lips and slipping out of the room without meeting Portia's eyes. Diana gazed on her departing friend in amazement, for she herself would not consider departing until Portia dismissed her. Portia felt momentarily angry with Susan for daring to undermine her superior feminine authority by catering to the whims of this male.

"Well!" said she, "I thought our Susan Ross was more liberated than that!" But Monty was pleased by Susan's sympathetic gesture and decided to send her flowers the next day.

"She simply understands that every man is not submissive, which is more than I can say for you," Monty snapped at Portia.

"Darling, if I did think you were really a submissive, you can be quite certain that I wouldn't bother to gratify you with this much attention," drawled Portia, letting loose with the flogger again. "No," she continued during a pause, "I only decided to punish you like this because I know you won't enjoy it."

"You're the one who should be punished," he replied.

"Oh? And why is that?" Portia changed to the martinet, which stung a good deal more than the flogger, having thinner and fewer lashes. The first stroke took his breath away. But he was obviously determined not to cry out, no matter how hard she whipped him.

"Because you're guilty of treachery towards your host," he rejoined.

"Treachery?" Portia stayed her hand. "How so?"

"This business of the strapping. You tricked me."

"Oh, is it still the strapping that's bothering us?" Portia pretended concern. "Or do you just keep bringing it up because you're anxious to get on with it?"

Monty clamped his lips shut as he decided that it was undignified to keep arguing with her.

"Diana, darling, go in the bedroom and get my camera," said Portia suddenly. "I must have a shot of this dear pirate for my scrap book."

When Diana brought the camera Portia took it from her and snapped Monty from several angles. In one instance she got right in front of him and he gratified her by glaring into the lens. "Perfect!" she crowed. "Now, Diana, before we get to my favorite part, namely unveiling the rugged he-man's backside, suppose you spoil our victim for a moment or two."

"Mistress?" Diana cocked her head in query.

"I want to see the outline of his cock against those riding pants," Portia commanded. Diana interpreted this to mean that she was to now inspire an erection for Portia's amusement, since the whipping had not done the job.

Sitting on the bed in front of Monty, Diana laid her hand upon his zipper. The solid form of a noble male engine suddenly sprang up behind it. The pants were so form fitting that Diana was able to trace the outline of his mushroom cap through the stretchy material.

"So the male is a slut after all!" Portia cried triumphantly. "I knew we'd find something to get your attention if we only persisted. But to think it was something as simple as the touch of a woman's hand."

Monty ignored Portia's sarcasm and smiled down at Diana, who gazed up at him earnestly. "I forgive you for betraying me now," he told her fondly. The sweetness of his address made her immediately unzip his trousers and begin the laborious process of hauling his penis out of the tight breeches.

"Just a minute, young lady," Portia cried, "what do you think you're doing?"

"I was just going to press my lips to it for a moment or two," Diana explained.

Portia was on the point of immediate refusal when the charm of this suggestion came home to her. What better way to observe whether Monty had the stuff to please a discriminating woman in advance of that awkward first date?

"Very well, but only for a moment! And this doesn't count as part of the whipping time," Portia declared. Diana now happily finished extracting Monty's full-blown erection and carried it to her lips as promised.

"Feather the knob and just under the knob with the tip of your pretty pink tongue," Portia instructed. "Deep throat is beside the point and only serves to give men an inflated opinion of themselves."

Monty could afford to smile at this observation. It was amusing to see how far Portia would go to prove to him that she was really a mistress.

Neither Portia nor Monty then realized that this was the first time the pampered college senior had ever pressed her lips to a penis.

"Very good, Diana," said Portia at length, causing the girl to look up. "But now I think it's time to return to fun and games, Portia-style. I'll have those pants down now. And bring his belt to me."

Monty sighed as his erection subsided and Diana followed Portia's bidding. Breeches and briefs came down with one sharp yank, revealing his firm, downy, temptingly rounded buttocks. "Very nice!" Portia heartlessly admired her depantsed victim. "So nice, in fact, that I can't stay away." Now Portia stepped up behind Monty and ran her hand across his backside.

Then, somewhat vindictively, she seized her wooden hairbrush from the nearby dresser and whacked him full strength, once on each cheek.

"Ow!" he intoned, quite unselfconsciously. "You might give a person some warning," he snapped.

"Oh dear," Portia sighed, "we're not going to have to put up with him topping from the bottom, I hope." But she put the hairbrush down and took up his wide leather belt. "How much time do we have left, darling?" she asked Diana, who looked at her black velvet watch and replied, "Ten minutes, mistress."

"Good! Ten minutes of hard strapping should finish this session off nicely," Portia declared, and began to lash his exposed backside with the belt, and not gently. But when all was said and done, it was only a strapping, and Monty was, after all, a man. If it hurt a good deal, he wasn't saying. Certainly, tears never came to his eyes, though Portia wore her arm out trying to elicit them.

When she finally threw the belt down, her brow was dewy with perspiration and Monty's backside was dark rose from hips to thighs. Towards the end she had him gasping for breath, but Portia felt he was nowhere near begging for mercy, whereas she was exhausted from the exertion of trying to break him.

"Diana, get the keys to the padlocks," Portia ordered and even came to help her unlock him. Diana was discreet enough to pull his breeches back up before this procedure had been completed, restoring full dignity to Monty.

"Thanks for an unforgettable evening," he told Portia, pulling his shirt back on without bothering to button it up. Diana handed him his crop shyly, then threw her arms around his neck. Monty smiled and hugged her hard. "You're a little darling," he told her, finally letting her go. "And you're a nightmare," he told Portia pleasantly. "Shall we set up a meeting for Monday?"

"Sure. My office, noon. We'll have lunch," Portia handed him her card, disappointed to realize how eager he was to be gone. And then he really was gone. Portia put away the toys thoughtfully.

"What a marvelous man," Diana commented, helping her.

"Do you really think so?" Portia asked her, a lump in her throat at the coldness of his parting nod.

"You two would make a beautiful couple."

"Except that he hates me."

Of course Monty didn't hate Portia. In his heart of hearts he was even flattered that she had gone to such lengths to prove how little she valued his good opinion, for it did in fact prove the opposite. And while it was true that her style of corporal punishment had been rather crude and careless, compared to that of a brilliant player, it was evident that she had attempted, to the best of her ability (the Diana touch had been inspired!) to give him a full, multi-dimensional scene.

However, the exact lesson she had been trying to teach Monty eluded him, for all he had learned was that both Diana Stratton and Susan Ross were completely amiable young ladies, whereas Portia was hell's newest vixen.

Portia was gravely disappointed to find Monty only disposed to discuss business over lunch on Monday. She had worn a striking Valentino suit and cocked hat and they were dining in the most exclusive restaurant she knew, which was saying a good deal. Monty was cool in a khaki suit that forcibly reminded her of the outfit he had worn the night of the party. But when she tried to ask him how he'd felt the morning after the party, the first frost of April set in.

"Sensitive about a certain subject, are we?"

"I wish you were wearing sensible shoes," Monty suddenly veered, peeking at her footwear under the table. "We're so near the park and it's a perfect day for a stroll."

"Well, the food is rather rich here," Portia agreed, "we could probably benefit from walking in Central Park."

"But your shoes."

"They're only 3". I've strolled around the Vault for hours in 5" fetish pumps. I'll be fine and I love to walk."

But half way through the tiny and exquisite salad, Portia looked at him suspiciously. "Wait a minute. I know why you want me to go into the park with you!"

"Do you?" he smiled.

"You plan to try something."

"Something, Portia? You mean, like stealing a kiss?"

"You know what I mean. You'll take the first fallen log that we come across as an invitation to turn me over your knee."

He smiled but shook his head, saying, "You've made it pretty clear that turning you over my knee is not an option." He threw this out for a reaction, for he himself was still not sure of her orientation. Her behavior on the night of the party had been very like that of a mistress, yet there was, at odd moments, a childishness in her that seemed to beg for a strong hand. Portia made no reply.

"I'm sure you're not afraid of me, Portia."

"I should say not."

"Then you'll come for a walk in the park?"

"Oh, very well!" she cried with a blush, for she had spent the rest of the weekend thinking of Monty, and by now was very nearly in love.

Monty spent the rest of lunch discussing the ad campaign. Portia nodded but found it impossible to focus on anything but his face. She leaned her chin on her hand and looked at him, noticing his fine, hazel eyes.

"Portia? Have you heard a word I've said?" she heard herself being asked several moments later. She shook her head and stared at him in surprise.

"What?"

"What are you daydreaming about, young lady?" he asked with amusement, causing her to flush angrily and take a long pull on her vodka tonic.

"Please continue, Mr. Powell," she advised him, opening her laptop to make a few notes.

Portia was extremely excited when they entered the park by the Columbus Circle entrance an hour later. Yet the truth was that Monty had no intention of trying anything in the park, or anywhere else with Portia, until she had signed a real contract with Chipper Knight. He hoped to make that happen later in the afternoon at his office, a cutting edge milieu that few clients could resist.

Monty entertained her as they strolled with anecdotes from the Saturday night party. Portia then warmly commended him for creating an atmosphere of elegant decadence that even she could enjoy.

Monty laughed, saying, "With all due respect, your standards couldn't be too high if you frequent The Vault."

"In boots, a cat suit and gauntlets, I'll play anywhere, but naturally I prefer an atmosphere where I don't have to fear flying sperm."

"Well, I'm glad you liked the party," said Monty, then changed the subject back to business. He was conscious of a warming trend, but at the same time he couldn't help but notice how often she seemed to reinforce the image of herself as a mistress in conversation.

Their walk ended in confusion and frustration for Portia, who realized that she was not, in fact, at all averse to being taken across Monty's knee. As they exited the park and Monty hailed a cab, Portia agreed to return to his office with him.

Portia took the contract home for her lawyers to look at the following day. Meanwhile, she set up a dinner appointment with Monty for the following night. Dinner proved even more pleasant than lunch had been, especially as it began with Portia handing him the signed contract in his renovated brownstone apartment on West 66th Street. This put Monty in the best possible mood.

"I knew it would be a good idea to throw that party," he said, pouring her a glass of wine. Then he looked at her and sighed. "How much formality do I have to stand on with you?"

"None," Portia replied, her heart throbbing with sudden excitement.

"Then I'm going to kiss you," he told her and took her in his arms.

Since Portia had no objection to making conventional love to a man she had fantasized about all weekend, she invited him to possess her. Yet throughout the standard foreplay, the thing that made her heart beat fast was the possibility that he might finally punish her for her haughty treatment of him on the night they met.

He did take her in such a way that might be termed forceful, and in such a position as allowed his hands access to her beautiful, satiny bottom. But when given the opportunity, he merely caressed her and squeezed her. This was the kind of tease she respected, because it increased the degree of her longing to actually go submissive to him.

Monty began to work on the campaign and date Portia. Their affair took hold quickly. They met to make love two or three times a week. She had a wonderful loft with a river view and a team of servants to attend to her needs. Monty felt comfortable at Portia's house, until she underwent a personality change on week two of straight sex and her behavior became intolerable.

Monty, who was fairly easy going, did not completely comprehend the concept of rampant sexual jealousy until he saw Portia react to a message from Diana Stratton on his answering machine. They listened to the message together on returning from a gallery opening:

"Hi, Monty. This is Diana Stratton. We met at the party. I'm sure you remember. (small laugh.) I was just calling to find out whether you'd recovered from the party yet and ... (she hesitated then continued in a rush) whether I can ever expect to submit to your divine bondage again. You have my number. I'm in the city every weekend. Call me."

"The little Vassar slut!" Portia scowled. "She's far too young for you."

Monty shrugged and smiled, "I can't help it if she liked me."

"You shouldn't take advantage of children who don't know any better."

"She's 21. And she knows what's good for her, which is more than

I can say for you!"

"Oh? And what is that supposed to mean?"

"That's all I'm going to say on the subject."

"Do you plan to see her?"

"Portia, she's a nice kid who's into bondage and whose boyfriend never ties her up. That's all she wants from me, I promise you."

"She wasn't averse to giving you head."

"Yes, but she never would have thought of doing anything like that if you hadn't dragged her and Susan into that ridiculous scene."

"Well, that was then and this is now and I insist you not play with Diana Stratton alone."

"Fine, I'll tell her that you'll tie her up instead. She'll probably like that better anyway."

"You will?"

"Sure. Anything to calm you down."

So Portia got her way and calmed down for a day or two. But there was still something lacking and they both knew what it was. Sometime soon Monty would have to assert himself.

Portia now had the key to his apartment and once she went there just to touch and inhale the fragrance of his collection of leather paddles, whips and restraints. Monty had a room set aside as a playroom and the walls were pegged with a variety of corporal punishment implements. She felt comforted handling his toys. Only a serious player would bother to have his own dungeon. Not even she had a playroom, she realized, and instantly vowed to remedy that situation.

"If only he would walk in now," Portia thought, "find me here, and do something finally!" But she saw how it was going to be. She would have to ask him for it, either verbally or by deed.

Then she suddenly got an idea and fairly flew back downtown to her loft to turn in an important roll of film for development.

Several mornings later when Monty arrived at work with the usual spring in his step, both receptionists, several interns, a junior account executive and his secretary either giggled or smirked at him in such a way that confused and disconcerted our hero. The reason was apparent the moment he arrived at his office and saw a very crisp, clear photo fax of himself, stripped to the waist and bound to a bedpost, glaring into the camera's lens. To the right were two smaller photo insets of the side and rear views. Mercifully, he had not yet been depantsed when the photographs had been taken. Monty jerked the paper off the door and crumpled it up as a hot flash of anger surged through him.

The next moment the color left his face and the anger was supplanted by a jolt of pure sexual excitement. Purposefully he strode to his desk and dialed Portia's direct line. She immediately picked up the phone and said hello. Monty hung up and walked out of his office. In a moment he was out on Madison Avenue. Portia's office was on Lexington, only two blocks away. On foot it took five minutes, elevators included.

Up in her office, Portia looked at the phone. She knew it had been Monty. Trying to still her pounding pulse she buzzed her intercom. "Walter, take an early lunch," she told her secretary imperatively.

"But it's only ten o'clock," Walter replied.

"Sweetheart, I'm expecting a visitor and I need to be completely alone with him."

"Oh!" Walter smiled. "I get it now. I need to buy a new umbrella at Barney's anyway."

"Get me one too."

But Walter had no idea that Monty would be showing up so soon and had barely straightened his desk when that gentleman strode in.

"Good morning, Mr. Powell. I'll tell Ms. Repton you're here," said Walter, touching the intercom.

"Never mind, she's expecting me," Monty said with confidence and walked into her office. Walter shrugged and was rather compulsively checking his tie and hair in the mirror before departing when he heard a noise the likes of which he had never heard or expected to hear issuing from his boss's office. Suddenly understanding why Portia had been so eager for him to leave, Walter slipped discreetly out of his office and locked the door behind him, safeguarding Portia from any further intruders.

Meanwhile Monty had pulled her out of her chair, dragged her over to the building's most expensive leather sofa, sat down and turned her over his knee.

"How dare you?" he accused, bringing his hand down hard and fast on either cheek, covered only by a pair of silk panties and a beige linen skirt. Smack! Smack! "You've violated the first rule of the scene."

"Oh? And what's that?" she looked over one shoulder, feeling the immediate sting, but more exhilaration than pain.

"You've blown my cover and at work of all places. How do you know my boss isn't an arch conservative?"

"I know I'm his first new million dollar client this month, and I'll be happy to remind him of that if he gives you any trouble."

"Always the manipulator!" Monty whacked her six times in a row and harder than before. Now Portia caught her breath at each smack. "What if I'd been the sensitive type?"

"But you're not. You're the Monty type."

"Oh, be still," he told her, and with focused determination pulled up the tightest pencil skirt he'd ever seen to expose her panties. They were a scrap of white silk, but as far as Monty was concerned, they only got in the way. He soon tugged them down to her knees.

"Considering the way you treated me when you had me at your mercy, I'd be scared now if I were you," Monty murmured, locking one arm around her waist.

"I am," she replied honestly, on tenterhooks as she waited for the first bare bottom smack to fall.

"I don't think I'll ever forget the particular sting of those two with the wooden hairbrush," Monty mused, beginning the spanking with a thrill of righteous indignation. He brought his big hand down hard and fast at least fifty times before allowing her a moment to gasp for breath. She didn't start to whimper or say "ow" till smack 40. Finally he gave her a break and rubbed her deeply pinkened bottom, but still held her fast to his lap. The spanking was not over.

"You just had to pull the tiger by the tail," he told her, renewing his grip on her small waist and administering another fifty smacks, but more slowly than the last. She made no protest and only wriggled to grind. He realized fairly quickly that his little mistress was no stranger to such attentions. Towards the end she arched to his hand, encouraging him to continue. Portia had a perfectly rounded bottom, though not a particularly ample one. In minutes the color changed from pink to magenta to rose under his hand.

"Now, see here, Portia," he soberly began, pausing to rub away the sting again, "I let you top me at the party for a lark-"

"And out of greed," she helpfully amended.

"–but I'm not going to let you make a habit out of humiliating me." Monty administered another dozen meaningful swats to her now wriggling bottom. It was starting to hurt.

"Ow!" she cried timidly.

"Ow?" he stayed his hand.

"It hurts, Monty."

"Nonsense, your hard little backside is hurting my hand," he said, finally pushing her off his lap. She stood looking at him and rubbing her bottom through her skirt, which had fallen back into place. He folded his arms and looked straight at her. "You and I are going to have to come to a better understanding, Portia."

"Understanding about what?"

"I won't have you knocking the world over every time you want some attention."

"I don't know what you mean."

"Oh yes you do. You've been wanting a spanking for weeks, but you've been too proud to admit it. So you thought up a trick so nasty that I would have no recourse but to react in the time-honored manner."

"It's your fault," she protested, sitting on his lap and putting her arms around his neck, "you called me a nightmare so that's what I became."

"I wouldn't have called you that if you didn't go out of your way to torture and humiliate me that night."

"Well, you put my back up, insulting me the way you did."

"How did I insult you?"

"By saying I needed a spanking."

"And yet, I was right."

"Perhaps I have been curious as to what it would feel like..." she admitted. Monty impolitely chortled. "What?" she demanded, pulling away from him.

"Are you asking me to believe that you never get spanked?"

"Well, almost never. Why?"

"You certainly weren't reacting like someone who almost never gets spanked," he observed.

"Well, I can assure you –"

"Quit lying," Monty cut her off. "You probably get that good looking secretary of yours to thrash you once a day, just to relieve the stress of managing your business."

"Go to hell, Monty," Portia jumped off his lap and set her skirt and white linen halter vest to rights in a mirror. Then she looked at him and smiled, "How decadent do you think I am?"

"That probably depends upon your mood, your outfit and the phase of the moon."

"The very idea of using my secretary for corporal punishment thrills is absurd," she declared, reapplying dark red lipstick in a mirror across the room.

"So who did give you the spankings?"

"What spankings?"

"The ones that seasoned you so well for my hard hand."

"Oh, just various dykes at the B&D clubs. Until now I've almost always been spanked by lesbians."

"And why is that?"

"I don't know, really. Men just naturally assume I'm dominant, I suppose."

"Gee, I wonder why they'd mostly think that," Monty grinned.

"No, seriously, Monty, you're about the first male who ever wanted to spank me."

"So why did you fight it so hard?"

"Oh, I was just in a mood. I get that way sometimes."

"I noticed."

"Once you get to know me, I'm not so bad," she promised.

"Except that you're irritatingly superior, insanely jealous and impossibly demanding."

"But I'm also young, sexy and rich," she reminded him.

"And spoiled rotten," he added.

"Oh yes! I'm going to be the hardest to handle girlfriend you've ever had," she promised happily.

"That's fine, so long as you realize that I'm going to be the least patient boyfriend you've ever had."

"Monty, I may have submitted once, out of curiosity, but don't think I'm going to let you spank me frequently."

"No, dear, of course not," he replied soothingly, taking her in his arms.

About the Author

In Random Point, everything is linked to spanking and this is true for the author of the Shadow Lane novels as well. Eve Howard has been writing and producing spanking erotica since the 1980's, when she began freelancing for one of California's largest fetish magazine publishers. While editing *Spank Hard* magazine (as Lizzie Bennett) in 1985, she was discovered by the video producer Nu-West and offered a chance to perform in spanking videos. In 1986 she published the first Shadow Lane story and the following year formed the video production company Shadow Lane with her partner Tony Elka. The Shadow Lane novel series, originally published by Eve in serial form in her magazine *Stand Corrected*, was brought out in paperback volumes by Blue Moon books beginning in 1992. There are nine titles in the Shadow Lane series and Eve is currently working on Volume 10.

Since 1988, Eve has written, directed and produced over 140 spanking videos, the vast majority featuring the same male-spanks-female dynamic portrayed in her novels. Female-friendly and designed to make people feel good, rather than guilty, about being into spanking, Eve suggests an irreverent alternative to the all or nothing B&D subculture portrayed in such beloved classics as *The Story of O*. Many spanking fans have discovered the real life spanking scene by following the same patterns of social networking as described in the Shadow Lane novels. And for almost twenty years, Eve's company Shadow Lane has been one of the primary social organs of the real life spanking scene. She lives with her husband Tony and three cats in Las Vegas.

Reader Reviews about the Shadow Lane Series

"I've become addicted to the "Random Point" series so much that I can't wait until the next chapter. I've ordered the first two Shadow Lane volumes and have re-read them over and over. I never tire of them. Eve is the only person I know who can make an enema sexy."

"I discovered Shadow Lane about a month ago via AOL. Prior to that time I thought I could write excellent spanking erotica. Then I ordered, "The Problem with Laura." This is just a note to commend Eve Howard's spectacular talent and to say thanks for an incredible erotic experience."

"I have just completed "Return to Random Point" and decided that I had to write about how much I enjoyed it. I have not been so aroused since reading my first discipline novel many years ago, about a girl raised in England and "coming of age" as I believe they put it. More recently I have enjoyed reading Grant Andrews' My Darling Dominatrix and Ann Rice's "Beauty" series. It seems that women, though, have the right touch when it comes to writing about this subject. Eve, especially, knows how to touch that erotic nerve and bring it to a pure, raw sensuality until one feels that he/she is near bursting with lust."

"I, for one, have always loved (and by loved I mean devoured... breathlessly) Eve Howard's novelettes. To read them... especially when I was just 'coming out'... was to feel completely validated. I truly identified with each and every heroine; the feisty, sassy ones, the shy, demure ultra 'subby' ones... the young ones, and the more mature. I loved the gentle yet firm "taken in hand" nature of the romantic variety of spanking D's that Eve always incorporated into the stories. I loved that the plots were not complicated... but, feasible nonetheless. I loved the depictions of sexual escapades after many of the spanking interludes. I appreciated that the girls were cherished and adored by the affably rogue-ish gents... that the submitting was willing and desired... that it wasn't like 'rape.'

I like the settings... having grown up in New England and living here almost my whole life. I LOVED the idea of the bookstore (which I always find sexy). Then and now. I could cite many passages too, but I fear I've rambled enough. Eve was/is always my favorite spanking author."